THE WICKER PALACE

To Connie
I hope you enjoy the book!

Anthony

Anthony G. Juarez

Copyright © 2015 Anthony G. Juarez
All rights reserved.

ISBN: 1514859742
ISBN 13: 9781514859742

1

WELCOME TO WICKER

Have you ever stopped, sat down, and really paid attention to the beauty of a curb? You know, one of those small-town curbs? Maybe just like the one right outside your house or the kind you'd find at an old gas station in the middle of nowhere. Have you admired a curb covered in dirt, cigarette butts, and maybe one or two bubblegum wrappers? I have. What's so beautiful about that? Everything. Well, to me at least.

You see, I'm the type of person who would much rather know where something began than where it ended up. It's a bad habit of my racy imagination to wonder who owned these cigarettes and pieces of gum before the items became mere litter. Did a seemingly shy, conservative soccer mom anxiously pull out a stick of gum while waiting outside the old 7-Eleven? Was she meeting with her much younger lover to let him know she could no longer do this to her faithful, God-fearing husband? He has been a great father to her two gifted children, she tells her lover. Did an outlaw on the run smoke his last stick, like the prodigal son in a western, one evening outside the Motel 6 across the street while debating his next move? The possibilities are endless.

The truth is those cigarette butts and gum wrappers are a lot like people. We can be alive in the world one day and be discarded the next. That's the beauty and tragedy of life: it can be so unexpected. And although there is no promise of life itself, it can be quite promising. That's why I believe that everyone has a story to tell. Whether it is of a heroic warrior, a journey to redemption, or simply an inspirational account, if you look deep down inside, you'll see that you have a story worth telling. Those who go through life without caring about anyone but themselves lose a chance to hear something marvelous. Every story that has a heart and soul can live on forever. No matter how short or long, funny or despondent, it is indeed the stories of others' lives that give us the courage to accept our own.

My name is Morgan. I'm twenty-five years old. My eyes are hazel with a light tint of green. I'm five foot four, tan, brunette, and petite. Though I do understand that I'm no longer a kid, I'd be lying if I said there weren't times when I still felt like one. In fact, I'll admit that I'm occasionally on the warning end of that waving finger. You know, the one indicating that not everything in life is a joke and that things should be taken more seriously. But I have my reasons for behaving the way I do. For one, my mother, who happens to be awfully intelligent, has always told me that laughter is the body's true source of youth. For another, my grandfather, without a doubt the most generous human being I knew, showed me that a smile is the greatest gift one human can give to another.

I'm a lot of things: witty, random, awkward, odd, vulnerable. I'm also stubborn, and at times I can be ignorant. But what I lack in persuasion, I make up for in patience and beauty. When it comes down to food, well, there's not much to say. It's quite simple: I don't eat fried foods. I hate chocolate and cashews, too.

I like rainy Mondays. They remind me of my childhood, and that always makes me happy. After all, those were my happiest times. The only thing I had to worry about then was not spilling my Apple Jacks on the rug while I watched cartoons. But just the thought of precipitation on a Saturday makes me sadder than the lonely, old gibbous moon. Then again, even on the clearest of days I've found myself with a bad case of the *mean reds*, when I'm sensitive, not wanting to hear the truth. I'm quite obstinate, you know? So whenever I don't want to hear a no or that something is foolish just because it's illogical, I raise my anchor and drift off into my own little world, where everything is nonsense and where everything that's beautiful isn't bad. It's a luxury we fortunately have. Or maybe it's just me.

While most people enjoy the finer things in life, I tend to enjoy the little things that often go unnoticed. But then again, I'm an unusual girl, one who isn't afraid to walk around with ribbons and flowers in her hair. I'm constantly carrying on conversations with my restless, wandering mind. And although I may not have any tattoos or crazy piercings, one thing is for sure: rock 'n' roll is all I know.

I've never really fit in anywhere, like a puzzle piece that provides more mystery than solutions. But I guess I only have myself to blame. After all, I tend to keep to myself. Of course, once you come in contact with my distinctive sense of humor, you can see that it is undeniably the best. And that's when I'll have you right where I want you.

Don't get me wrong. I'm not shy, just selective. However, I do have my bad habits and insecurities. There are times when I wish I could tie my conscience to a wild horse and send it millions of miles away, never to be heard from again, alongside my timidity and sense of remorse, because, truth be told, I'm pretty bad at being good. Now, I'm not saying I'm a whore or that I'm cruel in any way. I guess what I'm trying to say is I'm a girl who doesn't color inside the lines, a girl who doesn't always do what she is told. After all, what's the point of having a mind like mine if I'm not gonna use it?

My motto has always been "Do what you have to do, and trust no one while doing it." Believe me: you'll get more done that way, and who's not gotten farther by getting more done? It's not so much a spirit of rebellion as it is a spirit of sovereignty. I like doing whatever I want without ever thinking about who I have to answer to. It makes me feel like I am truly in control of the little situation I'm in called *life*. People will always have a thing or two to say as far as the decisions you make, so you might as well enjoy the rush of danger that comes with making your own mistakes.

I know what you must be thinking: A little wild thing like that, living life on her own terms, ought to be fearless. Well, I assure you that isn't the case at all. There are times when I get scared—terrified really. The truth is, I was born with a childlike terror that constantly lingers in the back of my mind. It scares me half to death when I allow it to.

Still, despite the fear I sometimes feel, I have high hopes. You see, I plan to become a writer someday, a famous one. It's not for egotistical reasons; I just dream that when I have a story of my own someday, it'll be worth sharing with millions. And if I can affect just one person's life out of those millions, the same way Edgar Allan Poe or Hans Christian Andersen affected mine, that would be a reward in itself. It's safe to say that anyone who has a dream as big as mine shares my fear of dying without ever becoming somebody, because becoming someone in this world is truly the hardest thing to do. Only a few accomplish it. I lost this dream for a while, as you'll see, but I've since managed to recover it.

So, now that you know my utmost fear, you're probably wondering, why writing? Well, it's my escape from a world where my imagination is sometimes all I've got and the one place I desire to be. Because the honest truth is, you're never too old to hope or crave something other than reality.

Speaking of imagination, it's my opinion that fantasizing takes faith. That means believing in something much greater than yourself, which I sure do. I believe that there is a God, creator of the universe. I believe He has purposely made Himself a mystery, just as He made the cosmos immense and made me a dreamer with an imagination as free and wild as a mad scientist. I believe He blessed me with the gift of revelation, the power of revolution, and wisdom beyond my years.

You wouldn't believe how many times the people I love have told me I'm an old soul lost in the wrong era. I simply laugh each time someone says it, because it never gets old to me. In fact, a man I once knew told me that I had the grace of Judy Garland, the heart of Jackie O, and the soul of Holly Golightly. Secretly I would have felt privileged to have lived and loved in the era of those greats and others, such as Elvis, Marilyn, and JFK. Sometimes I go as far as believing that James Dean would have had heirs to carry on his legacy had I been around. And although there are debates about these greats and their reputations, I find nothing but beauty in their flaws and struggles. After all, why else do we so relate to such fascinating people?

Sometimes I wonder how different my life would have been ordering ten-cent sundaes and dancing in a pair of saddle shoes at the local diner. Would I have appreciated living in the past, not knowing that the sense of innocence of the time wouldn't last? I don't blame the world for changing, because it hasn't really. Our world is still just as beautiful as it ever was. It's the people who have gone to shit. It scares me to death when I think about how much more ruthless and grotesque humankind's behavior will become in the next fifteen years.

But anyway, enough of my blabbering and sidetracking. I'm originally from a small town in Texas called Raymondville, where the drugs are cheap and the streets are territories. My hometown isn't Hollywood or the film portrayal of the small-town American dream, but there isn't one house in one hood that isn't a home. I grew up in the ghetto, surrounded by lowriders, pit bulls, graffiti gangs, and tattooed thugs, and as crazy as it sounds, we all took care of one another. That's the beauty of living in a small town: there is always an unspoken bond. I am blessed to say that I came from a happy home, one with a loving and caring family.

In August 2006, at the age of seventeen, I left my parents and my two brothers and two sisters behind to set out on my life's journey. I moved to Corpus Christi, Texas, to attend college. Although Corpus Christi is only a few hours away from home, it was far enough. The city is surrounded by beaches, which is the reason I was drawn there. I lived in Corpus Christi until an unfortunate event forced me to move back to Raymondville just before turning twenty-two. But now, at twenty-five, I'm back in the Double C. Yup, I'm back, along with my baby, Arson, a 1967 candy-apple-red Ford Mustang Eleanor with two white racing stripes. He is without a doubt my most valuable possession.

So, now that I've told you everything about me that you need to know, I'll tell you about my job, which is where my story begins.

I work at an old hotel called the Wicker Palace. Lucky for me, it's only fifteen minutes away from my apartment—on a good day, that is. There are 150 rooms, all suites. The hotel is one of the oldest buildings in Corpus Christi, and I'd be lying if I said it wasn't creepy. In fact, its eeriness is the reason I fell in love with it at first sight. Its outer stone walls always feels cool to the touch and are surrounded by dead trees. At the front stand two large doors that resemble the entrance to a dungeon. A corridor leads to the front desk, which is always stacked with large piles of unnecessary papers, including unwanted room receipts and a variety of old newspapers all missing the Sports section. As if the piles of papers weren't enough of an eyesore, adding to the cluster are small mounds of keys scattered all across the front-desk counter.

The Wicker Palace's interior layout has always reminded me of the Roman Coliseum, because every door to every room is visible from the atrium, which is located right in the center of the hotel. The hotel runs three stories high, requiring a total of four elevators, two near the entrance and the other two toward the back. The same goes for the stairs. But let's be real: Who uses stairs these idle days?

A large fountain stands in the atrium between the lobby and the hotel restaurant. The fountain, known as the Heart of Wicker, is made of metal, which has rusted over the years, and is in the shape of a dried-up oak tree. Four chipped and discolored crows that abide in its eerie branches pour mildew for water. For some strange reason, people tend to love that old thing, in spite of its lack of beauty.

Our guests pretty much consist of the rich, the widowed, and the ambiguously narcissistic. You know, your typical feathered hair, fur coat, pearls, and tailored suit types, those rich enough to afford hired help but cheap enough to be lousy tippers. They're the kind of people who seem to think the world revolves because they exist.

However, the people I work with are pretty cool and fairly interesting, to say the least. I guess it's safe to say that they are like my second family. It's hard enough to find yourself a good working environment, let alone a place where your colleagues are not just familiar faces but loyal friends. I'm very blessed to say that I have found both.

Michael Olivarez, the hotel night auditor, is the first face I see each morning as soon as I walk into Wicker. He keeps watch over the old building and seems to care for it the most. He is my idea of an outcast. His slacks are always too baggy, his tie is always too loose, and his glasses are duct-taped together in the middle. Michael's breath is always tart smelling, because all he ever drinks is grape juice. A lot of the other hotel staff belittle him for not fitting the standards of what our society thinks is cool. However, I don't think he's as weird as they make him out to be. I think the others are just too "normal" to appreciate someone like him. I'm not going to lie. There are times when he can be a bit awkward. But if he were any other way, we probably wouldn't get along as well as we do. Aside from that, Michael's sense of humor is classic and pure genius. He can make me laugh with a simple knock-knock joke. It has something to do with the way he manipulates the tone of his voice every time he's fishing for a chuckle. It takes true skill to make someone laugh without using profanity or sexual innuendos.

Joe Tapia and Judy Gallindo are the cooks responsible for the fairly interesting food served at Wick Oasis, the small hotel restaurant located in the heart of the atrium. We serve breakfast from six to nine, and then at eleven we reopen for lunch, which runs all the way until two. You'd have to be pretty brave to eat at our infamous little restaurant—and absolutely insane to actually enjoy it. The food is always raw and bloody, the eggs are served way too over easy, and everything you order is guaranteed to come with a side of rat shit or some sort of pest remains. Oh, and did I mention the grand pleasure I have of serving as a waitress there? I love it, sarcastically speaking. In fact, every morning I take a cup of steaming, bold coffee and use the heat to temporarily force a smile onto my face. I really can't complain though, because although everything else Wick Oasis has to offer completely sucks, that coffee sure is the best I've ever had.

Joe is the restaurant's comically cynical head chef, and Judy is his delightfully wacky cochef. They are both crazier than a pair of chipmunks on high doses of caffeine and crack. Joe's conversational skills consist mostly of jokes and punch lines, which send Judy's laugh echoing throughout the halls of the hotel every morning. They both have very short attention spans, yet they somehow manage to find enough focus to look after me like a daughter. They always remind me to smile and make sure I get a nutritious breakfast every morning.

From the first moment I met Joe, he reminded me of that one funny uncle every family should be blessed to have. Although he might look like a criminal in a chef's hat, with tattoos that only add to his already intimidating appearance, I assure you he is the complete opposite. In fact, he is as gentle as a lamb and as caring as a mother. Whenever I need to talk to someone, he is the first person I run to, because, like all good listeners, he takes the time to listen, not to mention he always offers the best advice.

Judy, Judy, Judy...What would I do without my Judy? To be quite frank, I probably wouldn't make it through a morning at the Wicker Palace without hearing her joyful "Good morning!" She is witty, flamboyant, and as beautiful as a sunrise. She is always looking out for me, always wanting what is best for me. After a long, stressful morning, she'll usually braid my hair in the break room while we talk about the naughty things we'd like to do to the rare fine-looking gentlemen we see during the restaurant's strenuous rush hour. Her nurturing tenderness sets my heart at ease and provides me with a feeling of a home away from home.

In addition to the cooks, Wick Oasis employs four other waitresses who work alongside me: Jesta, Emily, Cleo, and Derya.

Jesta Pickens is my best friend, because in addition to having a very sarcastic mouth in common, we share a lot of similar interests. For example, we both consider "Moon River," as sung by Audrey Hepburn, our most beloved song of all time. Moreover, *Breakfast at Tiffany's* is our favorite movie. It really is—cross my heart and kiss my elbow. I swear it's true. Why, we both can quote any scene by heart. And if that's not enough to prove the fundament behind our friendship, then check our music libraries. You'll see we have every single record the Blue Oyster Cult ever recorded, and everyone knows that love for classic rock is far stronger than any blood bond. Last but not least, we both share a rather wild fascination for body ink and beards. I really can't help but love the girl. The two of us are constantly getting into some sort of trouble at work. She is hands down the smartest cat I know—ambitious, opinionated, unobtainable, and easy on the eyes, with a slight pinch of Filipino in her.

Emily Hsu and Cleo Lei are a two-for-one. Those china dolls are inseparable. Their skin is as white as snow, and their hair is as black as a raven's feather. They are a pair of goofballs who spend more time getting into silly antics and then blaming them on their youth than they do working. I actually don't mind picking up their slack though, because whenever they aren't clowning around, they're usually making a mess—usually of my love life. For some strange reason, they have a habit of trying to pimp me out to anything handsome with a heartbeat that drifts through Wicker Palace. But no matter how many uncomfortable predicaments those silly girls manage to put me in, I'll always love them, especially Emily, who I have a soft spot for in my heart. I guess it's because my sister is also named Emily. So every time someone calls out for her, I can't help but think of home.

Derya Urun—boy, just one look from that Turkish beauty can make a grown man's heart melt like butter on a stove. Even though she's the center of customers' attention most of the time, she is definitely not the self-centered, stuck-up, backstabbing bitch typical of beautiful girls. In fact, she is the sweetest, most humble person I've ever come across. Sometimes I find it hard to believe that a girl as stunning as she is can be so genuine. Guests of all ages are constantly flirting with her, whether by serenading her with a crooner classic or simply leaving a phone number rolled up inside an awfully generous tip. It's rather amusing to hear some of the ridiculous things that guys are willing to promise when they know a girl is out of their league. We all get a good laugh out of all the cheesy stunts those lovesick scoundrels attempt in order to get Derya's attention. We've never really had a problem with any of the men getting too fresh, but if we ever do, Joe is always standing nearby.

Sometimes I feel so plain being in the midst of such exotic and driven girls, especially since we are all around the same age. However, I like to believe that I haven't always been this way. You see, there was a time when I *was* one of those wildly driven girls, full of life and ambition, with an outward demeanor that made me intriguingly unusual to all. It's funny how much can change over time, but it's quite sad when that change isn't beneficial.

Moving on to the rest of the hotel employees, thirty-five-year-old Kim McDaniel is the head honcho of our banquet department. However, the fun doesn't stop there for her. She also bartends the happy hour for Wick Oasis during our manic lunch rush. She has all the right assets for a good bartender: namely, a knack for giving great advice (if the advice you need pertains to either sex or alcohol) and incredibly perfect tits. She looks like good sex just waiting to happen, a femme fatale with the ability to bring any party to life. Kim is living proof that girls just want to have fun, constantly encouraging the girls and me to be the best sluts we can be.

Christopher Wolfe…How do I even begin to explain the big bad Wolfe? Well, for starters I guess I should state that Chris is Wicker's handyman, the go-to guy, Mr. Fix It. Whenever something goes wrong in the hotel, we all rely on Chris to fix the problem. No matter how ridiculous our requests are, he's always at our beck and call. Whether it's fixing a power outage or simply a jammed toaster, there isn't anything he can't do. There are two things you should know about Chris: (1) Don't ever refer to him as the "maintenance man," because he hates it and will definitely let you know it. You see, he feels like the title "maintenance" represses people's idea of his true potential. He sees himself as more of a jack-of-all-trades rather than your typical screw tightener, so he prefers to be called the "handyman" instead. (2) He is not as mean as he appears to be. His cold silence is usually a result of nerves more than anything else.

Chris has always reminded of me a bad boy in a teen movie. You know, the one who lingers in the background but draws more attention than the leading man himself. I guess it's because Chris shares himself only enough to remain mysterious—and the fact that he is dangerously handsome just leaves you even more curious. Most of my coworkers find Chris unpleasant and offensively sarcastic, but I think he's rather sweet. The girls at work are constantly poking fun at the idea that he fancies me. In fact, Jesta and Judy have both been playing matchmaker since the day he started working here. And even though I haven't budged on my stance, I must admit that it's absolutely adorable how bashful he gets when he's around me. Not even my pinkest blush puts as much color on my cheeks as that tattooed twenty-nine-year-old does. Last yet most important, there is something so mesmerizing about his diamond-blue eyes that they hypnotize my soul. They are rather animalistic, almost wolflike, befitting his name.

Liz Navarro is the wicked witch of Wick herself, the owner of the Wicker Palace, a position that only fuels her to be even more of a cynical bitch than she already is. Although she is only five feet tall, her words have the power to put you below her in a matter of seconds. In spite of her unpleasant attitude, not even the white hair covering every inch of her scalp can belie the beauty that once existed. She spends half her time at Wicker working our asses off and the other half spreading her money-hungry hospitality to the guests, shoving her head up their asses with cheerful yet bogus conversations and compliments. Sometimes it's too painful to watch. Still, at the end of the day, when all is said and done, we all realize there is no one better fit for the job than her.

Last but not least is Mr. Casanova himself, Wesley Dowdy. Wes is a thirty-one-year-old all-American boy in beat-up boots and faded jeans and with a smile that'll make you weak at the knees. He is the type of guy your momma warns you about, the kind of guy your daddy fears you'll come across. You can usually find Wes with a cigarette in his mouth and holding a cup of coffee with more whiskey than creamer in it. He's in charge of maintaining the hotel's botanical garden, which is one of our most popular attractions. I know what you're thinking: The gardener? Really? How cliché.

But hey, if the shoe fits, you might as well wear it. Standing tall at six foot two, the corn-fed southern cowboy is well known for his womanizing antics. But I gotta hand it to the guy, because he is indeed suave and debonair. It's such a shame that he chooses to abuse his God-given charisma by promising women the impossible just to get what he wants.

Don't let his pretty little brown eyes fool you. Just when you think you've finally found your George Strait, he'll show you that he's no better than the douchey country boys making cheap music and tarnishing what true country once represented. They're out there shaking their hips in skin-tight jeans while singing songs about beer and loose women. That's why romance is dead, because that's the kind of shit so many women have allowed men to sweep them off their feet with. And so I say, chivalry isn't dead; self-respect is.

Now that you know everything there is to know about the Wicker Palace, it's time to get into the real story.

On Friday, December 6, 2013, I was wiping down one of my tables when Chris walked by on his way back from getting his morning coffee.

"Mornin', sunshine." He nodded.

"Good morning, Christopher," I replied with a bashful smile.

He carefully took a sip of his coffee and said, "You do know that everyone else just calls me Chris, right?"

I looked up at him and quickly responded, "Oh really? And here I thought I meant so much more to you than everyone else."

"Touché." He blushed.

Out of the corner of my eye I could see Jesta eavesdropping from a distance while pretending she was attending to one of her tables. In reality she was only waiting for Chris to walk off so she could slither her way up to me with an impudent comment on how badly I suck at carrying on conversations with men.

Chris and I exchanged a painfully awkward "Have a good day" and "You too." Then he gently kissed my forehead and headed off toward his shop.

"Oh God," I said heavily under my breath as I spotted a smirking Jesta making her way toward me, her eyes bugging.

"What was that all about?" she asked, looking me up and down. "'And here I thought I meant so much more to you than everyone else.'" She mimicked me using the dinosaur's hands she always makes whenever she does an impression of me. I tend to use my hands a lot to express myself when I speak, and she states that there are times when I look like a T. rex carrying on a conversation.

I couldn't help but laugh. "I was just being friendly."

Jesta quickly sassed back, "Bitch, please. You forget that I know you."

An elderly woman nearby aggressively cleared her throat so that we'd be well aware that she was scorning us. Her old, clumpy mascaraed eyes made a silent but lethal statement that Jesta and I should be working instead of talking, and with such vulgar language at that.

"What's up her ass?" I quietly asked Jesta as we both moved away from the old hag.

"I don't know," Jesta grunted. "But I'll tell you what it's not—a big, fat, juicy cock." Jesta laughed as she made an obscene gesture with her hand, as if the man meat itself were in there.

"You're so gross." I laughed.

"Well, it's true." She laughed too. "A woman getting good dick doesn't go around scorning people."

I nodded in agreement. Although she could have found a better choice of words, Jesta had a point.

"Anyways…" She sighed. "All bullshit aside and going back to Chris, I just want to see you happy, babycakes. You know that."

This was Jesta's last day waitressing at Wick Oasis. I was going to miss her like crazy, because she was not only a genuinely good person but also a great friend.

"I am happy, J," I assured her with an unconvincing smile.

"No, you, my dear, are bitter," Jesta replied.

"Whatever. Help me with this table so we look like we're actually doing something instead of just talking before someone else feels the need to clear their throat."

"No shit, right?" she bemoaned.

As we gathered the plates and utensils from a table, we continued our little heart-to-heart.

"Look, Morgan, Christmas is right around the corner, and unless you still believe in Santa, you better expect that Christmas tree to be a few presents short. You're my best friend, and I love you to death. But I don't have a beard or a penis, so there's nothing I can do for you that you can't do for yourself. You're a young, gorgeous little thing, weird but gorgeous. And that ass!" She laughed as she gently groped my tush with a wink. Jesta paused for a moment and put her sass in the bag. "All I'm trying to say is that there is no reason a girl like you should be alone on Christmas day—or better yet, alone period."

I put my hands on her shoulders and pulled her toward me. "Well, lucky for me, I don't care for either a man's comfort or Christmas day. Look, I know you care, J, and it means a lot that you do; but I've done the whole dating thing, and guys these days are all the same: a bunch of spineless savages incapable of feeling a damn thing."

"Calm down, Ariel," she said with a groan.

I laughed at the fact that she caught my drift and then quickly continued with my feminist rant. "The truth is I'd much rather be content and alone than be miserable with some asshole who has me up all night tossing and turning, worried about his whereabouts. I don't know about you, but I kind of like the fact that I'm the only person I have to worry about."

Jesta rolled her eyes and sighed. "You are so annoying, but fine. Suit yourself. You're gonna end up all alone and bitter like that miserable old hag at that table, scorning and clearing your throat at young, pretty girls because they're still getting tons of dick while you're stuck with a cervix that backfires a cloud of dust every time you cough." She stopped and thought for a moment, adding, "Oh, and for the record, not every single guy is the same. And to be quite honest with you, if I was the one Chris was pursuing, I would have already been able to tell you how much that beard tickles. I mean sure, the guy's a complete asshole, but *woof*! Besides, it's not like he doesn't turn into a complete pussy whenever he comes around you."

"Jesta!" I made a show of looking around to remind her that we were surrounded by guests. I shook my head slightly in disbelief, trying to be serious. But before I knew it, we were both laughing like two silly, little high-school girls who accidently hit the hottest boy on varsity on the head with a volleyball in gym class.

Once Jesta was able to compose herself, she dried her joyful tears and continued with her little plea. "Just give him a chance. If it doesn't work out, at least you can say you tried."

As Jesta and I carried our bus tubs full of dirty dishes to the kitchen, we spotted Chris in the distance. He seemed to be having a very deep discussion with Liz. He must have heard the dishes in our tubs rattling, because for a moment he broke away from the conversation to look in our direction. When he saw that it was me, he smiled, and it was the nicest smile I had seen in a while.

"Aw, look at that smile." Jesta sighed. "I can tell he really does like you. There's no doubt about it." She then leaned in and whispered into my ear, "People can say what they want about him, but only the sweetest of guys will give a girl that kind of a smile any place, any time, without giving two shits if he comes across looking like a fool. Because even if he does, at least he knows it's for her."

I was going to miss Jesta so much. Her plane was leaving from Corpus Christi at five the next morning. She was heading off to a university in London to study medicine on a scholarship, lucky girl. There was no doubt in my mind that Jesta was bound for greatness. She knew what she wanted and wasn't afraid to go out and get it. I, on the other hand, am a twenty-five-year-old waitress with no plan to my name. It hasn't always been like this though. I once had big dreams of becoming a writer, one with hope, wisdom, and the slightest proof of magic. I dreamed of using my talent with words to share my experiences, showing others that love comes to those who wait. I believed with all my soul that our actions determined our fates and that we all ended up with the love we deserved. I wanted to travel the world, to experience it with my very own eyes, to live not just through the words of others but through words that were my own.

Sometimes it's hard to believe that only a few years ago, those dreams were still strong and well. And although they're gone, I've never blamed them for retreating. After all, you can't expect much to survive in the environment a lonely heart provides. What sucks the most is that everyone I now know seems to be getting married, starting a family, or receiving some sort of important work title. They all appear to have plans for their lives, and here I am pushing thirty, settling for serving tables and with no man, no degree, nor the slightest plan of action.

Once Wick Oasis was finally closed for the day, we all gathered in the center of the atrium to give Jesta our final farewells. We exchanged tears and words of wisdom, along with a few recollected memories that we'll surely never forget. As everyone took their turns giving Jesta their bests and good-byes, I stood off to the side, waiting to give my sayonara in seclusion. It's never easy saying good-bye to a good friend, and when it comes to crying in front of a group of people, I tend to get quite uncomfortable. Jesta and I headed out to the parking lot once everyone had cleared the atrium. As we walked toward Jesta's old Camry, I hooked my arm around hers and laid my head on her shoulder.

The weather in Texas never really gets very cool this time of year, but whenever we do get an occasional cold front, I get into this mood where everything around me makes me sad, such as crowded coffee shops, birds on power lines, even the mere thought of having to wear a sweater. Unfortunately, today was one of those days, and although it was only in the forties, just thinking of Jesta leaving was enough to break my vulnerable heart to pieces. Before I knew it, I lost my composure and began to sob like a child who had just lost her favorite doll. Jesta immediately hugged me and began to cry along with me.

There we stood, sobbing on each other's shoulders in the parking lot while the cold wind blew away all the things we came to know as two friends. And just as it rips the leaves off an autumn tree, it ripped one more friend away from me. After a while of crying, in the midst of nothing but our silent sobs, Jesta cleared her throat, forced a smile, and said, "You better call me every single day, OK?"

"Of course I will," I promised. "But I'm warning right now, if you ever forward any of my calls to voice mail, I will hunt you down and drag you all across campus by your pubes, ass naked! You hear me?"

Somehow we both managed to find the will, in such a bittersweet moment, to laugh through our snot. We dried our tears off and continued with our last face-to-face conversation while carefully leaning on the bumper of her car. Jesta raised her rosy-red nose up toward the pale, cloudless sky as she brushed an icy shiver from her body. "I can't even begin to tell you how much I am going to miss you." She sighed.

I laid my head on her shoulder again, pressing my cold left ear against the warmth of her polyester jacket, and softly whispered, "I can't believe you're actually leaving, and for London at that. Why couldn't you have just gone to a community college like every other normal human being?" I sorrowfully laughed. In the distance, soaring high in the colorless sky was a plane. And although it was awfully distant, it caught our eyes. "That'll be you tomorrow morning, baby girl: up above so high, sneaking away from a city that's sound asleep down below, out to fulfill your dreams while so many of us are only still envisioning ours. I am so proud of you, Jesta."

I could feel her staring at me but could not bring myself to look at her and continued to look up. She finally took her sights off me for a brief second to look at the plane too. After a while, she nudged me with her elbow and said, "Remember what I told you this morning. Promise me you won't turn into that miserable old hag, because there's no reason for a girl with your kind of soul to rot away in the arms of loneliness. You have a great guy right in front of you. Don't let him slip away, girlie. I know a good man when I see one, and I'll tell you what: that boy Chris is one in a million, a billion, a trillion."

I simply smiled. Although I wanted to, I couldn't promise her anything, for I didn't want to end such a sincere good-bye with a lie. She gave me one last hug, and her embrace alone could have defined the concept of bittersweet.

Jesta was one of a kind. In the last twenty-five years, I'd come across an assortment of people. I'd met the good and the bad. I'd raised a glass with the rich, and I'd danced with the poor. And in the midst of straddling the line dividing both worlds, I formed a sacred bond with the people who were fortunate enough to know the true meaning of struggle, because those were the people I could relate to; those were the people I understood. I knew why they did the horrible things they did, and I also knew that behind it all, they were simply trying to survive. Aside from teaching me how to pick a lock or steal a full case of beer, those were the people who taught me that the ugliest things in our lives are actually beautiful blessings in disguise. Even though I wasn't born into the beautiful life, I was never afraid of turning my life into something beautiful, because they were the courage that sustained me.

As I matured, I developed empathy and a thirst for the kind of people who had the power to turn molehills into mountains, people who were blessed with an instinctive ability to savor their rags as if they were riches. Because where I come from, it's not about how much you have; it's about who you have. You really learn to appreciate your life once you've been forced to pray to God for help. I've learned so much from the people I've met in my life.

I often wonder why the greatest people in my life have had to come and go, but I guess that's just the way the cookie crumbles. It wasn't only Jesta and a few high-school friends; there are hundreds of tracks in the dirt from the people who came into my life for a short period of time, only to provide their influence and then disappear. I'd be lying if I said this kind of life didn't make me sad. I feel cursed and aimless, like a Gypsy without a road. I can only hope that I have in some way served as an influence for others. But then again, you can never quench the thirst of a man who doesn't understand the full potential of his tongue.

As happy as I was for Jesta, I couldn't help but feel rather envious, envious that she still had her inspiration, whereas mine was long gone. I was gonna miss her, because with my luck, who knew if I'd ever see her again.

After my shift was over, I went home. Turning the key, I slowly opened the door.

"Home sweet home." I sighed. "Yeah, right."

When I walked into my apartment, a hint of cinnamon struck my nose. It was chilly, and all the lights were off. I put my keys and purse down on the kitchen counter. I don't like using much electricity, so I usually just open up the blinds and let the light of day in. After letting some light in my apartment, I jumped in the shower and washed off the toil of the day. I absolutely love how my skin smells like poppies after a hot shower. It's so invigorating.

Though I don't watch much television, I do have an eccentric habit of turning it on just for the sound. After all, they say that silence can drive a person absolutely insane, because it is in silence where we have the opportunity to analyze our darkest thoughts.

It gets pretty lonely around this memorabilia archive that I call my apartment, especially around dinnertime. Over the past few years, I've become sort of a health freak. Tonight I'm having baked salmon with a side salad. But in spite of my change of lifestyle, I just can't seem to give up my daily morning bagel topped with a thin layer of cream cheese.

I hate to admit it, but this is my life. I work, eat, and sleep. It's a routine, and it's always the same damn thing. What's worse is that it's my (unintentional) choice.

After dinner I usually make myself a cup of chai tea and head out to the balcony. I like to sit out there in the evenings and lose myself in the violet sky while I'm thinking of happier times. Have you ever just stared into the sky and allowed your thoughts to leave your body? If you haven't, you should try it, because it's actually very therapeutic. My thoughts mostly linger on those few seconds in life that I was never granted that could have changed everything.

It's crazy how fast the night sneaks up on you.

After my usual evening, I made my way to my room, where I pulled the sheets down and fluffed my pillows. I brushed my teeth and set my alarm for 4:35 a.m. I climbed into bed and pulled my diary out of the nightstand. She is my only friend outside Wicker's walls. In fact, our friendship just so happens to be the longest I've ever had. I tell her everything, because she listens without passing judgment, and her blank pages bring me release. She knows my past but never reminds me of it, unless I ask her to. Every night before I go to bed, I write. I jot down my quotes, my poems, and any other senseless thoughts that my mind comes across. I kept a regular diary since I was a little girl, but for the two years I was living back home in Raymondville, that came to a halt. When I moved back to Corpus, my father presented me with a brand-new diary as a gift. He hoped that it would be able to mend and reinspire me, but the sole purpose of his gift was just a reminder of why I was broken to begin with.

That night I wrote the following entry:

> Friday, December 6, 2013
> 9:55 p.m.
>
> Dear Diary,
>   Last night I dreamed that I was in the desert, and as I laid in the Sahara, I was

unable to move a single muscle. I then saw two seagulls soaring so high that envy smoldered in my eyes. They searched and searched for the sea but found nothing but grains of sand. As their thirst became greater, they soon realized that their only chance of survival was held in each other's company. They flew close to each other, so close that I knew it must be love, because I had no other explanation for what it was. When I attempted to join them, I realized that I was a prisoner held back by a pair of wings that had been clipped. In the midst of my struggle, the scorching sun tested me by calling out my name like a father does when guiding his child's first steps. I quickly gave up and settled back in the sand, feasting off the love the seagulls nurtured. As they soared, entwined, their rapture grew, and I saw truth being born for the first time in the summer's black-and-white sky.

They were two creatures in love in a cold world full of madness. They were two outlaws on the run, demanding freedom and adventure as their ransom. They were two unfortunate souls simply wanting a life together of both silver and gold; souls with a love as dangerous as a loaded gun in the hands of a child but as beautiful as a story waiting to be told for the first time.

I long for what they had, to come across my own summer's day, to have a taste of real life, real love, and all of the above. I want something so real that it can only be conceived by imagination and the make-believe. I want to feel alive and electrified by a simple sense of accomplishment until there is absolutely nothing left for me to desire. Above all, I want to be proven wrong, proven that even a shattered heart can be mended.

Good night,
Morgan

I turned off my lamp and let the darkness spread through my room like a plague. The city sounded so alive outside my window, and I could hear taxis blowing their horns, speeding midnight rendezvous, and the sound of police sirens howling through the night. The cars zooming by sounded like flies. The sound of Corpus Christi when darkness falls soothes me like a high dose of morphine, providing a slight wave of nirvana. The downy clouds scraping across the moon caused her to illuminate my room and then leave me in the dark. As I covered my cold body with my warm blanket, a wicked sense of solitude kicked in, and I started thinking about life. My life, to be exact.

I remembered when I turned eighteen. I thought I had my whole life figured out. I was so naive. But in all honesty, I'd give anything to be that naive again, because with innocence comes the power of belief. It's strange how things were so much easier to believe in then than they are now. I guess as you get older, you realize that it's one thing to believe in something and another to believe in yourself. I never had a plan. I simply relied on the magic that came with hope. I thought everything would fall into place, and in the beginning it kind of did. Without looking for it, I met the man of my dreams, and we fell in love. In fact, I fell in love so suddenly that I often wondered why people said love takes a lifetime to find.

Ever since I met him, I've never loved anyone in the same way or as powerfully. I saw my life as a glass that was half full, because the hard part was over. I was able to scratch "passion" off my list and focus on my ambitions. I began to push myself to become the writer I knew I could be, and with him as my muse, I felt indestructible. But in life nothing is certain. Life never hands you something without a price.

When I was younger, I constantly found myself wishing I were older so that I could enjoy life's advantages. But now that I'm getting older, I'm constantly wishing I were younger so that I could enjoy life's disadvantages. Since then, my dreams have become old legends, and love has become a myth.

I know that I said I didn't need a man, that I would be just fine on my own, but that's the kind of bullshit I like to hear myself say when I know I'm in denial. God Himself created two humans so that no one would be alone. The truth is I don't like being alone. It terrifies me, because when I'm alone, I dwell on the impression that my life will always simply be a routine, even as the years go by. There are often times when I feel as lonely as Norma Jean herself, completely hopeless and abandoned.

The thought of growing old is a force in itself, but I have come to terms with it. I know I'll be more than fine when my jokes start losing their shine and my charm starts losing its color, as long as I have someone unusual by my side when I start going through that metamorphosis.

My real problem is that I've shut out the whole idea of love, because I'm a girl with a broken heart who is stuck in the twenty-first century. Men have turned into nothing more than sexual savages. I'd be better off throwing myself into a lion's den than counting on a man to mend my wounds. I know it's the coward's way out, but you can only convince yourself for so long that you'll find love, until you realize it's best to leave it in the hands of God.

As my eyelids began to sink like two wounded pirate ships, I was sucked into a state of idle and pleasant contemplation that delivered my mind from its self-inflicted war. I slowly drifted away to the land where dreams are heavy and unsystematic.

Ring! Ring! Ring!

The sound of my alarm caused me to wake up feeling both startled and confused. It felt like I had just closed my eyes, and yet another day had come. As I reached for the snooze button, I looked at the time on the clock: 6:00 a.m. "Shit! I'm late! I'm very, very late!" I shouted. I rushed out of bed and threw on my hideous work uniform. I tied my hair back, grabbed my keys, and headed out the door. I could have sworn that I had set my alarm for 4:35 a.m. I couldn't help but think that something very strange was going on.

The fog outside was thick and opaque. There was no sign of life. There were no birds singing, no other engines running but mine. Corpus Christi looked like a ghost town, one that had been deserted after a nuclear disaster. I used my headlights to cut through the eerie fog. When I turned on the radio, the only thing playing on every single station was static.

I finally pulled up to the Wicker Palace, and I was shocked to see that the parking lot was completely empty. The old hotel is always a mad house.

"OK, something is definitely wrong," I muttered to myself.

When I walked into the lobby, I saw Michael throwing papers everywhere, like a madman looking for sanity. He seemed a bit hyped up and looked rather nervous.

"Michael, is everything OK?" I asked nervously.

He looked up at me, an indulgent gleam in his eyes. "Ah, Morgan, you're finally here!" he shouted. "A little late, but even that's better than never." He chuckled.

"Yeah, I'm sorry," I said, frowning in shame. "I had a bit of a problem with my alarm this morning."

He gave me a creepy smile and continued to ramble. "Anywho, I was given specific orders to inform you that even though the house is without guests, the house shall not rest. There is a mess waiting for you in the atrium. You will not be allowed to leave today until everything is situated. The mess is more than meets the eye. The task is more than a simple spot shine. But I assure you, everything you need will be provided to you; and before you know it, you'll be free to go home."

I gave him a funny look and then, half asleep, slowly made my way to the atrium, dragging my feet. The old building was dim and awfully cold. When I got to the atrium, I could not believe my eyes. Wick Oasis had been completely stripped. All the tables and chairs were gone, along with the menus, the silverware, even the coffeepots. I thought, *This has to be some sort of joke.* I stood grinning in the center of the atrium, waiting for the punch line, but no one came out and owned up to it. Suddenly a napkin fell from above and gently brushed my shoulder. When I looked up to see where the napkin had come from, I gasped. "You have got to be kidding me!"

The entire restaurant was turned upside down, with all the tables, chairs, and settings neatly hanging from the ceiling.

Freaking out, I ran back to the front desk, but when I got there, Michael was nowhere in sight. I shouted for him repeatedly but failed to get a response.

2

JOE AND JUDY

Bam! Crash! Loud sounds came from the kitchen. I dashed back into the atrium and pushed myself through the kitchen door.

"Oh shit!" I shouted as I ducked, dodging a plate that had been seconds from flying into my face. As I slowly removed my arms from shielding my face, I spotted the source of the commotion. Joe was in the kitchen throwing dishes left and right. He looked like a homeless person digging for food in a pile of garbage, and he was not alone. Judy was also there, sitting on one of the kitchen counters and laughing hysterically—and insanely.

"What the hell are you two doing?" I asked, raising my voice enough to get their attention.

Joe looked at me and smiled viciously. "We are looking for a map…Or was it a pot? Or a hat?"

Judy's laugh sounded exhilarated.

"You two have gone mad!" I shrieked, but they were tweaking so hard that they paid no attention to my remark. Instead, Joe passed Judy a large tray of teacups, and one by one, she began launching them into the wall.

"Stop!" I shouted. They immediately stood still. It was as if a sheet of silence had been laid across the room. I licked my lips and altered my tone. Looking directly at both of them, I said, "There is something very strange going on around here. And although I can't quite explain it or put my finger on it, something vile is lurking in the air."

Judy jumped off the kitchen counter and walked toward me. She tucked my loose bangs behind my ear and with an evil grin said, "You haven't seen anything yet, princess."

She went from being dead serious to chuckling again immediately, while Joe continued to break dishes. It was incredible how many more dishes he had left to break—it looked as though he had already broken hundreds.

"Oh, Morgan, did you see it?" Judy asked as she watched Joe. "Isn't it beautiful?" She sighed.

I knew exactly what she was referring to. "The shit hanging from the ceiling?" I asked, making a mockery of the question. "Judy, how am I supposed to get that down?" I whined. "I don't even know how ya'll managed to get all that shit up there."

Joe giggled and said, "It wasn't us, silly. It was you!"

Judy turned to me slowly and quietly, her eyes wide and her lips quivering as she tried to resist the one thing that now seemed as involuntary to her as breathing. And although she tried and tried, even the most trustworthy lips can fold under pressure. Soon she was curled on the floor, cackling like a psychotic hyena infected with rabies.

"Me?" I disregarded Judy's hysteria, looking at Joe in complete confusion. "When I got here, all that shit was already up there. How could it have been me?" I was utterly annoyed now.

Joe stopped dead. He looked at Judy and then looked back at me. "You know what, you got a point," he said. Then he immediately continued digging in the cupboards, carelessly throwing pots and dishes in my direction. "Ah, I found it!" he shouted. "Here it is! The map."

Joe handed me what seemed to be a distressed piece of paper. When I saw what it actually was, a sad sense of nostalgia struck me to the core.

"Joe, this isn't a map." I sighed in a low, doleful tone. "This is just an old picture of me when I was a child."

He looked at me as if I were the one acting crazy. "That's where you're wrong," he said. "It is a map, just not the entire map. For this is merely the starting point."

"The starting point to what?" I asked.

Joe looked at Judy as if he didn't have a response for me. Judy then looked into my eyes and softly smiled. Her smile always put me at ease. Sometimes I even referred to her smile as the sunrise of the Wicker Palace, because the equanimity that came with it was truly God-given.

"You have a lot of rearranging to do, and it must be done now before it's too late," she said.

"What are you talking about?"

"Your life, pretty girl. It's a mess. A big, big mess."

By the tone of her voice, I could tell she was back to her normal self. "What do you mean?" I asked her, even though I was already holding the knowledge in the palm of my hand.

"Come on. We both know that you aren't as put together as that pretty little smile makes you out to be. The sooner you can accept that fact, the sooner you will be able to move along on your little journey."

"Journey?"

"Yes," Judy replied. "Why else would you be here?"

I quickly responded with a loaded tongue. "Well, being that this is where I work, I'd say for work." I sniggered.

"Don't ever lower the standards of your words by giving them to a dumb mouth. After all, no matter how smart an ass is, you'll only end up sitting on it," she said, firmly crossing her arms in front of her as she scowled at me with her big, brown eyes.

"Oh my God." I sighed, completely mortified by her ruthless comment. "I was just kidding."

"Well then, shall we proceed?"

Judy was obviously irritated. I smiled at her sheepishly until her grimace turned into the smile I knew she couldn't keep from me.

"A great journey awaits you," she said. "And like all great journeys, you will face trials and tribulations." She took the picture from my hand and held it up to my face. "It is a journey you must complete in order to find this child's long-lost faith. Your body, mind, and soul will be challenged. You will be reminded of things you'd much rather forget, because even though you'd much rather forget such things, you must face your past in order to give a face to your future."

Suddenly Joe's voice came in from the distance, catching me off guard. "You have given up on way too much," he said. "Losing hope in love alone is already too much to count for as loss, but you, Morgan, have counted both your love and self-belief as losses. And when those two things are counted as losses, loss stops being a matter of privation and starts becoming a matter of defeat. Because although losing hope in love is understandable, believing in yourself should be like a war in which you never cease fire until death sucks the life from your lips. For if a man does not believe in himself, then he is a man with a heart as useless as a moon during the day."

Joe began smacking his lips together like an old man suffering from dry mouth. He continued to do so for a few more awkward seconds, and when he finally stopped, he eagerly look at me and said, "Being so, you will not be allowed to leave this place until you are able to let go of all the things holding you back from the person you were meant to be." He turned to Judy and began to chuckle. Before I knew it, they were both on the ground laughing in hysteria. Their laughs grew louder and louder and took on a sense of wickedness.

It frightened me so much that I ran out of the kitchen. I felt like prey running from a predator.

"This is just a dream, a crazy, crazy dream. I'll wake up eventually," I muttered to myself.

As I reached the lobby, I saw that a wall had gone up where the entrance used to be. *I'm trapped*, I thought. There was a wall in place of every single door leading in and out of the hotel.

I dragged myself back to the atrium. When I got to the center, I sat down on the floor. I began to pinch myself and blink my eyes repeatedly, but it wasn't helping.

"This has to be a dream," I said, feeling a slight sense of panic.

Then a familiar voice pierced the silence.

"That's not gonna help." It was Joe. "I already told you; you're not going anywhere until you get your shit together."

Joe and Judy made their way to where I was and sat down beside me.

Joe has always been a jokester, but even he knows that every joke must come to an end. After all, what's the point if there's no punch line? I've known Joe to have only two faces, one that is animated and one that is much more serious. And although he rarely uses the much more serious one, when he does, he is usually playing psychologist, giving advice about real life. It was that very face that he had on at that moment.

"Morgan," he said, "you are a very special girl, but as special as you are, you are also very, very lost."

"I guess you can say that," I mumbled.

"I've been told you once had big dreams." His eyes drifted off into the distance.

"Once…"

He continued, "I've also been told that your ambition at one point was even bigger than those dreams."

"Looks like you've been talking to someone who thinks they knew me," I sharply replied. His words left a bad taste in my mouth.

"What in God's name happened to you? Why did you give up on all those dreams? Was it because of *him*?" Joe asked.

"I do not want to talk about *him*!" I shouted, lashing out at him in a way I never had before.

Joe didn't say anything. He simply hung his head in humiliation. I felt so bad for yelling at him, but this was a subject no one was going to touch. Judy cleared her throat to break the awkward silence. Her sad eyes made me feel naked, because I felt like my pain had completely exposed itself to her. I turned to Joe with tears in my eyes and trembling lips and said, "I am so sorry. I didn't mean to be ugly. I'm just not prepared for all of this."

"It's OK, princess." He smiled softly. "It's OK."

Judy reached out to dry my tears, and as she gently wiped her warm hand across my face, she said, "Life has been hard on you, but in the eyes of a stranger, you'd pass for the happiest girl in the world. You are so beautiful and so graceful that no one would ever guess what you have been through, but it doesn't have to be this way. You've still got your whole life ahead of you. It's not too late to take charge of your destiny. You have a natural ability to shepherd words. Anyone can tell a story, but very few can tell a great story. And you have the gift of the few. A gift like yours should be shared with the world, because there might be someone out there who needs to hear your words of encouragement. Morgan, some people rely on the hope that words provide to them, because sometimes words can be so powerful that they permit people to escape their realities."

She paused and looked around the shadowy hotel. I could tell she was carefully sorting through the words in her head, trying to find the right way to ask the inevitable. After a brief silence she finally proceeded. "Morgan, the love that you mention in your writings is so precise that I cannot help but ask, who was he?"

"Please, I don't want to talk about it," I mumbled. I had no emotion in my soul and no desire to discuss my past with people who were only familiar with my present, because even if their ears would be able to serve me any use, their hearts would never be able to understand.

Joe raised his eyebrows and nodded. "The biggest mistake people make is believing that if they simply ignore something, it'll eventually go away. It doesn't go away; it becomes dormant. Sooner or later it will resurface. You can keep it bottled up inside, but at some point it will start scratching its way out, and when it does, it'll be against your will. Not only can the loose ends of your past destroy you; they can keep you from all the things your heart truly desires."

Judy stood up from the ground and extended her hand to me. I gently placed my hand inside hers, clutching it as she pulled me up from the ground. She then began slowly twirling like a ballerina inside a musical box, her eyes seemingly feasting on every detail that made the Wicker Palace so grand. After rotating several times, she finally stopped, and with a hopeful sigh, she said, "Facing our fears is never easy, but it's the only way to maintain our authority. Change always begins with baby steps, but only you can choose whether or not to take them. You don't have much time, because, yes, eventually you will wake up from this dream. So take action, because now is the only time you will be able to choose your fate of your own free will. You can stay here, lingering around the atrium until you wake up, and then simply go back to your life of solitude, or you can accept your quest and move forward toward a dignified life.

"Oh, and Morgan," she added, "if you do choose to accept this quest, keep in mind that this place represents you in so many ways." She giggled. "Just be careful what doors you open around here. These doors don't lead to your average custodial storage closets."

With that, Judy took the photograph from my hand and shoved it into my pocket. She faced me toward the lobby and gave me a little nudge. "Go. You haven't got much time," she said.

I looked up to the second and third floors. I had never noticed how gargantuan the hotel was until now. When I turned around to ask her and Joe where I should start, they both had vanished.

The hotel was dim. It looked haunted, haunted by the ghost of a tormented soul who was both withered and resentful. This Wicker Palace is so old that it has several books on its history. It's hard to believe how beautiful it used to be.

I walked to a bench near our infamous fountain and sat down with my nomadic thoughts. The hotel was so quiet, the only sound the scummy water flowing from the fountain's crows. I reached into my pocket to retrieve the photo Joe had referred to as a map. It was an old picture taken around Christmastime many years ago. I must have been about eight years old. In the picture I was sitting on my mother's lap, holding my favorite doll as my mother read me a book by Hans Christian Andersen. She was reading my favorite fairy tale, the one about a little mermaid.

I know it might sound crazy, but just looking at that old picture bombarded my senses with childhood memories of what Christmas used to be, once upon a time. I could *taste* the candy canes my father would hand out to the congregation after our church plays. I could *feel* the cold winter wind sneaking in through the cracks of the first home I ever knew as my grandpa and grandma's. I could *hear* "O Little Town of Bethlehem" playing on the musical lights as the midnight train drives by. I could *smell* the burn of an old electric heater warming up on the corner of Canal Street. And I could *see* the difference between the Christmases then and the ones now. I could see myself at Christmas.

Late December always gets the best of me. There is so much joy and hope dangled on the idea of Christmas, but a broken heart often refrains from peace and goodwill. As I walk down the winter streets at Christmastime, no warmth or feeling in my fingertips, I wish on the merriest of songs to grant me spare lips to share the candy cane I will falsely accuse of being impossible to finish. Yet I am left to wander alone as the bells ring silver and gold. Those bells always remind me of home. Where the stars burn their brightest on Vincent's Avenue. Where my cousins and I would tell scary ghost stories or play Cowboys and Indians when things got too boring. They say snow only falls outside happy windows and spreads out, taking the thorns from the roses.

My future looks like someone's past, and my present feels more like a debt than a second chance.

Our dreams are always polished for us when we are children, but once our features have matured, the polishing stops. We are stripped of our shine and left only a brush of the finest horsehair to keep those dreams from tarnishing. I have lost my innocence, and I have gained limitations. Time is no longer my peace, because it is my only war. Silence is not my cure. She is a disease that revels with all her friends.

Tick—you have stolen my shield and armor. *Tock*—you have taken my kingdom and my honor, along with everything I've come to know. Oh, I say that my life's clock *ticktocks* with an impetuous melancholy. *Ticktock*. In twenty-five years I have never heard it so clear. *Ticktock*—I am forced to take one step back for every minute that moves forward.

Way before my first kiss, my first sexual encounter, and my first party, I knew a girl whose heart sparkled with radiant iridescences like a crystal prism. Her hazel eyes were both young and full of innocence. She grew and grew, but she never knew what life would put her through. Then love came, with green eyes and a cigarette in his mouth. She cried for eight months for the taste of ash she'd never forget about. One, two, three years have passed, and now that I am older, I am a stranger to myself. I've lost my shine like a fading fabric and sold my heart of gold for one of plastic. *Ticktock, ticktock.* The sound hits me harder than a shot of liquor. *Ticktock, ticktock.* As I stand in front of the mirror, I see a girl who misses everything she used to be.

***

"Why is this happening to me?" I sighed and then began tracing my eyes along the black trim fencing the edges of the floors. I looked up. Above me, statues of daunting, vicious-looking gargoyles peered down. Suddenly I noticed a light coming from the door of the banquet room on the third floor. The door was slightly open.

I wonder if someone is up there.

I ran to the nearest elevator and repeatedly pressed its button, impatiently waiting for the doors to open. When they finally did, there was no cab, just the open shaft with hanging cables. *You have got to be kidding me!* I ran to check the other elevator in front of the hotel, and it was the same thing: no cab.

After having no luck with the two elevators at the back of the hotel as well, it finally clicked: *The stairs!* But even the door leading up the stairwell was sealed shut.

Suddenly a loud crash came from the third floor. It was the sound of broken glass—a liquor bottle, perhaps?

"Someone's up there. I just know it!" I mumbled to myself.

I ran back to the elevator I had originally tried, and when the doors opened, I grabbed the cables and began to pull myself up. I could feel the cables burning and chafing my hands, but I kept pulling myself up. When I finally got to the third floor, the elevator doors were already wide open. I carefully climbed out and immediately tended to my hands, which were sore and red. I had no idea who could be up there, so I began calling out for Michael, Joe, and Judy.

3

KIM

I was in such a hurry to find some company that I almost foolishly charged through the banquet door. It wasn't until I placed my hand on the doorknob that I remembered what Judy said: Be careful what doors you open around here.

Cautiously, I pushed the banquet-room door open. Its screeching sound sent chills down my spine. As I walked further into the room, I found myself with a bad feeling, and I knew then that whatever lurked ahead would be no bed of roses. Thus, I continued on with my guard up, quietly walking toward the back of the room.

The banquet room is divided into three compartments. The first section of the banquet room is basically used for storage. All our spare chairs and tables are kept there in case the hotel's occupancy ever catches us by surprise. The following section of the banquet room is filled with decorations from past parties that may come in handy for future festivities. Last and most important, the third section at the back of the banquet room is where we set up all the catered food when the ballroom is in use. It also happens to also be where the hotel's entire liquor supply is stored.

There is a side door located in the back of the banquet room that is designed for the private use of employees to enter and exit the ballroom during an event. Our ballroom is absolutely breathtaking. It looks like an authentic ballroom that you would find in an actual palace. Patrons use the ballroom for a variety of celebrations, such as birthday parties, wedding receptions, and dinners honoring anniversaries.

When I finally managed to get to the back of the banquet room, I heard the sound of crashing glass once more, but this time it came from inside the ballroom. My mind was telling me to run the other way, but my heart was daring me to be curious. I decided to listen to my heart for a change and pushed my way through the swinging side door that led into the ballroom.

I could not believe my eyes. The ballroom was no longer fit for a king but rather fit for a prisoner. Although it was cold and damp, it resembled the tales of Hades, a living hell, for the room looked like a dungeon in the castle of an evil king. It was dim and awash in dark colors. The smell of death in the air reeked, and the presence of loneliness weighed down my shoulders and attacked my soul. In the center of the room ran a long table in front of what seemed to be five afflicted ghosts. Seated in the master's chair at the center was the owner of the most perfect set of tits, Ms. Kim herself. On the table in front of her were bottles of liquor. Some were full, some were empty, and some were filled halfway, but none were alike in shape or size.

"Kim, what is this place?" I asked. I attempted to keep my voice from trembling, but it was impossible, because the truth was I was scared shitless.

Her eyes were dilated, and her pale, lifeless-looking skin was damp with a light layer of sweat. "You would not believe the day I've had." She hiccupped. "I don't know about you, but I could sure use a shot right about now." She smiled mischievously, her eyes venomous. "I've got rum, tequila, and whatever was in this empty bottle," she said, completely avoiding my question.

"No, thank you," I replied. "My lack of judgment seems to be doing just fine on its own. Kim, are you drunk?" I asked politely, though it was clear she was intoxicated.

Her giggles started off soft and playful and then broke out into hysteria. She wiped the drool off her mouth "No. How dare you accuse me of such a thing in front of all my friends? I'm fine," she slurred. "Really, I'm fine, because even if drinking can't bring you happiness, it sure does kill the pain." Her speech was completely distorted, and her composure was out the window. "Come sit next to me!" she shouted so loudly that it startled me.

I gave her a little wave, implying that I was just fine where I was standing. "Kim, can you help me get back home?" I asked.

She looked at me. Her mascara was running down her face. She said, "Home? What's a home when you've got no one to remind you that their love is the reason that your house is a home? Just stay here with us and drink." She smirked. "Yes, drink until you forget what a home is. Drink until you forget what it feels like, what it smells like, along with all the other little things that make it sweet. Blur out reality and feast on fantasy."

The scene at the table looked like a tea party that had gone terribly wrong. The five women, including Kim, carried heavy burdens that seemed to be the life source of the energy in the atmosphere. Each woman symbolized a trait that was visibly reflected onto her, and each had specific objects in front of her that represented her punishment, her curse, her affliction.

On the right side of Kim were two women. The first was beautiful, and she was exposing enough cleavage to make a mammographer blush. Her candy-red dress was so tight and revealing that it left nothing to the imagination. She ran a cube of ice across her bloodred-stained pout. She was hot as hell, but her eyes had no soul.

Kim's maleficent voice broke through the trance the woman in red had possessed me with. "Oh my," she said, "where on earth are my manners?" She turned to the women in red and said, "Morgan, this is my dearest friend, Lust. Isn't she lovely?"

"Charmed, I'm sure," I sarcastically replied.

"Now, now, Morgan, there's no need to be a bitch." Kim chuckled. "She's actually quite sweet once you get to know her. In fact, this little critter right here is quite fascinating, because, like a parasite, she lives off men, quenching her hunger with mere pleasure while remaining completely starved of affection. She has ruined the lives of many men with her malicious and manipulative ways, sullying their virtues with her salacious nature while condemning many more to their graves with countless plagues, such as disease and fatal vengeance, that abide within her loins. Sometimes it's hard to believe that once upon a time, she was just as sweet as you."

"What happened to her?" I asked.

"Men. Every man she ever loved merely saw her as an object. She gave herself, heart, body, mind, and soul, to each and every one of them. But in the end, when the time would come to reap some sort of reward for her time invested, each man left, taking his promises and leaving his false illusions, which cruelly held sentimental value. Maturing, each embarked on a journey to seek out his unicorn, his prized possession: the virgin every man secretly dreams of making a wife." She chuckled. "After all, it's hard to be the proud owner of something used."

Kim began to laugh harder. "Men are funny that way. They can fuck as many women as they want, but Lord forbid they ever end up with a woman who has the same number of casual encounters as they do. But those are the laws of physics. A man can be tainted, but women must be chaste." She sighed.

"After so many disappointments, one day the feeling of neglect broke Lust's heart, and she was not able to reassemble it. If you were to ask her what love is, she wouldn't have the slightest clue, because her knowledge of love was taken the night she offered Satan her loyalty for insensibility. She has no recollection of love. It's almost as if it never existed. And so now there is a hole that exists in her soul that she cannot fill, not even when the company of a man is well present between her legs. Night after night, man after man, there is an emptiness dwelling inside her that she cannot understand, for she has forgotten the essence of that emptiness."

As Kim talked, I could not take my eyes off Lust. She was such a vision, more beautiful than Aphrodite herself, or so I thought. Then suddenly she began to flicker like a hologram, presenting me with the opportunity to see her true form. She was rotten, dead, and ruined from the men who used her like a druggie uses a syringe, only to inject his fix, leaving her afterward without a drop of love, the men who left her without a taste of their slightest affections. She had been condemned to live a life without ever again knowing what it's like to feel cared for or loved. It was clear the only thing she would ever be able to grasp was the mere sensation of a cold and heartless penetration.

In front of her on the table were mounds of makeup, ashes, and cigarettes.

Beside Lust sat a woman dressed completely in black. She wore a veil that ran from the top of her head to the soles of her feet. Her tears, visible through the gauzy veil, were as black as ink and as constant as a leaking faucet. As they trailed down her pale cheeks, they left behind a coal-colored residue that resembled running mascara. She did not blink or speak. She did not even whimper. However, every time one of her tears hit the ground, horrific screams rang out from them and echoed through the room. The sound was bone chilling. A thin layer of fog surrounded her like she was a tombstone in a cemetery on a cold, moonless night. Draped in front of her was a thicker layer of fog that hung from the table like a grimy, downy tablecloth.

Before I could even ask who the woman was, Kim proceeded with her introduction. "My dear," she said, "this is Loneliness. Her biggest mistake was falling in love with a very, very bad man."

"What made him a bad man?" I asked.

"Infidelity."

"It happens." I was being realistic.

"Yes, it does," Kim agreed, piercing me with a sharp, scornful look. "However, not everyone concedes the way she did. Not one of his infidelities was with the same woman, but Loneliness forgave him every single time, no matter the tale, because deep down inside she felt that was the kind of love she deserved."

"Nobody deserves that kind of love. Why, in fact, that isn't love at all." I looked over at Loneliness. "When someone truly loves you, their thoughts are too consumed by you to have room for another," I told her.

"Well"—Kim grinned—"he may not have loved her, but she sure as hell loved him. Because even though he constantly came home covered in another woman's filth, she forgave him."

"How can someone keep forgiving somebody who chooses to be a constant disappointment?" I asked Kim.

She began to laugh. "It's the oldest story in the book, sister. The world is full of stupid women who think they've got the juju to turn a bad boy into a faithful husband. And what's sad is that some women die trying to prove that point to themselves, while the other half are left for dead by the men. In the end, they both eat shit, because the truth is you can't change a bad man. A bad man changes when he decides to change, not when you expect him to."

"So how did her story end?" I asked.

Kim sighed. "Well, one day in the midst of one of his infidelities, he fell in love. He ran off with his mistress and became a new man, the man Loneliness had always wanted him to be. She wondered every minute of every hour why he could never change for her after all the years she stood by his side while constantly blaming herself for his absence. He eventually remarried, popped out a few kids, and lived happy ever after with his new family."

"That's so sad."

Kim nodded in agreement. "Her heartache was so immense that she felt as though if she didn't remove her heart, she would surely die. One night while drowning in her sorrow, she decided to take matters into her own hands by summoning a crossroads demon by the name of Jaberiasu, keeper of contracts, and bargained for a favor. The demon agreed to remove her heart for the simple price of his custody over her soul. She thought she would be able to cheat the wrath of her one-sided love; but her actions had even greater consequences, for she was cursed with eternal loneliness."

Sitting at the table opposite Kim was an elderly woman with patchy hair and rotten teeth. Her eyes appeared to be as frozen as a lake in mid-December. And just like Loneliness, she too did not bat an eye; she simply carried the burden of a blank stare. I could tell that she was in deep thought and that whatever she was thinking of appeared to inflict a great sadness on her.

"My name is Regret," she said. Like a prisoner of a trance, she was unable to direct her eyes onto me. "I regret what could have been, because it should have been."

"If it should've been, why wasn't it?" I asked.

"Because," she said in a slithery, sibilant voice, "I lived my whole life satisfying the people around me, living by their choices, by their regulations, instead of following my heart and creating my own destiny."

"So you regret not following your heart?"

"No, I regret not using my voice."

"I don't understand."

She clamped her lips together like a snapping turtle, nearly causing me to piss myself, and said, "I was never able to use my heart because I chose to never use my voice."

"Who was he?" I asked.

"His name was Elijah."

"Did you love him?"

"Yes, and he loved me too." She sighed. "But my father was a man of greed, and my mother was a woman of pride. When they found out about Elijah, I was forbidden to ever see him again. They called him a thug, a street rat. They frowned upon him in disgust because he came from a family of peasants." Regret began sobbing hysterically. "I know he didn't have much, but his love was more than enough. And what kills me is that I had the chance, the chance to run away with him, the chance to live the life I wanted to live, but I chose to continue being a puppet on a string."

She paused, took a deep breath, and continued. "Eventually, my father made arrangements for me to marry a man who could afford me but could never love me. In fact, every time he beat me, I'd block out the pain by thinking of the life I could have had with Elijah. I died having spent my entire life in love with another man, wondering day after day what had become of him."

Various clocks were laid out on the table before her. Every *tick* reminded her of the man she loved but never belonged to, she said. Every *tock* brought her visions of the many ways he smiled, the shape of his eyes, and the way he smelled the day she said good-bye.

The last woman at the table was a corpse. She wore a velvet dress fit for a princess waiting to be charmed by a prince. Both of her wrists were bound by metal cuffs, and each cuff was connected to a monstrous chain that dragged across the table in front of her. I was so confused, as I could not figure out what she represented, and it didn't help that she wasn't alive for me to ask.

Kim's demonic laugh sent chills running down my spine. "Oh, I'm sorry. Please excuse her, my dear. She really doesn't say much. Some call it being bashful. I call it dead silence." She raised her voice so loud it echoed. "Her name is Failure!"

The whole room trembled. Kim immediately put her finger to her mouth and began to shush herself. She began looking over her shoulder and mumbling to herself like a schizophrenic. She looked horrified. Whatever was lurking in the shadows behind her terrified her.

"What's the matter?" I asked.

She began to giggle. She then pointed to the shadows behind her and said, "Look closer."

As I squinted into the darkness, the shadows became as clear as day. Two large men stood side by side, crossing their pitchforks. They looked like barbaric guards. Their flesh was transparent; every artery, organ, and bone was visible. Their skeletons appeared to be glowing in the darkness, which made them look like look ghouls that had ascended from the darkest dimensions of hell. As I looked at them, they stared back at me with tortured eyes. And before I could turn away, they redirected their eyes up at the wall behind them.

When I saw the object of the ghouls' fascination, I gasped. A demon of colossal measure was latched onto the wall behind the ghouls. The demon had the body of a dragon and the face of a disfigured bull. Its horns were similar to a ram's, and its wings were torn and severely burned. Its scales were as dark as tar, and its veins burned through its flesh like lava. The demon appeared to be in a deep slumber.

I quietly took a few steps back and prepared myself to run out the door.

"Leaving so soon?" whispered Kim.

I asked her why that demon inhabited the room. She grinned and replied, "That beautiful monster is Hate incarnate, and we are his prisoners. Those other two ghouls on guard are just his minions, Anger and Despair. Hate has condemned us to wither away in his chamber for all of eternity. But although it may be too late for us, there is still hope for you. Hate is a powerful force that mimics Love in so many ways. Whereas Love nurtures through joy, peace, and hope, Hate festers through anger, despair, and loneliness. Hate has a legion of allies that all serve a greater supremacy: Death. Death is a demon of the highest rank. He is privileged because he is favored. He is seated at the right-hand side of Lucifer, while Destruction sits at the other. You see, Morgan, Hate automatically seals the gaps in our lives that we do not allow Love to fill. Eventually you are consumed by one more than the other, and, well, you are what you eat. After all, serving two gods is impractical, because there will always be one who is superior when it comes to being practical. So come now; take a seat. Because I assure you that the path you're on now will guarantee you residency at this table."

Kim began to laugh like a woman possessed by a legion of sinister spirits. Her laugh frightened me so immensely that I didn't hesitate to run out of the ballroom. I could still hear her laugh as I ran through the second passage in the banquet room.

As soon as I stepped outside the banquet room, all my fear immediately subsided. My pulse began to slow, and my skin, which I could see on my hands and arms had turned pale white, began to regain its color. Eventually my fear turned into curiosity, and I had the urge to continue wandering around the third floor. Walking down the third-floor hallway, I tapped the door handles on rooms 312 and 313, testing them as I walked by. My thoughts were consumed with the five women at the table. *Love and Hate: nonfiction or fable? Can I really become a prisoner of hate if I continue to deny myself love?*

Love—I've tried to find it, but looking for love is almost as crazy as looking for something mythical. Our world has become so corrupt that our punishment has been the extraction of the beautiful things we once had that come the closest to magic, such as love, peace, and hope. Love, an emotion felt by the human heart. The human heart, a vessel created to recognize nerves, fear, happiness, and sadness. Most important, it's a daily confirmation of life.

I know exactly what it feels like to be in love. When you're in love, your mind becomes irrational. When you're in love, you believe your biggest dream can come true. I knew that I had to change my perspective on life if I ever wanted to feel that kind of love again, but I was so attached to my past that the idea of change frightened me. We hyperbolize what we have and sell short its benefits. As we get older, we may find ourselves validating our broken behavior more than modifying it, but to change something or someone requires more than behavior modification. It requires wiping out an old belief system and retrofitting the mind with an entirely new subset of instructions and information.

The Wicker Palace was so dark and quiet. The four lampposts off the corners of Wick Oasis were the only lights burning through the darkness. The hotel felt so peaceful for the first time since I had arrived today, and my thoughts of the treachery ahead were at bay.

As I looked down from the third floor to Wick Oasis, a tear unwillingly sprung from my eye. I had shut love out to protect myself, but in reality I was only hurting myself. Just then I had a thought: *Is it not breath that gives us life? For I can deny and deny, but a heart without love is a heart occupying a body without life. What is life if you have no one to assure you that you are alive? Foolish is anyone without anybody, for we are all fickle minded without the assurance of somebody.*

4

TWENTY-FIVE

I have always seen my father as one of the few wise men left living in this ignorant world. He leads by example, striving and sacrificing to be a reflection of Christ, not for self-glorification but to demonstrate hope and kindness to the weary. You see, he is blessed with the ability to nurture a wounded soul with his words alone. In one of our recent conversations, we spoke of change, and he said, "Everyone wants change, but no one is willing to break old habits or accept the challenge of change. Change isn't given; it's conquered. The size of your risk determines the size of your victory."

Those words have haunted me ever since, because deep down inside, I felt those words were meant for me.

He was right, you know. We are so blinded by living solely in comfort that we don't seek change until we see the dead end ahead that turns our sanctuary into our threat.

Could this dream be my beginning? I wondered. If I could find the girl I once was somewhere at the end of the treacherous maze the hotel had become, then that was a risk I was willing to take. It was obvious that these rooms held so much more than just sinks and beds. But did I have to go through each one, turning doorknobs until my wrists were sore? How would I find what I was looking for?

I began to linger on the third floor to look for a sign of what direction I should take. I kept my eyes and ears open, but only silence roamed through the halls. Just before I lost all hope, I overheard a conversation somewhere in the distance. I was on the hunt. I began to press my ear against every suite door on the third floor. When I finally reached room 322, I clearly heard the voices that were carrying on the conversation. I opened the door, feeling like an anxious and impatient child, and found myself in Wick Oasis. However, this was not the Wick Oasis downstairs, the restaurant that I knew. This was the Wick Oasis of another time.

There was so much commotion in the atrium. People were talking, chewing, and laughing loudly. As I stood and inhaled the chaos polluting Wick Oasis, a woman's voice surfaced from behind me. "Excuse me, madam. May I have some more coffee, please?"

I then realized there was a coffeepot in my hand. I thought, *I must be on the clock*. I quickly poured the woman some more coffee and then immediately began to look for my girls. I scanned the entire atrium, searching for

Jesta, but she was nowhere to be found. After having no luck finding her, I began looking for Cleo and Emily, but not only were they also missing; two very young girls I had never seen before were attending to their sections. *Where are they?* I was on the verge of a meltdown until I saw some beautiful, long, brown hair I would recognize anywhere.

"Derya!" My cry was louder than expected, catching almost everyone's attention. Derya turned her head and looked at me with a smile. I rapidly made my way over to her. "Derya, I'm so glad to see you!" I felt on the edge of hysteria. "Have you seen Jesta, Emily, or Cleo? I've been looking for them everywhere, but I can't seem to find them."

She looked at me with an utterly confused expression as she picked a few plates up from one of her tables. "Are you high again?" she asked in disbelief. "You know it's been about five years since those girls have worked here." She raised her eyebrows, looking concerned. She turned around and faced me, and it was then that I saw her baby bump.

"You're pregnant?" I muttered.

"Yes, this will be my second little bunny-bear." She smiled briefly. "Morgan, what's with you today? You're scaring me."

Without responding, I took three steps back and then walked away. By the time I got back to my section, I felt completely exhausted, as if I had just participated in a triathlon. As I looked around the atrium, I noticed that the layout of the restaurant was totally different from what it had been just a few minutes ago. The fruit bar and the coffee station had been moved. All the napkins were a different color, and there was a new girl now working in Derya's section.

In the midst of my confusion, I heard a laugh that could only belong to one human being on Earth. "Judy…" I uttered.

I quickly made my way over to the kitchen window, and sure enough, there she was, along with the cause behind her hysterical laughter. However, there was something different about her; she looked much older and a bit worn out. Meanwhile, Joe's crow's feet had grown in length and depth, resembling cracks on the desert ground. They were also both sporting more grays than usual. As soon as Joe spotted me at the window, he shouted, "Hey, princess, are you hungry?"

"No, thank you." I shook my head. "Have you seen Derya?"

He laughed. "Um, yeah, sure…about six years ago."

I then realized that time was causing the bizarre changes in the restaurant. Eleven years had gone by in only a matter of minutes.

The chaotic crowd eventually cleared up once Wick Oasis was closed for breakfast. I returned to my section and did the only thing I could think to do. Carrying on with my routine, I wiped down my tables, refilled the sugar caddies, and swept. Once my section was sparkling clean, I took a seat at one of my tables and stared stonily at nothing. "Eleven years…" I whimpered. "This isn't how

I wanted to spend my life. How could I have done this to myself?"

My mind was at war with my soul. An angry mob began running through my veins while a revolutionary riot formed in the center of my heart. Anger, disappointment, and self-blame waged a battle inside me and were winning until a familiar voice silenced the gunfire. "Hey, stranger. Why so blue?"

Jesta pulled out a chair and sat across from me. The second my gaze fell on Jesta's face, a smile found its way back to my heart, and for a moment the storm had cleared. "Jesta!" I gasped. "You look great!" I smiled with relief. "Like wine, you only get better with time." The sight of her filled my heart with such delight. She was wearing a black cocktail dress, her hair was slicked back in a bun, and her heels acknowledged her wealth. She smiled and reached for my hand from across the table.

"How have you been, girlie?" she asked. "Gosh, it's been such a long time. I've missed you. I've missed this place." She looked around, marveling at the Wicker Palace. "You know, I constantly find myself reminiscing about all the crazy shit that went down in this place. Ugh, we were so young, and so bad!" She laughed. "Anyways, what's new with you? I want details!" she playfully shouted.

"Um, not much," I awkwardly answered. "Still stuck working here. What about you?"

She anxiously bit her lip. Then she sighed and said, "My God, where do I begin? Well, two years after I left Corpus, I got married to a fashion photographer by the name of

Harper Hunnam. I met him while I was in Paris. He's so great." She paused as the thought of him brought a smile to her face. "It was love at first sight," she softly whispered. "Anyway, photography is just a hobby he happened to pick up. He actually manages a very popular fashion magazine in Paris, which is where we also own a beautiful home." She giggled with pride and then quickly continued. "I got my MD, along with four kids after that! Ah, can you believe it? Three boys and one girl. My God, Morgan, I have such a busy life."

She rolled her eyes at the self-indulgence of her own words and then gently slammed her hands against the top of the table. "However," she continued, "I still managed to do all the traveling I had told you I wanted to do. Sunsets in Aruba, sunrises in Aussie, and quiet strolls in Barcelona. Girl, I have seen it all: Tokyo, Moscow, Saint-Tropez. Oh, and I also own property in California." As Jesta rambled on about her successes and achievements, my stomach began to sink. I wasn't sure, but she seemed to notice that I was beginning to feel uncomfortable, because she quickly stopped midsentence and said, "Anyways, enough about me. Let's talk about you." She smiled, and although her smile was boastful, it was also sincere. "Do you have a husband or any kids?" she asked.

I wanted to break down in tears, because I had no one; I had nothing. Instead I mustered the little pride I had left to answer her. "No. No husband. No kids." I gave a pained giggle.

She looked at me with a repulsive pity. "Oh." She sighed. "Well, I guess we aren't all suited for children." She began playing with her earring. "Anyway, I'm gonna go say hi to Joe and Judy. I'll be right back." She looked at me up and down as if I were the result of some sick tragedy, and then she stood up and walked away.

I waited a while for her to return, but when ten minutes turned into twenty, I realized she wasn't coming back. So I took it on myself to go look for her. As I walked over to the kitchen window, I felt as if I were carrying a load of bricks on my back that were causing my steps to drag against the dull marble tiles.

When I finally got to the kitchen window, I did not see Jesta, Joe, or Judy. In fact, the only person there was a young lady in a chef's hat who I had never seen before. She was quickly counting down her drawer as if she were ready to go home and anxious to clock out. As soon as she saw me pull up to the kitchen window, she smiled and said, "Well, hello there, Ms. Morgan."

Even though I had no idea who she was, she sure knew who I was. When I asked her where Joe and Judy were, her face dropped in sadness. "Morgan," she whispered tenderly, "Judy no longer works here. Remember? Her family came and took her with them upstate to take care of her. And Joe? Well, he passed away two years ago." She sighed, looking at me sympathetically.

I felt my heart break. "Joe…" My voice was strained.

Every minute since I had stepped in the restaurant had reaped a year, as if the years were being conceived by the second hand on a clock. I promptly excused myself from the young lady. I needed to clear my head. I needed to be alone. As I walked past the juice machine, I caught a glimpse of my reflection and fell straight to my knees in disbelief. I was an old woman. My hair was gray, my skin was spotted, and my hands were wrinkled. I began to cry, catching the attention of several guests that were lingering around the first floor.

My life was on the brink of its last chapter. *How did I allow myself to stay working here for all these years? Why didn't I chase my dreams? I was supposed to be somebody. I was supposed to see the world.* The pain that came with my disappointment was unbearable. It was pain that I would not wish on anyone. My whole life had passed me by, and there was no going back. I began to scream at the top of my lungs, and I lay down on the floor like an injured animal. "Somebody wake me up now!" I shouted. "Please, someone wake me up!"

A crowd of guests began to hover over me, and the louder I cried, the harder they laughed. I felt as if life itself were mocking me as the crowd pointed and stared. This wasn't just a dream but a nightmare conceived by my fear and my predicament. I placed my hands over my ears to block out the crowd's ridicule. As soon as I shut my eyes, silence filled the air.

Fearfully opening my eyes, I found myself back in room 322. I ran to the closest mirror in the suite and found such relief. I was young again. There were no age spots, grays, or wrinkles; I was simply twenty-five.

Twenty-five is the age when our insecurities take on lives of their own. It's the age where our ambitions either do or die. Twenty-five is the fork in the road that reminds us that not only is the future real; it is near. It is the age when our ignorance of success hunts our goals and accomplishments. Age may only be a number, but even a number has the power to persecute. As young adults, we are showcased to society to display our offerings and benefits. We are judged on our statuses and fortunes. At such a wise age, being a single female is frowned on, while being a single male is glorified. Becoming a spouse is the bread, and becoming a parent is the butter. At twenty-five, you are put under a microscope and dissected in order to distinguish who you are as a person. Twenty-five is pure madness, but it is beautiful while it lasts.

5

DOUBT

I sat down in a corner of the room and placed my head between my knees. My entire body was shaking from the nightmare I had just experienced within this dream. I tried to fill my mind with happy thoughts, but no matter how hard I tried, visions of myself as an old woman lurked in every one. There was no way I was going to allow that to happen to me. There was no way I could.

Just then, I heard what sounded like an ocean breeze, with crashing waves, and then a few seconds later, I actually felt the breeze brush against my skin. When I lifted my head, I rubbed my eyes in disbelief. I was sitting on the shore of a beautiful island that was bathed in moonlight. The grains of sand shimmered like pixie dust as the crashing waves echoed through the night like the long-lost song of a siren. The moon was full and almost too big for the sinister sky. A halo made of stardust twirled around her like the rings of Saturn, rejoicing in her splendor. The clouds haunted the firmament. They looked like maleficent ghosts, perhaps of great men who died at sea. The stars were few but enchanting, hand-cut diamonds crafted by God's proficient hands.

I had no idea where I was, but I knew this was not Earth, because a place as magical as this could only exist in a fairy tale. This was a land of wonder and pure imagination, of fantasy and myth. *This is what it must look like when heaven throws up*, I thought. I looked out into the unending sea, expecting to see a mermaid or a pirate ship, but neither of them appeared. However, a legion of curious pixies fluttered around me like seeds of a dandelion, illuminating me with their lavender light. I couldn't help but laugh as a few of them tickled my skin.

Suddenly clouds swept over the moon, and the entire island, including myself, was cast in shadow. I could feel a presence lurking nearby, and I knew the pixies felt it too, because they quickly flew away. As the clouds gradually cleared, I saw the presence in its true form. Although it was merely a shadow of a man, my heart knew that silhouette very well. I quickly got on my feet, but before I could reach out to him, the shadow turned into a beam of light and descended into the jungle that rested in middle of this mysterious island. I made my way to the jungle, pushing through branches before I could reach a clear trail.

The jungle was full of trees and wildflowers. Some flowers were the size of trees, and some trees were as small as flowers. I could sense a source of life flowing through the vines and soil in the jungle that welcomed my presence.

Lurking in the shadows were the most beautiful creatures ripped from the pages of mythology and medieval times. Unicorns gathered around small ponds within the jungle. Their manes were the color of stardust, and their horns shimmered like pearls. Nymphs and satyrs hid behind the bark of the trees, while griffins and fauns observed my whereabouts from the branches above. Unlike the other creatures, the elves weren't so shy. They were so handsome that their stares stripped my nerves, and it didn't help that they were half naked. They stood out in the open, unafraid that their whispers were as loud as snapping twigs.

The jungle felt like the size of a small state. I had walked so far without knowing where I was going, but I was determined to find the shadow. Soon I was exhausted. I needed some rest, so I began looking for a spot to set up camp. In the distance I spotted a large tree with midnight-blue flowers that resembled starfishes. It seemed like the perfect place for a nap. When I reached the tree, I came across a lion with the bluest eyes I had ever seen. He was seated very properly beside the tree, and I could have sworn that he smiled at me. He didn't seem vicious. In fact, he seemed humane and domesticated.

"You are finally here," he said.

"You can talk?" I gasped.

He looked at me and laughed. "Of course I can, my dear. Everything in this world has a mind of its own, and every mind has a world of its own. My name is Cyrenius. I am the ruler of this world." His voice was stern.

"What is this place?"

He intensely looked around the jungle. "This is the land of your imagination. This is the land where your dreams and creativity take on a form of life. You are the creator of this land, and because you are the creator, only you can be the savior." He got up onto his feet. "Come now. Follow me. We have all been waiting for—"

"Savior?" I interrupted. "Whoa, I'm no savior. Believe me. I can't even seem to help myself." I giggled. "I'm sorry to disappoint you."

"Because you deny that you are the savior makes me certain that you are the savior," he replied.

"Well, I'm not. And even if I was, what exactly is my purpose?"

He laughed. "Why, to fulfill the prophecy, of course."

"What prophecy?"

He scrunched his brow solemnly and asked, "You've never heard of the prophecy?"

"No."

"Well then, allow me to enlighten you." He then looked into my eyes, almost piercing my soul, and said, "There is a prophecy written in the high stones of this west mountain that foretells of a savior, also known as the creator of this land, who will come one day and save us all from the wrath of the lamia."

"What the hell is a lamia?" I asked.

"Have you not heard of her?" He sounded concerned.

"No. Who is she?"

"It's more a question of *what* is she." As he raised his sights up to the stars, I gazed at his eyes, which glistened with grief as he said, "She is a dreadful monster created by Lucifer to serve him in the war between good and evil. The lamia is a serpent formed from the dust of hell."

"Dust?"

Cyrenius looked back at me. "Satan mimics God in so many ways, even with his creations. God's first significant creature was made of dust."

"Adam," I uttered.

He nodded. "Precisely. She is the very same beast that tempted Eve in the garden, the very same beast that has poisoned our land with loss, exchanged our hopes with fear, and filled our hearts with doubt." He turned and began walking further into the jungle. "Morgan"—he sighed—"she plans to destroy our land. Only you can stop her. You are our only hope." His blue eyes were then the saddest I had ever seen.

I wanted to find the bravery to show some compassion, but his words placed fear in my bones. "No, no. You've got the wrong girl, lion," I said, shaking my head.

"Lion? My name is Cyrenius, but if you insist on calling me lion, I will be forced to refer to you as plain girl."

"And the claws come out," I playfully provoked him. I took a deep breath. "Cyrenius, let's say I am the savior. How am I supposed to destroy such a powerful entity?"

He smiled. "Well, the question of *how* is always a start."

As we walked further into the jungle, Cyrenius shared his plan of attack with me. "I have assembled an army of the finest warriors in the land. We will all gather at Camp Simeon before heading to Far East Mountain, where the lamia abides. There is a very special sword in the lamia's possessions that you must retrieve. However, retrieving the sword will not be a simple task, for she guards the blade with her life. You see, that sword is the only weapon powerful enough to slay the beast. Without it you are just as hopeless as we are."

"Why haven't any of your warriors ever tried retrieving it?" I asked.

"Because you are the only one who can unleash its true power. But in order to unleash its true power, you must have faith like a child."

I looked into the lion's blue eyes, showing him my vulnerability. "Cyrenius, getting ahold of that sword sounds nearly impossible."

The lion gazed back into my eyes. He appeared to be immune to my fear and doubts. "Anything can be impossible if we believe it is impossible, but why would anyone waste their belief on not believing?"

"Touché," I whispered.

He smiled. "Very well. My troops and I will get you past the lamia's army of ogres and demons, but once you enter the mountain, you're on your own. How you choose to retrieve the sword depends solely on you."

A few miles later, we finally reached Camp Simeon. The camp's ground was covered with teepees made of buffalo skins and huts made of leaves and branches. As we approached the campsite, leagues of warriors began kneeling before me—a demonstration of their loyalty, I guessed. There were Minotaurs, centaurs, griffins, and elves all armed with swords, arrows, and spears. They saluted my presence and chanted for the hope I represented.

Wasting no time, Cyrenius took me directly to his headquarters to meet his general, Abidah. Abidah was an elf much larger than the rest, and he was the only one with a pair of wings. He was beautiful, his naked body chiseled and his heavenly eyes filled with so much desire. Although I have never seen an angel before, Abidah had the features I envisioned an archangel as possessing.

Cyrenius excused himself as Abidah pulled me aside. The elf seductively smiled at me and said, "So, I take it that Cyrenius has informed you of our situation?"

"He has," I replied, feeling bashful. "It's a bit overwhelming, if I may say so." I sighed.

"Well, if it helps, you're more intimidating than you think." He grinned.

"Let's hope this creature thinks so." I nervously giggled.

Abidah lightly grazed my face with the back of his hand as his big, beautiful, hazel eyes looked at my features with what seemed to be adoration. "Although the lamia seems like an invincible creature, her only source of power is doubt. She will try to poison your soul with doubt, for that is what she is; and if you let her conniving words question your certainty at any point, she will surely win," he said, tucking my hair behind my ear.

My eyes became spellbound by his perfectly shaped lips as he said, "I'm not too sure what Cyrenius has told you about the blade of prophecy, but allow me to enlighten you. The sword is useless in the hands of all humans but you, because you are the source of its power. Its handle contains the best of your past and the possibilities of your future. The gems that run down its shaft produce the magic that two lovers conjure when their love is pure and true. Last but not least, the blade is only as sharp as your belief. So believe, and you'll have a lethal weapon sharper than Chinese steel."

A few hours later, Abidah assembled the troops to prepare their winged horses and horselike wolves for combat. Soon the warriors were ready for battle, and their seeming capableness and numbers made me confident that I was capable too.

We cut our way through the darkness like cunning shadows. The moon's soft breath granted the night a gentle breeze. The flowers hummed while fireflies and pixies danced side by side. Beautiful, exotic fishes flew past us in the air like birds, setting an illusion of being underwater. I could hear the jungle chanting for victory as night-blooming orchids illuminated our path.

When I finally reached the end of the jungle, I laid eyes on the now infamous mountain. It sent chills down my spine, and for a second I could feel the presence of doubt. The mountain looked so out of place in such a beautiful world. It looked possessed by something very evil. Its jagged rocks were carelessly perched along the mountain's edges, and its steepness was terrifying.

I looked into Abidah's eyes, hoping they would be able to rebuild my courage. He must have seen the fear that was nicking me, because he was quick to comfort me. Gently putting his hand on the back of my neck, he said, "No matter what she says, her doubt cannot sow a seed without your consent. Being afraid makes you human, but facing that fear makes you a warrior. Fear doesn't defeat us; defeat only comes when the heart stops believing."

Abidah's eyes strayed quickly to the mountain as the lamia's army began to descend from the highest peak. They scattered throughout the surrounding plains like a swarm of ants. Abidah pressed himself so close to me that I could feel his lips brushing against my ear as he whispered, "She knows you are here, and although she may not show it, remember: she fears you more than you could ever fear her. Are you ready?"

"Yes," I replied.

He gently kissed my lips and then delivered a nod of confirmation to Cyrenius to signal the attack. Cyrenius inhaled deeply and then released a thunderous roar that shook the entire valley. The troops raised their swords and spears to the sky as we began to charge toward the mountain. Abidah and Cyrenius acted as my shield and sword, guiding and protecting me through the battlefield until I was able to safely enter Far East Mountain.

As soon as we had climbed to the entrance of the cave, Cyrenius looked into my eyes and said, "This is as far as Abidah and I can go. You are now on your own, my dearest friend." Cyrenius seemed saddened by the fact that he could not come along with me.

"I've never been so scared in my entire life," I admitted, "but I won't let my fear be the reason I disappoint you."

Cyrenius smiled. "There is a warrior inside you, my sweet little Morgan. There always has been. So I do not have the slightest fear that you will disappoint me, Abidah, this land, or yourself."

Before I could say anything, Abidah wrapped his arm around my waist and said, "We believe in you. Why else would we be willing to sacrifice so much? But this isn't about our belief; it's about yours, because once you step into that cave, it's all you're going to have."

For a minute all I could hear were the horrific sounds of the battle below: the cries, the destruction, blades crossing blades, arrows piercing through flesh. I could smell the bravery and belief in the blood of my allies as their nobility was splattered across the plains. The smell drifted into the wind. And then I realized, if spilling a little blood would help me reassure my belief, then it was time for me to bleed.

I looked at both Abidah and Cyrenius. "You must go. They need you," I said.

They bowed before me and then turned around and made their way back to the battlefield. I watched as they ran into the swarm of chaos until I could no longer see them.

As I entered the mountain, I noticed that the walls were sweating and pulsating with life, like breathing lungs. The air was thick and humid. Cobwebs hung from the ceiling like shredded curtains, and there was a heavy presence entwined with the darkness that tortured my nerves. Human remains were scattered throughout the tunnel, along with piles of sharpened bones that the lamia must have used to pick her teeth after gnawing the flesh off them. As I reached her lair, I could faintly hear the cries of innumerable souls. It sounded like they were being tortured. Then suddenly her demonic voice slithered throughout the room. "Come in, come in, my child. I've been expecting you."

I stood still, holding my breath, hoping she would assume that the sound of my footsteps had actually only been the noise of one of the many rats creeping around in the darkness.

"I know you're there, you foolish girl," she uttered in a bone-chilling voice. I knew she was nearby, but the darkness kept me from seeing anything. She began to cackle like a witch, and I could hear the weight of her body slithering across the loose gravel on the ground. "So, you are the girl who has been prophesied to slay me. I've got to say, I am quite disappointed. I was expecting more." Her cackles echoed through the cave, and I couldn't pinpoint where they were coming from. "Tell me, foolish girl: Do you honestly think you could defeat me? I am doubt! I am the demon who unleashed the first sin upon the earth. I am the reason one of the purest hearts chose to question and defy God. I simply convinced her to sink her teeth into an apple. I am the reason Lot's wife turned into a pillar of salt. I am the reason a rightful king was ridiculed with a crown of thorns. I have destroyed many, and I will destroy you just as well. In fact, destroying you will be easy. After all, your heart already seems to be full of doubt." She chuckled.

I quickly realized that this showdown was going nowhere if I continued hiding in the darkness, and so I gathered my nerves and shouted, "Show yourself, you monster!" I stepped bravely into the center of her lair, where she was bound to see me.

"My, my, my. You're even more foolish than I thought."

"You might think me foolish, but I'd rather seem foolish than intimidated, like you obviously are. Why else would you still be lurking in the shadows?" I asked. "Come out and show yourself, bitch."

She roared in anger and then blew fire at the ceiling, causing its surface to burn like hot coals and lighting up the dark cave. She then began to emerge from the shadows. Her scales were chipped and tarnished, and she had the horns of a ram. Although she was half serpent and half woman, her characteristics were of a dragon. Even though her face was severely burned and disfigured, I could see that her face was not that of a stranger. It was Liz, the witch who owned the Wicker Palace. I shook at the first sight of her. I began to look for the sword, but I could not see it anywhere.

"Looking for this?" she asked, grasping the sword with the tip of her tail. She flashed her fangs and attempted to strike me. I ran and hid behind a large rock and began picking up hefty stones and launching them at her with all my might. Somehow, despite having the worst aim, I managed to land a blow near her eye, causing her to drop the sword onto the ground. I ran quickly to recover the sword, but before I could run away, she began to circle around me like a shark.

"Look at you. You're pathetic. You can barely hold up that sword," she hissed. She looked into my eyes and said, "I know all about you, Morgan, and I know exactly why you are here. You doubt love, and I don't blame you. After all, love is merely a figment of our imaginations. There was a time when true love existed, but due to the curse Adam and Eve placed on themselves, it is no more. God gave them a choice; I simply guided them in the direction that was more convenient—for me." She chuckled.

"By biting the apple, they denied trust and innocence, the two main components of love. Their curse was passed on to their descendants, which includes you. The men and women in your world are led by the desires of their flesh. The name of love is used to disguise lust. Lust, the source of infidelity, promiscuity, and desperation," she hissed as she continued circling me, like a predator taunting its food.

"So tell me, Morgan, because I'm just dying to know. What hurts you more? Knowing you lost the closest thing to love, or knowing that you'll never, ever get it back?" She grinned mockingly and hissed. The louder she hissed, the heavier the sword felt. Eventually the sword became so heavy that it sunk me to the ground. I couldn't help but doubt myself. She was too powerful.

Just then something in the distance caught her attention. It was the shadow I had seen on the beach. The shadow I had been looking for. He flew around her in circles, like a pesky fly, before making his way over to me. As soon as he placed his arms around me, I was reminded of how much I had missed his embrace. And as he whispered in my ear, his voice brought tears to my eyes. "The curse is real, but you have the power to break it by rebuking it. Once you have rebuked it, the curse will be cancelled. Love does exist, but you need to welcome it into your life. After you have welcomed it into your life, you need to confess and receive it as yours," he said. "Don't ever doubt such a beautiful thing."

The lamia's serpent eyes viciously scrutinized him. He gently brushed his warm lips against my cheek and said, "And if there is ever an ounce of doubt, think of the many ways I looked at you when you belonged to me. And if you can doubt that, then by all means, you have my permission to doubt love." Then he whispered, "Come on, baby. You can do this. Do it for me."

With his words my sword began to glow, and fear began to rise in the eyes of the lamia. I swung three times before I actually pierced her torso. I knew the only way to defeat this beast was by decapitating her, and I was determined to do so, because I was not going to let my past have been lived in vain.

She became more aggressive toward me once she saw that trail of blood oozing from her torso. I knew she now saw me as a real threat, because her strikes became aimless and rapid. I tried to use my blade as a shield against her fangs, but she was too quick. Before I knew it, she had sunk her fangs into my right forearm. The pain was excruciating. I thought for sure my arm was gone, but fortunately it was still intact when she released me from her grasp. However, I now had two large holes pierced straight through my arm.

I was losing blood, and losing it fast. I felt disoriented, feverish. Puddles of sweat dripped from my brow onto the frigid ground. I knew I needed to rest if I wanted to regain my strength. So I began looking around the dark cave for a tight space big enough to take a quick break in but small enough to keep her out. In the distance I spotted two enormous rocks rooted to the ground with a perfectly sized gap between them, just big enough for me to squeeze in. I rushed over and tucked myself far between them to make sure she could not reach me. As I sat there trembling on the cold floor, completely covered in my own blood, I advised myself to suck it up. It was just pain, even if it was pain too severe to swallow; there was no way I was about to give up now. Besides, she had already pissed me off.

"Well, I've never known a warrior to be more of a coward than you." She laughed. "Why, even Judas had more balls than you." She hissed and coiled herself above the two enormous rocks that were my only sanctuary. Suddenly she began blowing fire into the cracks between the rocks to lure me out.

"Messy bitch," I uttered. "I'm gonna kill you! You hear me? I'm gonna kill you!" I could feel my sweat pouring from the heat of her fire. It was unbearably hot. She might as well have thrown me into an oven. I felt like she was literally cooking me alive. "I gotta get out of here," I whimpered. Her flames came closer and closer to where I was. "Come on, Morgan," I told myself, "you're not fixing to die without making this bitch bleed one more time." I waited for an opportunity to climb out from between the rocks, and once the coast was clear, I quickly climbed onto the side of the rock where her tail was dangling and took a clean swing.

"Arrr!" She yelled in pain as the tip of her tail flew into the air, falling to the ground, where it continued to spasm. She was clearly infuriated. Her eyes looked like those of a shark when it's on the verge of attack. "You're gonna pay for that!" she screeched. She began swishing around me, hissing thunderously as she moved from side to side, flashing her razor-sharp fangs in an attempt to evoke a primal fear inside me. When I failed to give her the reaction she wanted, she began striking her keen teeth in my direction, repeatedly missing each blow.

I knew there was only one way to kill her, and it wasn't gonna be pretty. If I could get high enough to take one clean swing at her neck, I knew that slithering wench would go down for sure. But how was I ever going to get anywhere near her neck? Then it hit me: the two large rocks where I hid before were high enough to face the beast eye to eye, but in order to get to those rocks, I needed to either come up with a great distraction or inflict some massive pain on her. I couldn't think of anything fast enough to distract her, so I shoved my blade into the center of the open wound where her tail was no longer attached. She screeched. Once I pulled out the blade, I ran to the rocks while she painfully attended to her abused wound.

I quickly climbed up onto the rocks. Once the demon and I were at eye level, she looked me up and down with a look of agony and said, "You stupid girl, I should have eaten you when I had the chance." Her scowl quickly turned into a scornful smile as she began to laugh, cackling like the demon she was. "Child, poor, sweet child, I really do feel so sorry for you." She grinned. "Foolish people who dream as big as you do have so much to lose. But that's right." She giggled. "You have already had your loss, and you will never, ever get him back!" she shouted.

Before she could send her laugh echoing throughout the cave once more, I swung with all my faith and cut through her neck. Once the sword had completely severed her head from her body, the sword exploded into a blinding beam of light, and I hit the floor from exhaustion. I was so weak that I could not move. My eyelids became as heavy as anchors, leaving me with a feeling of defeat. In the midst of my stormy haze, I heard him say, "Hurry, baby. I've been waiting for you."

When I opened my eyes, I found myself lying on the floor of room 322. I looked above me and all around, but he was not here, there, or anywhere. I looked at my arm, the wound the lamia had inflicted now gone. Then I got up off the floor and headed out the door. A bittersweet feeling swept over me. I was so happy that I was blessed with the opportunity to visit such a beautiful world, and any swing at Liz was also worth smiling over. But all in all, I had him so close but didn't have the chance to bargain for some time to tell him that I loved him. Dreams can be quite cruel when they aren't being sweet.

I slowly walked into the hall with a heavy heart. He was all I could think of, even though I was only able see his shadow. Suddenly I heard my name fluttering through the air. "Morgan…Morgan…"

I began to hunt for the source the faint voice. I knew it was his voice. It was undeniable. It grew louder and louder. When I reached room 314, it stopped. Little did I know that what lay behind that door would break my heart all over again so that my heart would have no other choice than to seek mending.

6

ANTONIO

Part 1

I really don't like sharing my feelings, but I'll always remember the day I lost one of the greatest things I've ever stumbled across in my life: his love.

We were both very private people. We never rambled about our love, and we never praised it; we simply respected it. I guess it was because we both had our fair share of inner demons, which reminded us that this love had come to us by chance, not because we deserved it. They were demons that were forced onto us during our childhoods. I was the only person he had ever shared his dark and brutal secrets with, because he was the only person who had ever seen the violated skeletons living in my closet. And although our souls were both vandalized, it never stopped us from trying to be better for each other, because we never allowed those incidents to define us.

Not a lot of people know our story, but just because it hasn't been told, that doesn't make it less beautiful. Some might say that our romance was a little risqué and maybe even wrong, because I was a lamb in the arms of a wolf, a young girl who happened to fall in love with a man in his prime. Some say he had too much knowledge for me, as I was just stepping out into the world, while he had already figured out how it worked.

He was my favorite person. There isn't a day that goes by when I don't wish more people could have had the opportunity to know him. Knowing that people like him existed makes me believe the world could have been a better place. He was like a hybrid: a truly good person with the outward qualities of a bad man. I had never met someone with so much soul, so much integrity. His perspective on life was rather intriguing. He never wasted time simplifying the complicated. Au contraire, he was constantly finding ways to make the simplest things complex, because he was always determined to find the beauty in everything.

He was my American dream, my red, white, and blue. His eyes were as mesmerizing as fireworks in the night sky, and his smile was as inviting as a slice of cherry pie on the Fourth of July. He had these pink, smooth baby lips that made his kisses so much sweeter than strawberry crème on a hot summer's day.

I can't even begin to tell you how much I loved him, because the God's honest truth is I loved him more than you or anyone can fathom. That being so, he was the inspiration behind so many things I did in my life. The day

I lost him was the day I lost my muse, my reason for being, the piece of me that made me extraordinary.

He used to say, "Nothing lasts forever. So if you ever get a chance to have something remarkable for even a split second, then you have no right to say your life is as bad as you think it is." He always came across as being brilliant in his own way. He called himself the Roger Waters of my life, and I guess he really was.

I miss him every day. Can you blame me? After all, that man's love still stands beyond ideal. Being loved by him gave me intense tingles. You know, the ones you get when you're on the verge of something dangerous and out of your element.

His love dared me, challenged me, and in that sense I grew into a woman I was proud to be. And in spite of how it might sound, our love didn't end on bad terms, even though saying good-bye was never my intention. Sometimes some things don't tarnish; they are simply interrupted. I begged him to stay, but he didn't—and I'll never really understand the reason why. I guess I should just be thankful for all that he taught and showed me while he was mine. Because, truth be told, he taught me so many things about myself that I would have never learned on my own.

I learned how to turn bargains into promises. I learned how much I hated chocolate. I even learned how to tell a lie while being completely honest. He taught me that a rose doesn't always have five petals and that a rich man is just a poor man who has embezzled. He showed me the importance of not being a stranger to myself and helped me discover the depths of my inner self. Most important, he showed me that life happens.

※

At the age of seventeen, I found myself in my new college dorm. My innocence smelled like fresh paint, and my heart still had the shine of the brand new, not a single crack or scratch. My eyes held no pain and had no story. They were simply naive and as happy as could be.

If you asked me now, I'd say that to dream would be a rich man's way to go down. If you were to ask me now if I believe in fairy tales, I'd say, "Only the ones where a poor man hurls his gold into a wishing well." But there was a time when I dreamed of things that could never be and believed they could, because in reality there was nothing that couldn't be if I felt it should. If there was ever a never or anything too crazy or clever, there was a man behind a cup of chai tea with a reason to believe.

I used to say, "Dream mad, because that's where happy wears a hat; and if happy wears a hat, then that's nonsense and the best place to be at." But that was then, and this is now. That was when, and this is how. It was a time when dreaming was as easy as breathing, because he made believing so simple. Unfortunately that simplicity has become just another tale for a once upon a time.

In my old dorm room, there were two pullout beds. One of them was mine, and the other belonged to a friend who could bet her life that she'd never seen me cry. If you looked around, you'd see an old radio, a wood-paneled TV, and all the other things that made me seventeen. My cell phone was resting fully charged on my pillow, and my bags were sitting by the window. I lay on my bed waiting for a call. When my phone finally rang and I saw his name on the screen, I quickly answered it with a blushing smile and a soft-spoken hello.

"Hey, I'm here," he said.

"OK, I'll be right down," I responded.

I looked out the window from the third floor, and there he was, leaning against the trunk of his 2005 charcoal Volkswagen Jetta. Though I was only seventeen, he was twenty-seven. As I watched him, I found it hard to believe that a man as magnificent as he was anxiously waiting downstairs for such an odd girl like me. Butterflies beat in my stomach while my nerves caused my knees to constantly knock into each other.

Once I grabbed my bags and my keys, I took a good look around the room and reminded myself to breathe. I locked the door behind me and headed downstairs, trying not to run.

That very moment haunts me whenever I think about it.

As I reached the exit door of the dormitory, I quickly thought of something cute to say. There he was. There we were. The only thing between us was a cold, metal door. As I walked out the door, he spotted me almost immediately.

I remember everything from that moment vividly. From the light breeze that had just blown in to the warm sun on my skin. From the trail of autumn leaves on the sidewalk to the sound of students coming in and out of the vicinity. And throughout all the commotion of foot traffic, he never once took his eyes off me.

He stole a kiss before I even had the chance to say hi. His mouth tasted like the spearmint gum he had just tossed into the grass. He quickly took my bags and locked them up in the trunk of his car.

Once we got into the car, I used my eyes to request another kiss. After my teeth released his bottom lip, we drove away from the campus and headed out toward our destination. The date was September 29, 2006, and the plan was simple: a whole weekend at his parents' lake house for my eighteenth birthday, just us two, something borrowed and something new.

Antonio Gonzales was born in Dallas, Texas, on September 15, 1979. The six-foot-one marvel was half German and half Mexican American. He inherited his mother's dirty-blond locks and his father's green eyes. His lips, however, were a gift from God all his own. Their shape was peerless, and they were always soft.

His looks had a diverse range. Sometimes he was clean-cut, with a close shave. Other times he grew a bearlike beard as a tribute to his careless hair. I loved the beard. All in all, that man was truly a vision. However, his pretty face never stopped people from raising questions, accusing him of a criminal background. Their judgment was based on the ink that covered most of his body. They made him out to be some sort of a thug, a drug lord, a gangster. But he was no criminal; he was an artist, an artist who used his physical presentation to express himself. I always found it to be his most profound quality.

He was a thirty-two by thirty-two and wore size eleven-and-a-half shoes, no matter what type of shoe. He loved Chinese food; it was his favorite. He had three major scars: one on the corner of his left eyebrow, one under his chin, and another under his right foot. Two of them were from his childhood, and one was from a bar fight back in 2002. He didn't like the taste of coffee but was fond of the smell. He hated lizards and loved the sea. And if he ever had to choose between the sun and the moon, he'd pick the moon in a heartbeat. He liked dogs because he had no other choice; cats freaked him out. If you really wanted to piss him off, all you had to do was bad-mouth Freddie Mercury. If you ever wanted to see him smile, all you had to do was mention me. He had such animosity toward television that he used to say that the shit passing for shows these days was the government's way of keeping America stupid by influencing us with false expectations. But in spite of that, he was proud to be an American.

There wasn't anything about that man I couldn't tell you.

Three hours later we finally arrived at his parents' lake house in Austin. I must have dozed off when we passed San Antonio, because the only thing I remember after that was waking up to the sound of the loose gravel on the driveway as we pulled up to the house.

I turned my head in his direction. He was gently tapping the steering wheel and softly humming along to "Just Like Heaven" by The Cure.

I sat up straight in my seat, catching his attention almost immediately. He quickly lowered the dial on the radio and said, "Well, hello there, sleepyhead."

"Hi," I said, smiling through my embarrassment. "How long was I asleep?"

He squinted, thinking, and replied, "Hmm...about forty minutes or so." He looked at me and began to chuckle, like a child with a secret too big to keep.

"What?" I asked.

"Nothing." He giggled.

"Tell me," I demanded.

He threw his head back, laughing like a little kid, and said, "You were snoring so loud! You sounded like a sea lion with asthma."

"Whatever. You are so full of shit...Was I really?" I nervously chuckled, hoping it wasn't true.

He busted out laughing. "I'm just kidding!"

"Ugh! That's so not funny," I said, laughing along with him.

He unbuckled his seat belt and leaned over toward me. He gently pecked my lips and whispered, "We're here."

When I first saw the house, it reminded me of a small cottage in the woods from a story I once heard as a child. The roof was scattered with autumn leaves, and the walkway was bathed in evening shade. He gently tossed me the keys and said, "Check out the house while I unpack."

I remember walking into the lake house for the very first time. I remember hearing my footsteps echo like sighs of relief from the silence that had been waiting to be broken. The small brick house had two garages in the driveway and one gigantic porch in the backyard. It consisted of three bedrooms and a living room that connected to the dining area. The floors were wooden, the china was fairly new, and there were more windows than walls. A pile of scented gel beads on the kitchen counter made the house smell like spring. I made my way into the living room, where I caught my first glimpse of the lake through a large window. As I ran my fingers across the black leather divan, I envisioned the future.

In the future I saw an old woman in an old lake house taking care of the old man who gave her the best years of her life. The old man loved her, because he always knew that she'd give him the best last days of his life. And they lived happily ever after in a quiet and settled routine that involved gazing out onto the lake every evening to remind themselves of all the beauty they had accomplished in their youth. And although the years had changed the both of them, their grays never changed the fact that he was her strength and she was his weakness.

I quickly ditched the fantasy when it occurred to me that I should go out and help Antonio with any of the luggage that was left. The front door was wide open. I must have forgotten to close it. Antonio's car was still in the driveway, but he was nowhere in sight. I could hear the wind rattling through the branches of the oak trees. The setting sun filled the sky with various shades of lilac and tangerine. It was an evening capable of making any neighborhood look friendly. I took a deep breath of fresh air and made my way back into the house. I checked the living area, the kitchen, and the nearest guest room but didn't see him anywhere. However, it wasn't too long before I finally found him.

Antonio was lying facedown on the mattress of the master bedroom. The bedroom was enormous. It had two large windows, one facing the driveway and the other facing the lake. The window that was facing the lake had a built-in seating area, where Antonio's mother kept a pile of books from her favorite American authors. I slowly approached the nearest bed pillar and gently leaned my face against it, admiring the grain in the dark chestnut wood. Antonio suggestively patted the bed and said, "Come lie down." His voice sounded muffled from having his face buried in the pillow.

I tossed myself right beside him. The smell of lavender from the sheets hit my nose like a thousand butterflies on a summer night. He looked into my eyes, and I looked straight back into his. At first his eyes looked very hesitant. And although he never said it, I knew he was very afraid of being hurt, because beneath the tough exterior, there was a man looking for a taste of real love. But even so, there was always something about his eyes that made me want more, more out of life, more out of love, more of the impossible. They held a force like magic that made me feel invincible every time they gazed upon me. And so, I looked for them, more than his lips, more than his hands, more than any other part belonging to a man.

He rolled himself over toward me and simply said, "Hi." He smelled like Christmas. He always did, with the way he gorged himself on peppermints. To this day, it still fascinates me that he never had a single cavity. He bashfully smirked, quickly pulling me into his big arms. From that moment on, his arms became my safety net, my parachute, the only thing in this crazy world that wasn't based on illusion.

The following day I woke up to the smell of sizzling bacon and buttermilk pancakes. I made my way to the kitchen, where he was cooking in a pair of black swimming trunks. He had a pair of baby-blue shades resting on the top of his head and was shirtless, proudly baring more of his symbolic tattoos than usual.

Although he had many tattoos, I'll only share a few of my favorites with you. My absolute favorite was the baby-blue rose that covered his right fist. It was a simple indication of his mother's love of roses and his love of the color blue. His most interesting tattoo, however, was of a raven wearing a suit on his left forearm, inspired by the story of Coronis's affair with Ischys found in Greek mythology. Antonio favored what he believed was the moral of the story, as far as the raven was concerned. That tattoo was his reminder that you are pretty much damned if you do and damned if you don't. As for the nineteenth-century suit the bird sported, well, that was just a little touch of his weirdness that I loved so much.

On the side of his right hand was a replica of James Dean's signature. He loved Jimmy because he felt that Dean had paved the way for a different kind of man. Antonio saw a lot of himself in James Dean, and so did I. They both shared a heavy look in their eyes that's almost too agonizing to describe. He had 1979 going across the knuckles on his left hand and 1931 across the knuckles on his right. I always thought those two tattoos made him look like a heavy hitter. He said those were the two years that two of the greatest men were born, Antonio Gonzales and James Byron Dean.

The year Antonio's father passed away, Antonio got the exact tattoo his father had gotten when he had first joined the service. It was a tattoo on his left hand of a blue sparrow carrying a heart with his parents' first initials. In the center of his chest was a very detailed tattoo of a human heart done in black and blue to represent all the things that his actual heart had been through. His back was covered by a large pair of ravaged angel wings, because he believed that we were all fallen angels living on Earth until we proved that we deserved to regain our wings. He had both his sleeves done with mixtures of skulls, guns with roses, a reaper, two Bible verses, and a melting pocket watch with the quote "Sometimes forever is just one second," which gave the illusion of a chain.

He was covered by the things he loved and the people he respected. I never planned to settle for a man like Antonio. Love just happened. I never had a problem with his tattoos. As a matter of fact, they only embellished him in my eyes.

"Well, good morning, beautiful," he said, smiling at me from over his shoulder.

"Good morning, handsome." I smiled while still clearing the morning haze from my eyes.

I pulled out a barstool and watched him as he juggled a few pans and a spatula. Once all the commotion had come to a rest, he slyly stuck a cigar in his mouth. I literally did a double take, because I had no idea where the hell he had pulled it out from—but there he was, lighting it.

"You smoke?" I asked in disbelief.

He smirked with the cigar hanging from his lips and said, "Baby, you ain't seen nothing yet."

"Oh God." I sighed, rolling my eyes.

"What? You don't like it? I think it makes me look rather sophisticated, like an old-school gentleman. You know? More of a Cary Grant than a Gary Cooper, of course." He chuckled while carelessly waving his cigar in the air. "C'mon, you don't think so?"

I simply smiled and nodded.

"Anyways, I just started cooking breakfast, so it'll be a while. Do you want to start off with a bagel?"

"No, thanks. To be quite honest with you, I don't think I like bagels," I said, scrunching my nose in dislike.

"Wait, what do you mean, you don't think you like bagels?"

"Well, I've never actually had one before." I laughed.

He looked at me, obviously shocked, and said, "What? Are you serious? No way! You have got to be kidding. Right?"

"No, I'm serious."

"Why?" he asked.

"I don't know. They just look odd. Besides, I'm not a big fan of bread, unless it's sweet, of course."

He quickly ran over to the counter and grabbed the bag of bagels. He then took a one out of the bag and popped it into the toaster, making his way to the refrigerator shortly after to grab the cream cheese. Once the bagel popped out of the toaster, he took a butter knife with a good amount of cream cheese and gave the bagel a good spread.

"Here, try this!" he said, holding out the bagel as though he were an anxious child. As I reached out for the bagel, he quickly pulled it back and said, "No, no. I'm feeding you."

I bashfully consented. "OK." I could feel my face flushing from embarrassment as I took a bite out of the bagel. As soon as the bread and cream hit my taste buds, I was unable to contain myself. "Oh my God...This shit is amazing!" I shrieked.

"Didn't I tell you? You can thank big daddy for that one," he said, laughing with so much enthusiasm. He took a big bite out of the same bagel and placed the rest of it on a plate in front of me.

"Wait!" I said, stopping him before he continued on with breakfast. "You got cream cheese all over your mouth." I laughed as I wiped off the cream from the side of his lips. I then licked the cream cheese off the tip of my thumb and waited for an expected kiss.

I was so awkward around him at first, almost like a baby deer trying to walk for the first time. I had never had a boyfriend before him, not even a real kiss. So in the beginning I overanalyzed every one of my movements and words.

After breakfast, we cleaned up the table, and I volunteered to help him with the dishes. Every now and then, he would splash me with the dishwater, and I splashed him back. I'll never forget how his laugh echoed throughout the lake house.

I had been begging him all morning to take me out to the lake for a swim, so as soon as we got done with the dishes, he had me change into my swimsuit. He waited on the couch as I slipped into my coral-pink bathing suit. When I walked into the living room in my two-piece, his jaw dropped to the floor. I guess those squats and sit-ups had paid off after all. I took his baby-blue shades off the top of his head and seductively put them on my face. I then dangled my tight, little body in front of him and said, "Catch me if you can." I ran out through the sliding doors that led out to the back porch. He chased me all the way out to the lake, and when he finally caught me, he threw me over his shoulder and spun me around. I screamed with joy. It was a moment of pure bliss. I honestly felt like I was in the scene of a romance movie.

It was such a perfect day for testing the power that an itty-bitty bikini can have over a grown man. The sun was shining bright in the cloudless sky. The birds were singing, and the bees were buzzing. The grass was greener than emeralds, and the daisies were more potent than a man's pheromones. I felt such a sense of nostalgia every time the wind caused the tire swing to sway. But the most enchanting thing I saw that day was that man's beautiful face.

Antonio stared at me seductively as he began walking backward toward the lake. When he got to the boardwalk, he expanded his arms and shouted, "Come on, baby! What are you waiting for?" I ran up to him and jumped on his back. Before I even had the chance to brace myself, he plunged us over the ledge. We both surfaced from the water, laughing at the top of our lungs. He wrapped his legs around my waist and pulled me toward him. I could taste the lake water on his lips as his heavy breath escalated our kiss.

I looked at him and said, "Can I tell you a secret?"

"I would want you to tell me a secret," he replied. "After all, they can be quite dangerous if they're kept from the wrong people."

"Do you believe in magic?" I asked.

"That sounds more like a question than a secret."

"There is genuinely a point. Believe me." I chuckled. "So answer the question. Do you believe in magic?"

"Yes…I do. Do you?"

"Of course I do. And now that I know you believe in it too, here is a little secret from me to you." I smiled, leaned in, and whispered, "Every once in a lifetime we are all fortunate enough to meet someone who isn't just anyone, who isn't like everyone else, and when we do, we encounter a spark that ignites into an instant connection. Science calls it chemistry, but I believe it's magic. I believe that God allows two people to find each other when He sees that their souls are truly in need of each other. The spark is just the seed, but the love, that's the real magic. And the more you tend to that magic, the stronger it becomes." As I looked into his eyes, I could feel my heart practically pounding through my chest as I said, "I believe we were given that seed. And I know it sounds crazy, but ever since I met you, I've felt my heart spinning around inside me like a carousel."

I won't lie. I definitely felt a sense of panic when he remained speechless and his eyes stared off into the distance. At the time I couldn't comprehend why the silence went on for as long as it did. I just automatically assumed that he simply didn't feel the same way about me. I couldn't help but feel that maybe I had come on a little too strong. If he had not smiled at that moment, I swear to God that my heart would have shriveled up and died.

"Do you want to know a secret?" he asked.

"I would want you to tell me a secret," I replied. "Because I heard keeping them to yourself can be quite dangerous."

Suddenly he submerged himself in the water. When he resurfaced, he swept me into his arms and said, "For the last few weeks, I've been feeling something happening inside me. And I've found myself constantly obsessing over it, but I could never quite put my finger on it—until now. Because you have taken the words right out of my mouth." He pressed his cheek against mine and uttered, "It sure does feel a lot like a carousel, doesn't it?"

I kissed him so hard that he had no other choice than to kiss me back even harder.

We spent the rest of the afternoon talking about our dreams and ambitions, our goals and aspirations. I knew he was truly passionate about becoming an entrepreneur the moment he went on and on about his dream in precise detail. He said that he had been saving up some money for the past few years and was only a few bucks away from making his vision a reality. Although he loved managing the oil rigs, he wanted his life to count for something greater. He talked about opening two restaurants in Corpus Christi. He wanted a seafood restaurant and Mexican restaurant, and he made it clear that he wanted both of his restaurants to be affordable for everyone. He also mentioned opening his own tattoo parlor. In fact, he had already recruited a few of his close friends to run his shop, because he trusted their artistry. After all, they were responsible for most of his body art.

He was instantly intrigued when I shared my dream of becoming a writer. I told him that it wasn't about being the best; it was about inspiring others and simply making a little money, enough to travel the world and actually see it with my own eyes, because I could never be satisfied with just hearing about it through other people's words.

After dinner that night, I was so stuffed I could barely move. As a matter of fact, I made him carry me all the way to the bedroom. When he tossed me on the bed, the cold sheet felt so good against my body. He took his shirt off before he hopped in next to me. I immediately begged for those big arms, and he quickly surrendered them to me. I could feel his scruff rubbing against my skin as he threaded his fingers through mine. I looked out the window and saw the crescent moon swimming in the flat, calm lake.

"Hey, wake up!" he said, when I began dozing off. "I know your birthday isn't until Monday, but I just can't wait until then." He cleared his throat and began to sing in a low, melancholic voice. "Happy birthday to you. Happy birthday to you. There is something about you, beautiful, that makes me happy on your birthday too."

I knew from that very moment that this here was what I wanted. That weekend at the lake house is a memory I'll hold on to for the rest of my life. I'll never forget how the seconds turned into days, how the silences turned into late-night conversations, and how his laugh was the first thing I ever loved.

I met Antonio at a coffee shop around six fifteen in the morning on August 29, 2006. The semester had just started, so fortunately I was safe from homework that day. I was too shy to be interested in the life on campus, so for the first few days, I stayed locked up in my dorm room, far away from the annoyingly peppy sorority girls. But for some strange reason, on that particular Tuesday, I had the urge for a breath of fresh air. I didn't have friends in the city. Wherever I went, I'd be going alone. I had no idea where I was going. I just knew it had to be off campus. Then I remembered an old coffee shop about ten minutes away and how I was always curious about it whenever I drove by. I thought for sure it would be a perfect environment for me to processes my thoughts in and maybe even write a little.

Sure enough, when I got to the old coffee shop, there were only a few people there, all with their noses drawn to their books and laptops. Although there was only a fat man with a fanny pack ahead of me in line, he was ordering enough pastries for an army, and being quite selective at that. I began looking around at the details of the coffee shop's interior, admiring its antique touches as I impatiently waited to place an order I had yet to decide on.

Seconds later the bell on the door jingled. I turned to see who had walked in, and there he was, making his way toward me and then taking a spot in line awfully close behind me. He was the most beautiful man I had ever seen, but I didn't pay much attention to him. I figured a guy of his stature would never even give the time of day to a girl like me.

As my turn came up in line, the quirky girl at the register seemed more concerned with getting his number than taking my order. I literally had to clear my throat to get her attention.

"I'm sorry," she said. "What can I get you?" Her eyes were still fixated on him.

"Um, this is actually my first time here. Do you have any recommendations?" I asked, awkwardly scuffing the ball of my shoe against the wooden floor.

Before she could give me any of her recommendations, the gentleman standing behind me leaned over my shoulder and said, "You should try the chai tea. It's the best. Definitely my favorite."

I looked over my shoulder at the handsome man behind me and smiled. "Really?" My cheeks felt hot. I was sure they were redder than roses. "Well, in that case I guess I'll have to try it." I smiled at him once more, and to my surprise, this time he smiled back. He was so cute. Thank God that I had done my makeup that day.

I got my chai tea and took a seat at a corner table off to the right. I looked out the window. The sky was getting darker, and the coffee-shop lights were dimmed. Although my eyes were focused outside, my ears were hanging on to every one of his words as he laughed and joked with the cashier. He had gotten his order, a chai tea along with an apple-raisin muffin, and was about to walk out the door when suddenly he hesitated. He took his hand off the door rail and then made his way to the table across from me. He smiled at me as he raised his chai tea as a sign of cheers, and then he went in for his apple-raisin muffin. With a mouthful of his muffin, he asked, "So, are you from around here? I've never seen you before."

I nervously played with the rim of my mug as I responded. "No, I actually just moved here a few days ago for school. What about you?"

He picked up his napkin and wiped his mouth before he answered. "Yeah, I'm from here, unfortunately." He laughed.

My next move really caused me to step out of my comfort zone. "I'm Morgan, by the way. Would you like to join me?" I pointed at the empty chair in front of me.

He quickly set his drink on the table and crumpled his muffin wrapper with a smirk. "I thought you'd never ask." He pulled out the chair, but before he sat down, he extended his hand to me and said, "I'm Antonio, or Anthony, whichever one works for you. So tell me a bit about yourself." He took his seat. "What are you studying for?"

I playfully rolled my eyes. "You just had to ask me the one question I can't answer."

"Aw, is that so?" He chuckled.

"Yeah." I sighed. "I mean, I more or less know what I want to do, but right now I'm just focused on getting my basics out of the way."

"Ah, nice." He nodded. "Well then, let me ask you something that you can answer." He raised one eyebrow. "What's your favorite movie?"

"And so the cliché questions begin." I grinned.

He bashfully smiled. "No, not necessarily."

"C'mon, everyone knows those are the type of questions you ask when the conversation's running dry." I pouted my lips.

"Well, if you must know, I personally can tell a lot about a person just by knowing their favorite movie. It's a gift." He shrugged and then pointed his finger aimlessly in the air. "You see, you can ask someone about the kind of music they like, hobbies, foods, and eighty percent of the time, I guarantee you, they're lying. Because let's face it: when you first meet someone, your natural instinct is to win that person over. And some people might not even realize it, but they begin morphing into a character, versus themselves. So to prevent that from happening, I ask the previous question specifically. Just one, that all-time favorite. Now that takes thought, and everyone knows a limited answer always relies on some form of truth." He firmly placed his elbows on the table, intertwining his fingers, and said, "And so I'll ask you again, but this time, you only have ten seconds to answer. What is your favorite movie of all time? One...two—"

"*Breakfast at Tiffany's*," I quickly responded, interrupting his almost demeaning countdown.

"Hmm...Never seen it." He pressed his lips together, frowning slightly and shaking his head.

"Well, isn't that funny? Because I can tell a lot about a person who hasn't seen *Breakfast at Tiffany's*. It's a gift." I tauntingly grinned.

"Well, with that being said, I guess it's safe to assume that you aren't trying to impress me." He smirked.

"How can I be when you're hogging up all the effort to impress me?" I smiled, pressing my thumb against my teeth.

We talked for about an hour and a half. It was strange. I felt so comfortable in our conversation that I almost forgot I had been shy my entire life. And what's more bizarre was how honest I was with him throughout the whole conversation—that is, until he asked me about my age. He told me that he was twenty-six going on twenty-seven in September. So when he asked me how old I was, my first instinct was to lie. I told him that I was nineteen when in fact I was only seventeen. I knew it was wrong, but I didn't want my age to be the reason he didn't give me a chance. We exchanged numbers and set a date for our very first official engagement.

Two weeks had gone by since our encounter at the coffee shop. And within those two weeks, I saw Antonio almost every single day. He would come scoop me up after my classes, and we'd go either to dinner or to the local cinema.

On the day of his birthday, we went back to the old coffee shop and celebrated with a cup of chai tea. We'd stay up all night, every night, talking on the phone until one of us fell asleep. I literally had to clear my inbox several times a day from our text messages alone. It was a beginning that felt too good to be true—and I would soon find out that it really was.

On September 18, 2006, he called me as I was on my way to class. He was very quiet and distant. I knew something was wrong, and it scared me. I thought of all the ways he was capable of disappointing me. "Is everything OK?" I asked, knowing in my gut that something was terribly wrong. "You don't seem like yourself," I added, pausing and waiting for his response to set me at ease, but all I got from him was a long silence that sent my heart racing.

"Morgan," he finally said, "there is something I have to tell you." By the sound of his voice, I knew that whatever was troubling him was about to destroy us both. I stopped walking and sat down on a nearby bench, where I waited for the worst. He took a deep breath and then said, "Morgan, I have a girlfriend. Well, I mean I had a girlfriend."

"While you were seeing me?" I asked, my voice beginning to crack.

"Yes," he responded, sounding ashamed.

I immediately felt sick to my stomach. That was the last thing I expected him to say. I had no idea what to do or what to say, so I simply stayed quiet as the wind blew past me and through a few trees nearby.

"Hello? Morgan, are you still there?" I could hear the panic in his voice as he pled for a response. "Look, I had just started dating her two weeks before I met you. It was nothing serious. It was nothing like us. And to be completely honest with you, I haven't even seen her in over a week. You gotta believe me when I say that I'd rather lose her before ever losing you. Because the honest truth is I don't want anyone else but you. And that's exactly why I ended things with her this morning. I'm so sorry." His voice wavered. "I didn't mean to drag you into this. You gotta believe me, kiddo. This wasn't intentional. I never in a million years expected to meet someone like you, and when I did…"—he hesitated—"I knew I couldn't let you go, even if it wasn't the right time to be holding on to you. Please forgive me. Give me one chance to prove to you that I am none of those horrible things you think of me right now. All I'm asking for is a fresh start, me and you, just us two." He sighed.

I could hear his breath rattling on the other side of the phone as he waited for me to say anything at all. I looked up at the evening sky, and without any hesitation, I simply said, "Good-bye," and hung up the phone. And even though I was sad, I didn't cry. I simply reminded myself that my life had been better when I was a recluse.

That Monday, I received a total of thirteen missed calls and twenty-two text messages from him, none of which I responded to. He continued to call and text for a week straight. And for a week straight, I continued to not respond. In spite of what he had done, I couldn't get him off my mind. I found myself constantly thinking about that smile and those pretty eyes. I missed him. And you can call me stupid, but something told me that he was worth one more chance.

I finally decided to respond a week later, on the night of the twenty-seventh. My text went through at exactly 11:21 p.m. I asked him to come over. I told him that I was dying to see him and that it couldn't wait for tomorrow. The rain was pouring hard that Wednesday night. I remember standing by my window as I waited for him to arrive, hoping every pair of headlights driving by were his.

As soon as I saw his car pull up to the side of my building, I ran downstairs. He was standing in the middle of the pouring rain, wearing one of the saddest faces I had ever seen. I ran as fast as I could into his open arms. It wasn't necessarily to feel his arms around me but rather to feel my arms around him. He continued to apologize, uttering "Sorry" over and over again like a broken record. I had to drag him under the canopy of the building in order to get him out of the heavy rain. I stopped him before he even had the chance to give me the explanation he felt I deserved. The truth was I didn't need an explanation. What I needed was a promise.

"I don't want to hear about her anymore, ever. I don't even want to know her name," I said, gently placing my hands on his wet cheeks. "What we have starts right now, right here. I just need you to promise me that, from now on, it's just me and you, just us two. And if you can promise me that, I promise to never bring up the past."

He was soaking wet, and his entire body was quivering. He tucked my hair behind my ear and in a soft voice said, "I promise. It's just me and you, just us two."

We went inside into my dorm room and talked for about twenty minutes before he reminded me that my birthday was coming up. "So, have you made any special plans for your birthday?"

I shook my head. "No, not yet."

"Good!" he said. "I wanna take you to my parents' lake house for the weekend."

Part 2

We spent our first Christmas together with my family in Raymondville. That Christmas had all those things you hear about in happy little carols. The weather outside was frightful, but Momma's hot chocolate was so delightful. Our neighbors' houses were all covered in lights that sparkled like the hope of a world waiting for peace on Earth. The yuletide was in the air, and its beauty was everywhere. There were lanes of candy canes, red-berry mistletoes, and a nativity scene in every Christmas play we went to. There was old-fashioned wrapping paper, holly jolly carolers, and some of the ugliest polyester sweaters I had ever seen.

My parents had already been in Antonio's company several times by that point, so bringing him around on Christmas didn't rack my nerves whatsoever. In fact, my family had immediately fallen in love with him the first time they met him. My father gave Antonio his approval and even named Antonio one of his fishing buddies. My mother thought he was handsome and always told me that she could see in his eyes how much he cared for me. Antonio was always respectful toward my parents and nothing less than a gentleman around my siblings.

On Christmas Eve I had the honor of watching *It's a Wonderful Life* for the first time, and Antonio was right there by my side. That night, we stayed up playing card games and bingo with my family while carrying on full conversations over hot chocolate. My siblings were all so curious about Antonio. I guess it's because he was the first guy I had ever brought home.

Around one o'clock in the morning, my brothers and sisters headed off to their rooms for bed. They all still lived with my parents, because my sisters weren't married and my brothers were still too young to move out. I stayed behind in the living room with Antonio, where my mother had left some pillows and a blanket on the couch for him. I wasn't ready to tell him good night just yet. All the lights in the house were off. Only the lights on the Christmas tree were twinkling. He took out his cell phone, checking for any missed calls, and asked, "What's your favorite Christmas song, baby?"

"That's easy. Judy Garland's version of 'Have Yourself a Merry Little Christmas.' Ever heard it?" I gently drew circles on the peak of his knee with my fingertip.

"Of course I have." He yawned. "*Meet Me in St. Louis* is my mother's favorite movie."

"Really?" I smiled. "It's my mother's favorite as well."

"Yeah?"

"Yeah."

He sighed, positioning himself more comfortably and then pulling me deeper into his arms. "Well, in that case we definitely have to listen to it now." He got up and rummaged through my parents' Christmas-CD collection, which was scattered on the coffee table. Finding the right disc, he popped it into the player, keeping the volume low.

I remember lying in his arms while I looked around my parents' living room. It was a quiet night, and only the voice of an angel rang through the room as two hearts were stirring, one through a shirt and one through a blouse. The stockings were hung with care, while presents of all sizes reminded us that Christmas would soon be here. Even Antonio had a few presents under our family tree. One of his presents was from my family, and the other three were from me.

As we lay in the darkness, we didn't utter a single word, because there was nothing that we could say to make the moment more beautiful than it already was. I believe they call that *golden silence*. The smell of cinnamon and pine soothed my senses. As my head sunk deeper into his chest, the sound of the ghost train passing through my hometown iced the night. Its *choo-choo* spread through the night, awakening the ghost of my Christmas past. I felt like a kid again, a kid whose troubles were miles away because all was calm and all was bright. A few minutes later, I kissed Antonio good night. I made sure he was comfy on my parents' couch before I headed off to my room, waiting for a morning that couldn't come too soon.

We woke up early the next morning, around five forty-five. Although we had only gotten a few hours of sleep, we were wide awake because it was Christmas day. That morning, I took him to my favorite bakery in Raymondville. After all, he had introduced me to the bagel and cream cheese, so it was my turn to introduce him to the best doughnuts in the world. At Lara's Bakery you can buy a slice of heaven for under fifty cents. When I was a child, my mother would take me there every morning before school. The pumpkin-filled pastries were always my first choice.

We got a mixture of pastries and rushed back home to get the coffee brewing. Antonio and I wanted to have breakfast ready by the time everyone woke up. He started cooking the bacon, and I cooked the eggs. Eventually, one by one, my entire family made their way to the kitchen. My parents looked so happy to see us all there that morning. They had always been big on Christmas and its traditions. After breakfast my sisters and I cleaned up the kitchen. Once we finished cleaning up, we all exchanged gifts and reminisced about a few childhood memories.

After we all had opened our gifts, Antonio pulled me aside and said, "I have one more gift for you." He pulled out a small, robin-egg-blue box from the pocket of his hoodie. "I wanted us to be alone when I gave this to you." He seemed rather nervous, keeping his eyes on the little box he continuously rotated in his hand. "I know how *Breakfast at Tiffany's* is your favorite movie," he whispered, "so I figured it was about time that you actually owned something from Tiffany's."

"Aw, bumblebee, you shouldn't have." I opened the box and found a beautiful silver necklace with a heart-shaped charm that had our initials engraved in it.

"Oh," he said, "before I forget, I wrote you a little something on the inside of the box top."

I checked the box top. The message read: "My heart keeps me alive, and you keep my heart alive. So promise me you'll always be mine so that I always know my heart and I will be just fine." He took the necklace out from the little blue box and gracefully placed it around my neck.

That Christmas was both silver and gold. The *choo-choo* from the passing train that night became the chorus to my Christmas carol. The frost on my childhood window made North Eleventh Street look snow laden. And even though Texas kept us from walking in a winter wonderland, we still frolicked and played the Eskimo way. No matter what they say, there is no place like home for the holidays.

As a child, dolls and coloring books brought me the merriest of Christmases, but at a wise age, being in the midst of his presence showed me the true meaning of merriness.

It's Christmastime in the city. The church bells are ringing, "Silver and Gold." Their peaceful chimes bring magic to every home, no matter how young, no matter how old. On a quiet night, on a quiet street, there is a house almost too small for a Christmas tree. And in that house, there are two glasses of warm cinnamon milk. One glass is half-empty, and the other glass is half full. Tony Bennett is singing my favorite song. God, I love it when he sings along, because no, they can't take that away from me.

He holds me, and he holds me close. He leaves no space or cracks in between. His lips graze my neck as he gently hums to a small-town girl dreaming of New York City and how it never sleeps.

I ask him to blow out the candles, all but one. He asks where I've been on the bumpy roads of love, to which I simply reply, "I have no memory of…"

"Well then," he says, "Merry Christmas to all, and to all a good night."

※

A year went by after that Christmas, and plans were made, dreams were conceived, and a future was born. Although we had our fair share of ups and downs, our love never let us down.

There were times he pissed me off, and there were times I really pissed him off, but no matter who was at fault, we never said good night until one of us apologized.

※

Antonio's father died in 1996 in an industrial accident. His family received a small fortune from his father's company to compensate them for their loss. Antonio's mother saw the small fortune as an opportunity for a fresh start. After all, she wanted nothing to do with the city of Dallas because of all the memories she had made there with the only man she had ever loved. She grabbed her two boys, and they made their way to Corpus Christi, Texas, in 1997.

Antonio was very protective of his mother and his younger brother. He felt that it was now his responsibility to take on his father's role as the man of the house. His mother, Elena, was as sweet as pie. She had so much love to give for such a tiny woman. She was as caring as she was compassionate. She always told me I was like the daughter she never had, and still to this day, I truly believe that we shared that bond. She was a great mother who had the best interest in mind for her two sons. I'll always remember the time she told me that I had fixed her boy and that for that she would always be grateful.

Alejandro, "Alex," was Antonio's twenty-year-old football-scholar baby brother. Alex was quite the ladies' man. And who could blame him? He was just as handsome as his big brother. Alex had the best of everything, because that's the kind of life Antonio had provided for him. Antonio never wanted his brother to feel like there was something missing, even though there was. He didn't want Alex growing up angry at the world like he had, so Antonio made sure to be the father figure that his little brother needed.

I knew his father's death had a lot to do with Antonio's troubled soul. Elena told me that Antonio was very close to his father. They were the best of friends. She said that the day his father died, Antonio went from being such a happy child to a rebellious teen. "And although my baby was smiling and joking around most of the time, I could always see the pain in his eyes. There were many nights I witnessed him waking up in tears. Dreams of his father haunted his thoughts and preoccupied his subconscious. They never stopped even as the years went by. 'Sometimes dreams are so sweet,' he'd say, 'I often wonder if they should be considered nightmares.'"

Antonio worked for Bay Coast Drilling, a company that managed a few oil rigs in South Texas. He worked as the assistant manager in the main office, which was located on the outskirts of Corpus Christi. Although the job paid very well, he had bigger dreams for himself, and so did I. On the days that I didn't have class, I would pick us up some lunch and drive out to his office, where I'd spend the whole hour of his lunch break with him. At the time I was the owner of a jungle-green Geo Prism. I hated it. Antonio would constantly tease me about it. He called it the Green Goblin. And even though it was great on gas, I was ever so happy when I finally got rid of it.

I could always hear his collection of old classic rock blaring from his office down the hallway. It was always chilly in his office, but that really didn't bother me much. My constant complaint was instead the fact that it perpetually smelled like an old, greasy mechanic shop. But all in all, I really do miss going and surprising him at work, because as soon as he would see me standing in the doorway, his smile just beamed. He would turn down the radio, give me a kiss, and then go straight for the bag of food. He was such a goofball—one of the many reasons why I loved him.

Thursday, April 5, 2007
9:46 p.m.

Dear Diary,
My class was cancelled today, so instead of spending the afternoon alone, I decided

to give Antonio's mother a call to see what her plans were for the day. She said she had spent the entire morning cleaning and was just lounging around the house at the moment all by herself and with nothing to do, given that Alex was at the university working on an assignment with his study group.

As soon as I told her my class had been cancelled and that I also had nothing planned until Antonio got out of work at five thirty, she insisted that I come over for a late lunch. I headed for Flour Bluff around one. I was hauling ass to get to Elena's, because I hadn't eaten all day and I was starving. Lucky for me, it's only about a twenty-minute drive from the university to her house. You know, I never really understood the whole concept of Flour Bluff, because it has its own name as a small town but is actually still considered a part of Corpus Christi.

Anyway, when I got to Elena's, she had prepared us some delicious strawberry garden salads with grilled chicken for lunch, along with a large pitcher of iced mint water. We ate out in the backyard under the little Bali hut that Antonio and Alex had built for her. Her backyard is breathtaking!

I must say, Elena's home is hands down the most exquisite out of all the houses down Otranto Street. Down the road, if Antonio and I ever get married, I want a house just like hers. After all, it's all I really need: three bedrooms, a spacious living room, and an in-ground pool in the backyard surrounded by a beautiful garden. Oh, and I wouldn't mind having my very own Bali hut where I could spend my quiet evenings writing about my God-given, bizarre dreams of strange worlds inhabited by mythical creatures while waiting for my husband to get home from work. Don't get me wrong. I don't plan to get married anytime soon. But hey, a girl can dream.

After lunch, Elena asked if I would like to see some baby photos of Antonio. I won't lie. I was pretty excited at the fact that she had even asked. After all, it's a pretty big deal when a mother is willing to share with her son's girlfriend such intimate photos of him. I quickly gathered up all the dirty dishes from lunch while she went and fetched Antonio's baby-photo albums.

Every photo she shared with me seemed to have such a compelling story behind it. And although there were many, I couldn't get enough. She told me that Antonio was her miracle baby, because after she'd had two miscarriages and a stillborn, the doctors told her that the possibility of her actually giving birth to a healthy child was slim. But that didn't stop her. In fact, she and Antonio's father, Fernando, tried again only seven months later, and that's when they conceived my little rebel. She told me that she had a lot of complications while she was pregnant with Antonio and didn't know what to expect at the time. The day she finally went into labor, the doctors had to perform an emergency C-section, because Antonio's umbilical cord was tangled around his neck and he was slowly being strangled. She admitted that when she first heard the news, she doubted her faith in God for a minute, but once she was able to hold her breathing baby, she swore to herself that it was the last time she would ever question her conviction.

Once we got past his newborn pictures, we were able to laugh about the silly things that little menace did throughout his childhood. If we ever have kids, I sure hope they don't take after him, because by the sound of it, he was quite a handful.

Kids? Hmm…maybe two boys and a girl. I definitely want to name one of my boys Dean, after the Winchester brother, and my baby girl Emma, an amalgam that's a tribute to my sisters, Emily and Amy. Emma Riot—I really like that name.

I had a lot of fun today, and I learned a lot of new things as well. But I think the most memorable thing about today was when Elena shared with me her family recipe for her famously delicious banana cake. That was pretty much her sealing the deal with me as far as welcoming me into the family.

"Elena's Banana Cake Recipe"
¼ cup of butter
1¼ cups of sugar
2 eggs
2 bananas (sliced thin)
1 cup of buttermilk
2 cups of flour

And that's all you're getting from me. Besides, it's a secret family recipe.

Anyway, I'm off to bed. Goodnight! Sleep tight! Dream of all that's sweet, like banana cake, rich frosting, and 1¼ cups of sugar without the hassle. After all, dreaming isn't anywhere near as complex as Elena's recipe, and unlike her banana cake, even the sweetest dreams are fat free.

Love,
Morgan

I eventually told Antonio the truth about my age. And although he was disappointed, the little things are always too late to matter when you're already in love. In fact, he even took it on himself to light the nineteen candles on my cake that year.

When the people around us asked him what our secret was, he simply answered, "There is no secret. She's a Pegasus, the only one that exists, and she is mine, all mine."

In autumn 2007 we spent most of our spare time at the lake house with Antonio's brother and my two sisters, carving pumpkins and indulging our appetites for seedless watermelon. And while our siblings splashed around in the lake, Antonio and I sipped on freshly squeezed lemonade as we rocked back and forth on some old chairs on the back porch. In the evenings we would chase each other around and push each other into large piles of golden leaves we had raked together hours before. It was our version of tag, with a twist. Every time Antonio tossed me into a pile of leaves, he made sure to fall right next to me. I made him promise me over and over again that this was how it was always going to be, because this was everything I wanted it to be.

He loved autumn. It was his favorite season. He said it reminded him that change was something infinite and that as long as we were living, it was never too late for a transition. The brown leaves, those orange skies, they live so comfortably vivid in the back of my mind. If I close my eyes, I can still smell the light scent of pomegranate that sailed through the wind on those quiet evenings. If I dare close my eyes, I can still see him carelessly rocking back and forth on that old chair of his, clumsily strumming the strings on his father's old Gibson as he gently sang the sixth verse of "Stairway to Heaven," concentrating on every chord, lost in a world that not even I could be a part of. And while he paid his form of homage to Led Zeppelin for writing what is possibly the greatest song ever written, I stared at the sky wondering why so many people are convinced that love is only something we are supposed to dream of.

After all, if we can love the seasons, the thought of change, and a rock song as much as we do, then why is it suddenly impossible for love to exist between two human beings?

Autumn, you used to be a dear friend of mine, but now your skies make me question everything I was so sure of.

Monday, December 24, 2007
11:27 p.m.

Dear Diary,

I just got done baking a batch of sugar cookies. Well, a second batch of sugar cookies, since I burned the first ones. Unfortunately I'm not very good at baking. As a matter of fact, I even made an effort to shape my second batch of cookies into little reindeer, and they just ended up coming out looking like disfigured jackrabbits—but at least they still taste good. Anyway, can you believe it'll already be Christmas again tomorrow? Where did the year go? Oh my God! I just realized it'll be mine and Antonio's second year together. Wow. It's hard to believe we've made it this far. I feel like the luckiest girl in the world.

OK, so I did something kind of bad, and I need to get it off my chest. But you gotta promise not to say a thing...I may have taken a peek at one of my gifts. I know. I'm a horrible person, but I couldn't help it. I was home all alone, and when I'm all alone, I have no self-control. Besides, the wrapping paper was already coming undone, so technically it was only a matter of time until I saw what was in there. And it's not like I didn't already know they were the earrings I was hoping for.

Gosh, it's so cold outside. I have the heater on in the apartment, but I'm still freezing. I'm wearing a sweater and some thick wool socks. But I'll be fine, because Antonio will be home any minute now to warm me up. He's out putting gas in the Jetta, because we're heading out to Raymondville bright and early in the morning, so I'd better head off to bed. I want to pretend I'm asleep when he gets here, because I left him a little surprise in the living room. In order to make sure he sees his little surprise, I left on the musical lights on the Douglas fir. In fact, right now they're playing "O Christmas Tree," his favorite carol. And by the singing tree are a batch of questionable cookies and a tall glass of milk, along with a letter I wrote that reads, "Dear Saint Nick, Thanks for making me believe again."

Anyway, I'm off to bed. Good night. Don't ever be afraid to dream a little weird, a little happy, and a little hopeful.

Love,
Morgan

That Christmas Day, Antonio gave me a beautiful musical figurine of a young princess dancing in the arms of her charming prince. It played the most mesmerizing song. Its depiction of innocence was a perfect description of our love. To this day, whenever I miss him, I wind up that figurine and play its song over and over again for hours.

July 26, 2008, was a hot summer day in Corpus Christi. Antonio and I had just smoked a little hydroponic before making our way out to Bob Hall Pier. It surprises me how faithful and clear the images of that day have been to my mind. The dirtiest of blond locks tied back in a bun, a color so precise in shade that some would call it filthy, ravaged. Shades kissed by the child of blue haven't aged a day in spite of all the summers they've seen. Cherished, they rest accounted for on the back of his sun-freckled neck as he licks and tucks the jagged ends of the grape cigarillo he cut to fill with our relentless thoughts, potent thoughts that raised questions about the universe and all its mysteries. Potent thoughts that dragged me by my will, back to my youth, where they raped me with an uncut innocence over and over again until they knew for sure that I was indeed satisfied.

It wasn't an addiction or substance abuse; it was a liberation. Every huff was sultry, and every puff had its artistry. The contact between our lungs and the cannabis gave us a freedom that people like us normally weren't privileged to have. The smell of the cannabis on his skin combined with the lingering lavender on mine was like a rush of cocaine to my senses. To this day, every time I catch a whiff of cannabis carelessly drifting in the wind, I hear his childish laugh, because it's the one thing I refuse to lock away in that safe place we as humans make in an attempt to forget the unforgettable.

I had been waiting all week for that Saturday to arrive, because it was the only day we were both free to hit the beach. I was in desperate need of a tan, and to be quite honest, so was he. On the way to the beach, I took a few sips from my coffin-shaped flask, because a little warm whiskey always helped me relax. We kept the windows rolled down all the way past the JFK Causeway. I could smell the salt of the sea in the air. I could see flocks of seagulls everywhere. Angel birds, that's what he called them.

As soon as we got onto the island, I began to scroll through my MP3 player like a lunatic, looking for "Maps" by the Yeah Yeah Yeahs. It was my favorite song to listen to whenever I was soaring high from the golden quality of his drugs. Every time I hear that song now, it haunts me like that beautiful summer day.

We spent that whole day chasing waves and putting life into the clouds that rolled by in the Caribbean-blue sky. At 6:53 p.m. the waves had eased, and the sun began to set. A slight breeze set the mood for an unforgettable conversation. My poor baby, he was completely worn out by the end of the day. He buried his back in the sand and looked up at the evening sky with so much wonder in his eyes. With the sun almost gone, the breeze was beginning to feel a little chilly, so I threw on an old, sleeveless Boston T-shirt he had stashed in the trunk of his car from the band's Third Stage Tour. I then sat in the sand and propped his head on my legs. As I brushed his hair back with my fingertips, he began to ask me questions that I could not firmly answer. "Baby, have you ever tried to grasp the concept of how long forever truly is? I mean, I know forever is forever, but have you actually ever tried to imagine what it would be like to live forever? I mean, really think about it. It's kind of weird, isn't it? Or maybe I'm just kind of weird."

I leaned over for a kiss and said, "Well, now that you mention it. You probably are the weirdest person I know, but then again, I think your weird is sexy. So I probably don't fall too far behind you when it comes to being weird."

"You're such an ass!" He laughed. "But in all seriousness, how can people say that there is no God when we are surrounded by so much beauty? Look at all the stars. Look at all the clouds. Look at all the birds in the sky and the fish in the sea. How does the sun know where to set? And how does moon know when to shine? How does the ocean know it's only supposed to come this far?" He sighed, looking exhausted from his own train of thoughts. "I don't know. There's just so much mystery in the universe and so many questions to those mysteries that I find it hard to believe that there isn't a greater power out there keeping the unknown. Are we alone? Are there other realms or worlds where magic exists? And how do we as humans get the opportunity to visit these lands like Dorothy and Alice, without the acid?" he asked. He rubbed his eyes, both red from the saltwater. He then looked up at me with a frown and said, "I'm sorry, babe. I don't mean to ramble on about random shit. Just have a lot on my mind."

I used my fingers to force his frown into a smile and said, "Don't ever refer to your thoughts as 'random shit,' because the moment you do is the moment they become just that. If it's any consolation, I think your thoughts are rather glorious. Random? Well it's only normal for a vigorous soul to have an active mind, and almost every active mind has a tendency to be untimely."

He smiled, and this time on his own. "Darling, do you think it's possible that somewhere out there in this whole wide world someone is doing this very same thing at this very same moment?" He moved his rough hands up my thighs.

"There better be," I whispered. "It would be a damn shame if there wasn't, because then how else would anybody know how happy I am at this very moment?"

"How the hell did we get so lucky?" He groaned happily.

I gently flicked his nose and said, "Easy, tiger. You should never question a good thing."

He took a deep breath and said, "I know, baby, but think about it. Some people spend their whole lives looking for what we have and don't even come close to something as special. Yet here we are."

He sighed as his eyes sailed off into the endless sea. "I guess I just feel like God's been a little too sweet on me, and I'm not quite sure if it's by mistake or design. But hey, never question a good thing, right?"

"What makes you say God's been a little too sweet on you?"

"C'mon. I was a bad man, kiddo."

"You weren't bad. You were angry."

"Yeah." He nodded. "So angry that I drank until I was numb, and once I was numb, I went looking for trouble because I wanted to feel again. I knew exactly what I was doing, Morgan. I could have dealt with that anger another way, but I chose to show the world what I was capable of." He nervously laughed and said, "Shit, I've been in jail so many times; I don't even know how I was able to land such a good job. I messed up. I messed up a lot, on the drugs, on the women. I made things so much harder for my mother than they already were. I didn't even give her a chance to mourn my father's death the way she should have. There were cops at her door every single night, because her junkie son had to start shit at every bar he went to." His eyes watered as his lips quivered. "I just wish I could give that back to her."

I placed my hand on his forehead. "But you have given her something so much greater by being the man you've become."

He broke into a smile that expanded from ear to ear. "I fucking love you, kiddo."

I smiled and said, "You better."

"I sure do, my little riot." He bit his lip and placed the palm of his hand against my face.

I pressed my lips firmly into the center of his palm, replying, "Good, because I think I just might love you as much as I love rock 'n' roll."

"Wow." He raised his eyebrow, evidently impressed. "You just said a mouthful there, young lady." He quickly stood up and reached out for me, lifting me off the ground. I threw my arms around his neck and wrapped my legs around his chiseled, tattooed torso. I then kissed him over and over again for reminding me why my summer was the best. "Look at the sky," he said. As he continued to whisper in my ear, I could hear his words becoming one with the wind. "Do you know why the sky turns orange and why the clouds turn lilac in the evenings?"

"No. Why?"

He slyly smirked and said, "Because that's when the sun and the moon secretly meet for a kiss. So whenever you see the sun and the moon in the midst of their rendezvous, always remember how lucky I was to have found you."

I'll never forget that day, every word he said, or how he smiled when he looked at me with no words to follow after, no worries big enough to matter. God, I can still feel him twirling me around in the sand, waltzing with me like a madman. I can still see our poor sketches and love letters scattered across that warm summer sand. Oh, you've got to believe me when I say I loved that man.

"Honey and Bumblebees"
I hope you remember me like this,
From my sunbathed eyes to my brown skin,
To vanilla ice cream trailing down my lip,
To yellow daisies in my hair,
To dancing in circles around you, leaving footprints in the sand,
Footprints that'll later serve as stories for all our tomorrows
While the seagulls sing and bumblebees buzz
Buzzing, because you've made my life so sweet
The waves are crashing as visions of love gracefully flutter in the wind
I'm only a few feet ahead of you
Secretly dreaming of a better life in a world of black and white
Constantly turning back just to make sure you're still there
Even though I know you're still there
I don't utter a single word
I simply continue to walk
Walking, as if I have hope that heaven lies ahead
And all I can hear is silence, because all I see is golden
And I am happy, and by the looks of it, you are too
And it's at this very moment I realize
I want to spend my whole life being your happiness
Because like honey, you've made my life so sweet

Monday, September 15, 2008
8:01 p.m.

Dear Diary,

    There's a pile of dishes in the sink that I am in no rush to get to and tons of leftover food in the kitchen that I am in no hurry to put away. I am so stuffed. I can barely move. In fact, I'm still sitting at the kitchen table asking myself why I ate as much as I did. Antonio is in a food coma on the living-room couch. It's been such a long day, but everything went as planned. Today was Antonio's twenty-ninth birthday. At twenty-nine years old, my old man is slowly but surely climbing over that hill. But shit, I'm not complaining, because his strong features are right behind him—and boy, are they coming along nicely.

    Today I had originally just planned to take him out to a fancy little restaurant downtown for dinner, but this morning when he woke up, he seemed a little gloomy. I asked him what was wrong as soon as I noticed the mood he was in. He simply but sadly responded, "I'm almost thirty." He then guzzled the rest of the coffee left in the pot and headed for the shower.

Before heading off to work, he gave me a kiss on my forehead. As he picked up his keys and moved toward the door, I stopped him. I gave him a big hug and said, "Nobody likes getting old, but it's not something that should make you sad; it's something you should be thankful for. There are people all over the world right now wishing that they could have just one more birthday, wishing that they could live just one more year, one more day. And here you are worried about turning thirty. You know what? I hope you do get old. I hope God gives you many more birthdays to come. Because I plan to live a long and healthy life, and I wouldn't know what to do without you here by my side." I finally wished him a happy birthday, and he was able to break into a smile. I just couldn't send a man who had to work on his birthday out the door in such a doleful mood. I pulled him in by his collar for a kiss, and while I kissed him, I thanked God for giving the man who gave me butterflies, knots, and shivers another year of life.

As he walked out the door, I softly sang, "There's something about you, handsome, that makes me happy on your birthday too." I'm pretty sure I sent that boy blushing all the way to work.

I only had one class today, and I knew that I would be out by two o'clock at the latest. So I decided to do something for Antonio that was a little more special than just a cheesy dinner, something that would make him really happy on his big day. I called my sister Amy before class and asked her if she could come to Corpus to help me set up a little surprise party for him, since Antonio was the biggest fan of her homemade lasagna. She said both she and Emily would be here by the time I got out of class.

After class I rushed over to Antonio's apartment, where my sisters were already waiting for me in the parking lot. We quickly made our way to the grocery store to get the stuff we needed for dinner and decorations. We had no time to waste. Antonio's boss was letting him out early because it was his birthday, so we needed everything ready by four thirty. I called Elena and asked her if she and Alex would come over to surprise Antonio with us, and she said, "I'll bring the banana cake."

Elena and Alex got to the apartment around three forty-five. Sure enough, Elena had brought her baby his favorite cake, freshly baked. And as for Alex, well, he also had his hands full with a twenty-four-pack of his big brother's favorite beer. Emily and Alex blew up some balloons while Elena and I prepared the salads and garlic bread. Everything was ready by 4:15 p.m., and at exactly 4:23 p.m., Antonio's key began turning the lock.

When he walked through the door, his smile was from ear to ear. He was so happy to see us all and what we had done just for him. Amy, Elena, Antonio, and I ate at the kitchen table. Emily and Alex had to eat in the living room, because Antonio's table is only built to seat four. But all in all, we enjoyed ourselves, Antonio especially.

I really wish my sisters could've stayed, but they both have long days ahead of them tomorrow. I know I should really get to these dishes, but I think I'm gonna take a quick little nap before. So in case I don't wake up until tomorrow, good night! Dream big, abundant, and of nothing small at all, 'cause even in your dreams, the smallest things should be bigger than you. With that being said, unleash your darkest fantasies and allow them to run free, because it's within that freedom that we discover the most beautiful possibilities.

Love,
Morgan

Sunday, February 15, 2009
4:13 a.m.

Dear Diary,

It's four o'clock in the morning, and I'm wide awake. I can't sleep for the life of me. I thought a warm bath would help, but even after that I tossed and turned for almost an hour. So now, here I am at my last resort. After all, a warm glass of milk and a diary entry have always provided me with a steady sea in which to drop the anchor attached to my wandering, restless mind.

There's a full moon out tonight, shining big and bright. Her azure light is peeking through the open blinds and crawling across the room, spreading an illusion that makes me feel like I'm under the deep, blue, mysterious sea. And although she is so beautiful here and now, I bet she'd look far more gorgeous outside an eighteenth-floor window down Lamar Street in Houston, Texas. After all, that is where Antonio and I should have been tonight. I won't lie. I'm a little bummed out that we couldn't make it to our romantic Valentine getaway, but I could never and would never ask him to leave his mother behind in her delicate condition.

Elena suffered a massive heart attack Friday morning. She has been in the hospital all weekend. The doctor said it's gonna be a slow recovery. He said it was a miracle that she even made it, and if she isn't careful, next time she might not be so lucky. I love Elena, and I hate seeing such a strong woman like her in such a fragile state. It really broke my heart to see two grown men cry for their mother's sake. Antonio was completely devastated. Why, he even asked my parents if they would come pay his mother a visit at the hospital to join him in prayer, and so they did, first thing Saturday morning.

Even though my nose did not smell a single rose, and even though I spent the entire day alone, I'm glad we stayed. Because if anything had happened to her while we were away, I would never have been able to forgive myself. Besides, Valentine's wasn't all that bad. Antonio got home from the hospital around nine o'clock dressed up as Humphrey Bogart, the dangerously handsome saloon bandit, one of his latest personas concocted for the collection of explicit characters we use in our adult monologues. The truth is you don't need to be in a fancy hotel room in order to unleash your imagination.

He started off with a little striptease and then went straight to the pistol whipping. Afterward we popped open a bottle of champagne and ate red velvet cake in bed while we watched *Breakfast at Tiffany's*, as we traditionally do at the end of every Valentine's Day.

He thanked me over and over again for being so understanding of his situation. He said he was sure I was the girl he wanted to spend the rest of his life with, and those very words are always the best a girl can hear a man say on Valentine's Day. He lit a cigar and then debonairly requested I place my head on his chest. Once I was settled, he gently squeezed my body against his and said, "I love you, Ms. Whoever-You-Are."

To this I replied, "I love you too, Freddy baby."

Anyway, I'm off to bed. This milk and entry are already working their magic, and the more I yawn, the lower my eyes get. So good night and (like always) dream sweet and (like always) sleep tight. Happy Valentine's Day, whether or not you're a "yours to a mine." Life is a fact, and it's a fact that eventually two people do fall in love and that eventually those two people end up belonging to each other. It's only a matter of time. So until then, don't be afraid to splurge on the fiction of dreams while waiting on the facts of life.

Love,
Morgan

"I Love Lucy"
I know it's only May, but I swear, I swear it feels like Christmas morning
Maybe it has something to do with the thermostat being so low
Or the fact that you made yourself a cup of chai tea before December
You're watching *I Love Lucy*
You've always been a big fan of black-and-white TV,
Just as I've always been a fan of all those little details
You are so intrigued, that I pretend to still be asleep
While secretly watching you
Constantly attempting to restrain your laugh
By trading it in for a much quieter, boyish smile
I think it's quite silly that my eyes can't be yours, for just one second
So you can see just how beautiful you are to me

And so I say, it feels like Christmas every day
Well, at least in the mornings I wake up next to you
Maybe it does have something to do with the thermostat being so low
Or the simple fact that you feel like my gift from God Himself
It's only 6:51 a.m.
And so, I have all the right to pretend that I am still asleep
Even though the truth is I'm watching you
And I'm trying not to smile, but I can't help it
It's absolutely adorable to see you so focused on something other than me for once
And although I know it's only May
Merry Christmas in every single language
And a good morning in just one single kiss

※

Elisabeth Lena Gonzales passed away at 3:07 a.m. on May 14, 2009. Doctors said it was bound to happen. There was so much damage done to her heart the first time around that she had been practically living with only half a heart for the past few months. Of course, I believe that Elena had been living with only half of her heart long before the first attack; the infarction just finished what was left of it.

Antonio cried every night and every morning for months. Alex, however, didn't shed a tear, as far as anyone witnessed. In fact, he really didn't say much after the light of his world left him with nothing but darkness. After the burial, Alex packed up all his things and moved somewhere upstate. He never said where he was going. He sort of just disappeared. That was the last time Antonio heard from his little brother. And although he tried and tried, he never could get in contact with his brother after that.

I know what you're probably thinking by now—that my story is just some other cheesy tearjerker waiting to be made into a movie for one of those channels for hormonal women. Well, it's not. Don't go thinking we were a boring couple, because we weren't. I'm telling you the sweet side of the story, because, as a girl, I can't help but like that sentimental crap. So bear with me, because this story actually gets pretty gritty.

I grew up in a very sheltered home where I wasn't allowed to do a lot of things that the other kids were doing because I had two conservative parents who were completely devoted to their religious faith and its moral views. And anyone who has been in my situation knows that you tend to go balls to the wall when you are finally given the slightest freedom to make your own decisions and create your own mistakes.

On October 2, 2009, I left an awkward seventeen-year-old girl far behind when I officially became a confident twenty-one-year-old woman. That year Antonio and I celebrated my birthday with my family at my parents' house in Raymondville. Antonio was willing to take me anywhere I wanted to go for my twenty-first birthday, but I told him that I just wanted to enjoy turning one year older in the company of my family. It's funny. I remember when I was younger, I wanted to get out of my parents' house so much, but as I got older, I kept running back to that little house like it was a sanctuary.

Antonio and my father threw some steaks on the grill while my mother and sisters stirred up some sides to go along with our late lunch. After lunch they all gathered around the kitchen table to sing "Happy Birthday" to me. As my sisters lit the candles that were nearly buried in strawberry frosting, Antonio shouted, "It's a cake, not a genie! You only got one wish, angel bird, so make it count!"

I laughed and said, "Well, maybe next year you'll get me a genie instead of cake!" I closed my eyes because I wanted to convince everyone I had made my wish when I blew out the candles, even though I didn't. Instead I kept my wish for someday when I'd really need it, because at the time, I already had everything I could wish for. There was no point in wasting a good wish.

Shortly after everyone had eaten their slices of cake, Antonio pulled me aside. He had a blindfold in his hand and a mischievous look in his eyes. "Easy there, tiger. We're at my parents' house," I whispered with sarcasm and a dirty mind.

He rolled his eyes and said, "It's nothing like that, you pervert. Well, at least not yet." He winked. "Anyway, hurry up and turn around so I can blindfold you. And don't worry." He giggled. "Your parents are in on the surprise."

As he placed the blindfold over my eyes, I could hear my brothers and sisters giggling among themselves. Soon everything was pitch black. He placed his hands on my waist and slowly began directing me toward my surprise. After taking a few steps forward, I heard the screen door open, and he carefully led me outside. As soon as I made my way out the front door, my sense of sound was struck by all the life in my neighborhood, from lawn mowers to unattended children playing carelessly on the streets, from the bass of the lowriders passing by the block to the ice-cream truck on its daily route.

Suddenly I felt Antonio's lips graze my ear. "Just a little further, baby." His words gently fluttered off into the wind.

As humans, I believe we have a natural instinct of knowing when we are supposed to capture a specific moment, because for some strange reason, I knew to take in every second of that moment in every way possible, just as effectively as a video or a photograph.

"OK," he said, "when I take the blindfold off, keep your eyes closed. Do not open your eyes until I tell you to, OK?"

I nodded. "OK."

I could feel him tugging on the blindfold as he struggled to untie it. As soon as the blindfold slid off my face, he said, "You better not be peeking, you little shit."

I playfully nudged him in the gut. "I'm not."

He led me a few steps further ahead before his whisper traveled to my ears like a symphony. "OK, open your eyes."

When I laid eyes on my surprise, it was love at first sight. Antonio had always put so much thought into the gifts he gave me, but this was beyond anything I could ever imagine. Most guys usually just give their girlfriends ridiculously expensive jewelry or tacky designer purses for their birthdays, but on mine, my man had parked a 1967 Ford Mustang Eleanor in my father's driveway.

"Oh my God! He's perfect!" I shouted.

As I wrapped my arms around Antonio, he kissed my forehead and said, "The paint's new, the interior's new, and it's even equipped with a full audio system. Oh, and check out the rims on this bad boy. They're customized."

I've had a thing for hot rods and muscle cars since I was thirteen, and this was absolutely, without a doubt, my dream car. The candy-red body paint was gorgeously glossy, and the two white racing stripes finished it off to pure perfection. It was everything I had ever told Antonio I wanted in a car. I had thought I could only dream of it. "Thank you so much, baby! I love it!" I shouted. I couldn't refrain from thanking Antonio over and over again, because this was hands down the best gift I had ever received in my entire life.

Before I could thank him again, Antonio looked at my father and said, "Whoa, whoa, whoa. Don't give me all the credit. It actually took your pops and me about a year to track this bad boy down."

I turned to my father and watched as his face lit up when I said, "Aw, Dad, you're the best. I absolutely love it." I gave my father a hug. "I love you, Pops."

He smiled that famous smile of his and said, "I love you too, my little sunshine"

My father cleared his throat and then raised his brow, cocked his head toward the car, and said, "I don't know about Antonio, but I'm pretty curious to know. What are you gonna name him?"

As I began to carefully examine my car, his name came to me almost immediately. "His name is Arson," I said. My father and Antonio both looked at me as if I were crazy. I knew that they were both wondering why I would give my car such a name, and so I explained. "I'm gonna name him Arson because he looks like he's ready to raise as much hell as rock 'n' roll." They both laughed and nodded in full agreement.

When we got back into Corpus that day, Antonio and I took Arson for a ride down Ocean Drive. That evening, without request, I tossed Antonio my keys, because I knew that he had secretly made the investment to spend some time behind the wheel as well. The sun setting across the bay made me feel like I was in the ending of an old mob movie. The rows of palm trees and the ramshackle mansions always reminded me of a younger Hollywood, when fame wasn't spoiled by rotten children and when talent didn't rely on sex or scandals to fatten its credibility. Lighting a joint behind the wheel of the fantasy he had made into a reality, the man of my dreams looked like such a badass that I almost didn't want to interrupt the magnificence of the moment, but I simply had to. "So," I said, "I've been thinking, and

I really want to make the year of the big two-one into something memorable."

"Yeah? How so?" He clamped the joint between his lips.

I had to cast my gaze on the glamour and grittiness of the downtown scene one last time before I was able to firmly reply. "I want to break out of my comfort zone. I want to meet crazy, careless people. I want a chance to hear their insane stories," I said, running out of breath. I looked over at Antonio, who seemed intrigued, and said, "You know what? Screw that! I want to be one of those crazy, careless people. I want to have my own crazy-ass stories to tell. C'mon, what do you say, badass? Let's be young. Let's be wild. Let's get into some trouble. Let's bend the law and break a few rules. Take me to questionable bars. Show me the ropes. I want chills, cheap thrills, friends, adventurous weekends!"

I had to take a deep breath in order to simmer down. Once I felt capable of carrying on a rational conversation, I gently squeezed Antonio's thigh and said, "Look, I know it sounds insane, but it's a desire that I need to get out of my system. Just one year, baby. That's all I'm asking for. Let's ignore all the warning signs. Let's take a walk on the wild side." I looked thoughtfully out at the setting sun before I said the only thing I had to say in order to convince him. "I just don't want my youth to slip away before I have the chance to create memories that I can share as stories later on in my life when I'm an old, old, old lady."

As I continued to ramble on about how I wanted to spend the coming year, I noticed that Antonio had been selfishly taking hit after hit from the joint, nearly causing it to roach. So before he could take another hit, I ripped what was left of the joint out of his fingertips and took two big hits. I let the smoke linger in my lungs for a while before I slowly released it from between my ruby-red-painted lips. Once the smoke had cleared, I turned to him and asked, "So, what do you say? Are you in or out?"

He snatched the joint from my fingertips and then grinned and said, "Count me in, kiddo. If you want crazy, I'll show you crazy."

He quickly killed off what was left of the joint and then flicked the butt out the window, floored the gas pedal, and picked up momentum in a matter of seconds, causing my entire body to sink into the brand-new leather seat. As he gazed over at me, laughing like a lunatic, I couldn't help but smile. And so I smiled. I simply smiled.

Part 3

Before Jesta and Emily, before Cleo and Derya, there was Ruby and Jaceil. Long before the Wicker Palace, there was a place called the Wall.

The night after my birthday, a Saturday, Antonio took me to downtown Corpus Christi at around ten thirty. The city lights were burning their brightest, and the commotion was at its rowdiest. I had never seen the streets or the night so alive. A swarm of drunken people fell in and out of the clubs that infested the nightlife of the strip. Taxis lurked in every corner, while minors prayed to pass for adults. The night was still young, but the police were already enforcing the law. There was graffiti on the sidewalks and on older buildings that were high enough to cover pieces of the sky. The alleys were dark and uninviting. It was obvious that they could not be trusted. The mixture of music flowing throughout the air met in the sky, evolving into a ruckus that sounded like angry gods at war. Everyone was dressed in their best, ready to impress. Even the homeless wandered in the midst of the crowd, hoping that the people's alcohol levels would amplify their compassion.

That night I wore a tight little black dress that hugged me in all the right places. My eye shadow was smoky, and my heels were from hell. In fact, I had to hold Antonio's hand as we walked down the street to keep my balance in those dreadful heels. But I won't lie. It was worth it, because I felt like a total Betty. Antonio wore a button-up shirt with some fitted blue jeans that made his ass look incredible. He had just gotten a haircut earlier that day, so as you can imagine, he looked like such a stud that night.

He planned to take me to a fancy terrace and lounge called Skyros, because he had heard of its very chill and laid-back atmosphere. I guess he didn't want to overwhelm me, since it was my first time out. When we got to Skyros, there was a huge line. As we waited in line, I began to notice that all the people waiting in line with us to get into the lounge consisted of prissy skanks and greasy-haired douchebags. After processing what could possibly be waiting for us inside if this was what was waiting with us outside, I turned to Antonio and said, "Hey, babe, this isn't exactly what I had in mind."

He wrinkled his nose and said, "Yeah, I didn't think so. Let's go somewhere else."

We got out of line and continued walking down the strip. After walking for a few minutes, we stumbled across a club called the Wall. The building was old, gritty, dark, and dingy. It instantly lured me. There was something about it that was both intriguing and inviting. I grabbed Antonio's hand and rushed over to get a spot in line. When he caught a glimpse of the old building, he laughed and said, "Of course you would."

When we finally got into the bar, I felt like I had entered another dimension. There was rock 'n' roll blaring through the speakers, welcoming us to the jungle. It was so crowded that people were constantly bumping into one another. In the center of the club was a huge bar with two platforms off to each side where two busty strippers flaunted their perky, naked breasts, saluting those about to rock. The pool tables, the dartboards, and the jukebox were all just bonuses. The crowd was the real gold, because it was made up of misfits, outcasts, and thug blood. They were the kind of people I could relate to, as they were the only kind of people I had ever known my whole life.

I quickly dragged Antonio to the bar, where four bartenders were working that night, three guys and a girl. The guys looked like they should have been sterilizing tattoo needles instead of mixing drinks. However, the girl was actually really cute. She definitely wasn't as hardcore as the other bartenders, but she did look like she could be pretty sloppy after a few drinks. Antonio had to wave down the bartenders a few times before the girl behind the bar finally made her way over to us. She must've been either tipsy or coked up, because her eyes were way too giddy for such a busy night. "Hey, what can I get you guys?" she asked as she adjusted her melon-sized tits into her bra, which was two sizes too small.

Antonio had to raise his voice in order for her to hear him over the loud music. "Yeah, I'll have a rum and coke and a Jack and coke!" While she made us our drinks, he dropped a five-dollar bill into her tip jar. The girl was fast. Before I knew it, she was handing us our first round. After taking a sip of our drinks, Antonio and I raised our glasses toward her in cheers to show our satisfaction. And although they were strong as hell, boy, were they good.

She winked at us and asked, "So, is this y'all's first time at the Wall?"

"Yeah," I answered.

She opened her eyes wide. "No way! Well, in that case, allow me to officially pop your cherries! My name is Natalie, but you can call me Natarita, because I make the best mango margaritas in all of Corpus Christi!" She laughed as she grabbed and shook her ginormous tits. Her laugh reminded me of an evil queen who found immense pleasure in abusing her powers. "Anyway," she continued, "we have a live band every Friday, along with Open Mic Night. On Saturdays we have the jukebox going until twelve, and then DJ Rave is in the mix from twelve till three. Last call is at two, and the bar closes an hour after that. So make sure you come get all your drinks from me, because I'm the best bartender in this damn city. Oh!" She shook her head. "Last but not least, make sure you check out our girls, Malaya and Mercedes." She pointed off to the sides where the two topless strippers were rolling around in dollar bills.

We thanked her and then made our way around the club, looking for a good spot to chill. We eventually found a couple of bar stools near one of the pool tables, but before I could take my seat, Antonio leaned in toward my ear and said, "Hey, babe, I need to take a leak. Will you be OK?"

I nodded. "I'll be fine. Go ahead, babe," I assured him with a smile.

He chugged his drink before he left and said, "I'll stop at the bar on the way back to get us another round."

"OK."

He kissed me and said, "I love you more."

I pinched his ass and said, "I love you best." He chuckled, amused by my quick response to his *more*, which most people say after the first person says it, in order to one-up them. "Was that a setup?" I asked.

"Sure was."

"Nice try, bumblebee, but don't forget; I'll always be two steps ahead."

"It was worth a shot!" he shouted as he walked away.

As soon as he disappeared into the crowd, two frat boys approached me. I could tell that they had already thrown back a few cold ones, because their speech was slurred and their eyes were all over the place.

"Hey there, pretty, pretty. My name is Blake, and this is my buddy, Matt the Mighty Wingman." Blake licked his lips. "I've been watching you from across the bar, and I've gotta say, you look good enough to eat." He smelled my hair and said, "Why don't you let me buy you a drink, baby girl?"

"No, thanks," I said, quickly brushing him off as I got up to walk away, but before I could get too far, his friend Matt quickly blocked my path.

Blake then got uncomfortably close to me and said, "Come on, don't be like that, baby. I just wanna show you a good time, if you know what I mean." He grabbed his balls and made a sexual facial expression, causing Matt the Mighty Wingman to chuckle behind his beer. Blake put his hands on my waist, pulling me toward him, and asked, "Do you wanna see it? It's nice and thick, perfect for those pretty little lips." He rubbed his thumb under my bottom lip.

I pushed him off me, completely fed up with his bullshit, and said, "Look, if you don't back off, I'm gonna take Matty-boy's dick and shove it so far up your ass you're gonna wonder why you went without it for so long."

Blake took me by the arm, aggressively pulled me toward him, and then grunted between his teeth, "You stubborn little bitch!"

Suddenly Matt went flying back into a chair, landing flat on his ass. At first I thought it was Antonio coming to my rescue, but when I looked to see who had dropped the dumbass, I saw that it was a girl. She was wearing some blue-jean booty shorts with ripped pantyhose and a shirt she had craftily cut herself. She looked at both Blake and Matt with a pair of crazy eyes.

"Is there a problem here, gentlemen?"

"Nah." Blake shook his head, clenching his pride with his jaw. He then quickly helped Matt up from off the floor and waited for Matt to dust himself off before they both walked away. It was almost as if they knew who she was. It was almost as if they had dealt with her before.

She pulled me toward her and asked, "Are you OK?"

"Yeah," I quickly responded. "Thank you."

She rolled her eyes. "No problem. Those guys are idiots."

"Yeah." I chuckled.

"Besides"—she smiled sweetly—"what kind of world would we live in if us girls didn't help each other out every once in a while, especially from persistent little pricks."

I nodded. "I guess some guys just aren't used to hearing no."

"Yeah, tell me about it." She laughed and then scrunched her forehead and asked, "What's a pretty little thing like you doing all alone in a place like this?"

"I'm not alone. I'm actually here with my boyfriend. He ran over to the restroom, but he should be on his way back." I looked around at the crowd. "I'm Morgan, by the way." I extended my hand to greet her.

She shook my hand and said, "I'm Ruby." Scrunching her lips, she looked around the club and said, "Well, I hate to be the bearer of bad news, but I think your dude might have gotten lost." Then she looked me up and down and said, "I'm going over to the jukebox. Come with me. I'd feel really bad if I left you standing here all by yourself."

I looked around the club yet again, and Antonio was still nowhere in sight. So I thought, *What the hell.* "Yeah, I'll go with you."

She placed my hand over her shoulder, and we swiftly made our way through the crowd. Once we got to the jukebox, she began digging in her pocket for quarters. "So, chica, are you from here?"

I leaned against the jukebox and said, "No, I actually moved here a few years ago for school."

"Oh, college kid, how fancy." She giggled.

"Well, not currently." I frowned a little. "I'm actually taking the year off. I'm bumming off my boyfriend in the meantime." I laughed.

"Why did you ditch the books?"

"Oh no, I didn't ditch the books. I'm planning to go back after the year is over," I assured her.

"Why a year?" she asked.

"Because I just turned twenty-one, and I want to enjoy it the best I can, without any worries or distractions." I smiled.

She smiled back and said, "That's badass. I kinda dig that."

"What about you?" I asked. "Are you from here?"

"No, I'm actually not from anywhere." She sighed. "I'm a nomad, a gypsy. I go wherever the road takes me. To be honest with you, I've only been in Corpus for a few weeks now. As crazy as it sounds, I enjoy the perks of not having a place to call home, because when you're bound to something or somewhere, you limit how far you'll go down a road. I've been called a road dog, a hitchhiker, and even a tumbleweed, but I wouldn't have it any other way. After all, those names have the hardest creditability to gain." She smiled.

I could tell this chick was deep. Although she was a loaded pistol, I could tell that she had a sweet side to her. She had the face of a beauty queen with a pair of eyes that were as comforting as apple pie. Her black eyeliner complemented her rosy cheeks, and her bright-red lipstick made her lips look like cherries in the spring. She must've been the reason men love cold beer and rock 'n' roll. She carried a persona both daring and candid. Her words were like poetry on a summer's eve, because when she talked, she had a way of making you believe that she had the answers to everything. In fact, there came a point when I was quite sure she did. All in all, she was the badass of all badasses.

Suddenly I heard Antonio's voice shouting in the distance. "There you are! You scared the shit out of me," he said, sounding awfully worried. When I turned back to look at him, I saw that he was being followed by a guy and a girl. Antonio ran toward me and placed his hands on my waist. "I'm sorry I took so long. I ran into an old friend of mine." He smiled, looked over at the couple following him, and said, "Morgan, this is my buddy Kenny and his girlfriend, Jaceil."

I politely waved and said, "Hi. Nice to meet y'all."

Kenny and Jaceil nodded and smiled as they both waved back and said, "It's nice to meet you too." Kenny and Jaceil looked like rock stars, a pair of heavy-metal lovers whose relationship was fueled by sex and jealousy.

Antonio began to laugh uncontrollably as he wrapped his arm around my neck and said, "Baby, Kenny and I gave our administration so much shit back in the day, constantly in detention when we weren't suspended."

Kenny Salvador was about Antonio's height and was also only a few months older than my baby. He had a trucker's beard and a dope-ass Mohawk that was only a few inches from the sky. His ears were gauged, and his ink raised questions of a possible loyalty to the dark side. With those brown eyes and that jet-black hair, he was the definition of a bad boy. His teeth were freakishly straight, all but one, which happened to be plated in gold. It was on the bottom row toward the front. I constantly found myself staring at it when he spoke to me. I thought of velvet curtains, cigarettes, and ashtrays whenever I saw Kenny.

Jaceil Martinez looked like a 1950s pinup girl. She had these big, brown cartoon eyes that were so intriguing. She laughed like a villain and cursed like a sailor. She had tiny gauges on her ears, a bull ring through her septum, and a few hippie tattoos here and there. She had the manners of a man, and she didn't give a damn about how she came across to anyone. She was absolutely insane, and her body was just as crazy as she was.

I looked at Antonio from over my shoulder and said, "Well, you aren't the only one who made a friend while you were gone."

I directed their attention to Ruby, who had her arm leaning against the jukebox. "Everyone, this is Ruby."

Jaceil quickly ran to Ruby and me and wrapped her arms around our necks, looked at the boys, and said, "I think you two boys should get us lovely ladies some shots."

The guys looked at each other with goo-goo eyes and laughed as they both nodded toward the bar. As the guys walked away, Jaceil shouted, "Surprise us!" belching louder than Homer Simpson shortly after. While Ruby and I continued to scroll through the jukebox, Jaceil began to shower me with compliments. "Dude, you are so fucking beautiful, and that dress—oh my God! You gotta let me borrow it sometime."

Ruby looked over at Jaceil and said, "Dude, isn't she a total babe? She has that Old Hollywood glamour."

Jaceil agreed, and shortly after, they both began throwing out names of Old Hollywood starlets—Sophia Loren, Bette Davis, Dolores Del Rio, Audrey Hepburn—matching almost every one of my features to those belonging to the queens of the silver screen.

Suddenly Ruby's face, staring at the jukebox, lit up. "Oh shit!" she shouted. "Y'all better buckle up, *jotas*, because shit's about to get real!" She giggled. "This one's for you, M." She winked at me, smacking her bubble gum, and dunked her quarters into the old record machine. As soon as I heard "Cherry Bomb" by Joan Jett and The Blackhearts come on, I knew that we were gonna be the best of friends. Before the song was able to reach the chorus, the guys came back with their hands full of shots. Once all the shots had been distributed, I raised my glass and said, "Cheers to the beginning of a wild night."

One shot quickly turned into three. Three shots quickly turned into eight, and eight quickly turned into a wild night, as predicted. Before I knew it, Antonio and I were off in a corner making out and dry humping on an earth-shaking speaker. Jaceil and Kenny were both drenched in sweat from grinding on each other on the floor. Meanwhile, Ruby had her tongue down some random guy's throat who she had pinned down on a pool table.

We all met one another at the Wall the following weekend, as we had planned for a night that was just as wild. The weekend after that, Ruby met the love of her life. He was filling in for the drummer of a band called Radio Riot that was performing that Friday night at the Wall. His name was Markus Castillo. He had his eyes glued on Ruby the whole time he was on stage, and after the performance, he made his way over to her and challenged her to a pool match. I saw sparks fly that night. They were the same sparks that had ignited the day I met Antonio.

Markus was covered in tattoos from his neck to his sleeves. He looked like a walking piece of art. I found it quite fascinating. However, people outside the Wall constantly stared at him, and some even cringed as if he were some sort of freak. In spite of what some closed-minded people thought of him, he was a total babe. His eyes were greener than the Emerald City, and his pale skin was vampire-like. He reminded me a lot of myself, because he also had the tendency to keep to himself. He wasn't shy; he was selective. He had a big heart and a beautiful way of seeing life. He was such a goofball, definitely the funniest one out of all of us.

In truth, no matter how stable a facade I projected, on the inside I was the biggest misfit. They all had a genuine notion of who they were, while I was still on the brink of self-discovery.

Markus and Kenny both had choppers, so, as you can imagine, Antonio was quick to want one for himself. But instead of buying one, he settled for borrowing one. After all, Kenny had a small collection of three from which he insisted Antonio choose. That week our guys took us on multiple rides from Ocean Drive to North Padre Island, but the girls and I wanted more. The guys were willing to take us on a voyage. The only problem was we had no destination. And then it hit me: Raymondville. I had a cousin back home who threw the craziest parties on the outskirts of town. The girls literally jumped for joy when I told them that we had an open invitation to one of his shindigs. I called my cousin early that Saturday morning to ask him if we could crash at his place for the night, and not only was his response affirmative; it was warm and welcoming.

Ever since we were little, my cousin Sam and I had always been close. He was one of the few of my cousins who actually made me feel like family, because he actually acknowledged me as family. He was twenty-six, a farmer by day and a much-feared racketeer by night. His blood reeked of the thug life, for it was the very same blood that had been staining our *cholo* streets like motor oil since he was thirteen. He was a different kind of different, but I understood him. After all, I'd known him my whole life, so I accepted his violence, although I favored his peace. His skin reminded me of walls in a dirty, old bathroom stall that had been vandalized with graffiti, though the graffiti on his body stood as a sign of allegiance to his heritage and nationality. Anyone who knew him knew that the Mexican flag was his pride and our family name was his joy.

Sam lived in a three-bedroom house that was way too big for just him. It was an old-fashioned house with a squeaky porch, a swinging door, and a pinch of the good ol' South. He didn't have any neighbors, but what he lacked in neighbors, he made up for in acres. He had a huge barn in the back of his house. That's what most of his investments went to. He had spent thousands transforming that colossal shed into a nightclub, one that had no rules and owned no regulations. The cops never raided Sam's parties, because his house was so secluded on the outskirts of town that the noise never bothered anyone. Besides, he gave the people of the small town something to look forward to on the weekends.

On October 24, 2009, we all met at Antonio's apartment around seven forty-five at night. The girls and I sat on the curb and smoked some Kush while the guys inspected the steel horses before we hit the road. The sound of the rumbling engines gave the girls and me erections of anticipation. Meanwhile, our legs in daisy dukes gave our men erections of the flesh. We had each packed only a small bag of overnight necessities. After all, we only needed a spare change of clothes and a toothbrush, since we were driving back in the morning. Jaceil had thrown all of her stuff into a plastic grocery bag along with Kenny's toothbrush and a pair of his tighty-whities. I packed Antonio's clothes with mine in one of my old messenger bags. I remembered to pack everything—everything but his underwear, that is. Markus wasn't too fond of packing, even if it was just for an overnight trip. He simply threw all his shit into one of the compartments on his chopper. Ruby, on the other hand, wasn't much of a light traveler. She had an old, black JanSport covered with signatures written in whiteout, and that bad boy was jam-packed. When I saw her struggling with her bag, I laughed and said, "Bitch, are you relocating?"

She busted out laughing and said, "No, asshole, it's just my mini boom box. I take it everywhere I go, because you never know when life is gonna hand you lemons and you're gonna need a good record to pull you through. Besides, I ain't too fond of the crap that's passing for music these days."

I blew her a kiss as I saddled myself onto the chopper. She winked and blew one back. I loved Ruby, because although she didn't have the best of everything, she made the best of everything.

Antonio and I would always quietly bicker before our rides, as I always refused to wear a helmet. However, our silly little arguments never lasted long, because eventually he'd get so frustrated that he'd just let me have my way. I knew that he was just looking out for my safety, but sometime you've got to take risks if you want to feel the wind in your hair.

Once we got out of Corpus Christi's city limits, the freedom of the open road welcomed us with open arms. There were no more buildings, no more traffic, no more city noise. There was nothing left but the quiet, windswept countryside filled with cattle, wild daisies, and rusty automobiles. I could feel the cold air in my lungs and the power of the motorized machine rattling between my thighs. I felt both vibrant and electric. And I know it sounds crazy, but there are times that I can still feel Antonio's body clenched between my arms. The feeling I had on that night from being young, being his, and being me will forever be indescribable.

It was a quiet night, and although the sky was starless, the moon was at her best. She looked so beautiful hanging high up above that, alas, the silence was broken when Jaceil began howling at the moon like a lonely coyote lost in the desert. Then, before I knew it, they all were howling at the moon, like wild animals that were rabid and completely delirious.

At the entrance of Willacy County are two rows of palm trees that run for nearly a mile, signifying a gateway to being home. Ruby later often referred to this landmark as the palm trees of paradise. As we entered Raymondville, I let go of Antonio's waist and threw my hands in the air. I closed my eyes and pretended to fly, because I knew that was the closest I would ever come to flying without pixie dust or a magic rug. Life is about living, not just being alive.

When we arrived at Sam's, the party was already in full force. When we walked into the barn, I couldn't believe my eyes. I had never seen so many kegs in my entire life. There were shot tables, bong tables, and beer-pong tables. There was a disco ball surrounded by strobe lights in the center of the ceiling. There was also a huge platform at the back of the barn where Sam had installed seven sturdy stripper poles. If I hadn't walked through the barn doors myself, I could've easily been convinced that this was indeed a nightclub, because Sam even had his very own disc jockey. It was a complete madhouse. People of all ages were dancing like they had been infected with indiscretion. Meanwhile, others lurked in the shadows distributing high-quality party favors for reasonable prices.

After making a few rounds in the barn, I finally spotted Sam at one of the shot tables. I could tell he was happy to see me, because he was smiling—and he hardly ever smiles. When I first introduced Sam to Antonio, I was scared. In fact, I was praying the whole time that Sam wouldn't feel the need to threaten Antonio for my heart's sake. Sam's threats weren't bullshit, and Antonio wasn't the kind of guy you wanted to threaten, either. Once Sam had given me his nod of approval, introducing him to the rest of the gang was easy.

Sam was so fascinated with my little entourage. I had never seen my cousin so interested in a group of people before. I could tell that he liked my friends. After all, Sam would never pour a shot of tequila for someone he disliked. Once we each had a full shot in our hands, Sam raised his glass in the air and said, "Cheers! To family, friends, and one hell of a night." After we downed the liquor, he quickly began to pour us another round. I guess he felt like we needed to catch up.

As Sam handed us our shots, I noticed that Kenny began looking at the ground in amazement. It wasn't too long before he said, "I just noticed that there's tile on the floor." Sam began to laugh. He patted Kenny on the back and disclosed the fact that the shed also had central air. Kenny looked at me like a kid at a candy store and said, "Dude, this joint is sick."

It was only a matter of time before the guys were doing keg stands and the girls and I were gyrating on the dance floor. I remember being completely drenched in sweat and soon on the border of being shit-faced. Eventually I had to stop dancing in order to cool off. As I looked around the party, I saw Antonio in the distance throwing up in one of the trash cans in the corner and Jaceil on one of the stripper poles flashing her tits to the whole party. Meanwhile, Ruby was sitting on the edge of the stage clearly trying hard to sober up, drinking a bottle of water and gently slapping her face to get her focus flowing in order to drink some more.

One by one, I gathered the whole gang and took them to a corner in the back of the barn where Sam was waiting for us with an Indian pipe stuffed with White Widow. We passed the pipe among the seven of us until we cashed the bowl. After the smoke session, I overheard Kenny and Markus begging Ruby and Jaceil for a little girl-on-girl action. I know that it sounds crazy, but I actually felt bad for the boys, because I knew it was all in good fun. So I made them an offer they simply couldn't refuse. "Tell you boys what. The girls and I will make out for one whole minute if the two of you make out for twenty seconds." I grinned and then hooked Jaceil under my arm and seductively cupped her tit as I added, "And I promise we'll make it worth your while."

"How so?" Markus asked and then hiccupped.

"We'll strip down to our bras and panties."

The guys looked at each other and shrugged. Then, without hesitating, they swapped spit. My jaw dropped. I couldn't believe that they were actually going through with it. Sam and Antonio teasingly cheered them on. When the kiss heard around the world was over, Kenny and Markus signaled me to hold up my end of the bargain.

I immediately began undressing as promised, and with no need for persuasion, the other girls quickly followed suit. Once the three of us were stripped down to our delicates, I grabbed Jaceil and Ruby and aggressively shoved my tongue into their mouths. The crowd went wild. All the guys at the party began hollering like gorillas in heat, along with a few girls at that, but I don't blame them. After all, in my opinion we were the hottest chicks there that night.

It's rather fascinating how much fondling three women are capable of doing in one minute. To say the least, it was pretty intense and quite enjoyable, if I may say so myself. After our little peep show, the seven of us headed out to the back of the barn to take a piss. As we made our way behind the shed, Sam locked his arm around Antonio's neck with brotherly love and slurred like I had never heard him slur before. "I'm having a Halloween party next weekend," he said, pacing his words as if he were allowing his brain to process them. "You guys should come. It's a costume party. It'll be fun."

"Fuck yeah, we'll come!" shouted Antonio, slurring even worse than Sam.

The sound of zippers unzipping echoed in the darkness. The guys peed alongside one another, trailing their piss all over the dusty barn. The girls and I popped squats behind some nearby shrubs. Jaceil was so shit-faced that she lost her balance and landed into her own puddle of piss. And that was the last thing I remember from that night.

About a week later, we went to Sam's party. It was the first time I had ever celebrated Halloween, and that night was first time I had ever done any other drug besides weed. On that night, a little purple pill helped me complete one of my biggest acts of kindness. And although the quality of my actions that night is debatable, one thing is for sure: ecstasy is one hell of a drug.

Kenny was dressed up as a heavy-metal Frankenstein, and Jaceil, of course, was a seductively dressed killer clown, her twist on Harley Quinn. Ruby and Markus were dressed as darker versions of Jack and Sally from Tim Burton's *The Nightmare before Christmas*. They looked so cute together. Markus's makeup was insane. He looked like the Grim Reaper himself. Sam's costume wasn't too far from his real persona. He was a Mexican bandit. He wore a colorful poncho with an oversized sombrero and had two fake toy guns, which he constantly shot into the air while mimicking the *gritos* that he had heard in his favorite *corridos*. Antonio, dressed as a convict, wore an orange jumpsuit with a pair of broken handcuffs. His beard was grown out longer than usual, and he had drawn a tattoo on the center of his forehead that read, "Luke 23:34." He looked like a very dangerous man. But to be quite honest, I've never wanted him more. I hate to disappoint, but in the midst of monsters and murderers, I was an angel, inspired by Claire Danes's beautiful, angelic costume-party getup in *Romeo and Juliet*. And although it was a simple costume, it had a powerful statement, for it represented the yin and the yang that formulated my relationship with Antonio.

Around ten fifteen, Sam came up to me at the party, looking a bit tense and awfully worried. When I asked if everything was OK, he eagerly responded, "No, it's only ten o'clock, and these bitches have already gone through more than half of the beer." He wiped the sweat from his anxiety off his brow and said, "The kegs are on their way, but they won't be here until about twelve thirty; and I doubt the beer on hand will hold up until then."

Kenny was standing nearby and had overheard Sam's small dilemma. "Is everything all right?"

Sam shook his head. "I'm gonna need someone to do a beer run."

Kenny volunteered. "I'll go."

"Are you sure?" asked Sam with a hopeful tone.

"Yeah," Kenny assured him.

"I'll go with you, Kenny," I said, knowing he would need my knowledge in order to maneuver around Raymondville.

Sam looked at us with a sigh of relief and said, "OK then," and then began digging into his pocket before pulling out a stack of money. He handed me three hundred dollars and said, "Morgan, go to the Quickie Market on the corner of Seventh and Holloway. A guy named Carmichael should be working. Just tell him that I sent you, and he'll hook it up. Here, take my car." He quickly reached into his pocket for his keys and then tossed them to Kenny.

"You're gonna let me drive your Cadillac?" Kenny asked, completely baffled.

"Yeah, but hurry up before I change my mind." Sam laughed. He then looked at Kenny, pointed his finger at me, and said, "And do not, under any circumstances, let her drive. Women and cars do not mix."

I looked at my cousin with complete disgust and said, "You are such a pig."

He sarcastically smiled and said, "I love you too."

As soon as Kenny and I walked out of the barn, we spotted Ruby and Jaceil outside sharing a cigarette. "Hey!" I shouted. "You two hoes wanna go on a beer run with me and Ken Ken? Sam's letting us take the Caddy." I tried to emphasize the excitement.

Ruby laughed and said, "Yeah, I wanna go."

"Me too, bitch!" Jaceil shouted.

Once they were done smoking their cigarette, we raced to Sam's car like a herd of buffalo, raising clouds of dust and filling the night's lungs with trails of our youth. Crying "Shotgun!" we left our carefree tracks on that sacred dirt road where many had walked who would never forget the nights they did but would never remember how they managed to do so.

As soon as we walked into the Quickie Mart, I made sure the clerk's name tag was a match, and it was. I told Carmichael that we were there on behalf of Sam's SOS, and sure enough, Carmichael hooked us up with five free cases of beer on top of the several cases we bought. It took the five of us four trips in and out of the store to load it all into the trunk. I then noticed that Kenny had wandered off. Something in the distance had captured his attention. "You all right, Ken Ken?" I asked as I tried to figure out what could possibly be so intriguing.

"What's the story on that pink house that's on the other side of the railroad tracks?" he asked. "It's pretty creepy."

"Oh," I replied, "that's the old Doyles' house. It's been abandoned since 1979. My aunts used to tell me stories about that house when I was a child. There are so many versions of the story that I just stick to the version my aunt Gloria told me." I took a deep breath. "The Doyles were a young couple that had moved to Raymondville from California around the late seventies. If I remember correctly, their names were Tommy and Rose. My aunt said that she had encountered Rose a few times and that Rose was just as sweet as she was beautiful. Rose was a stay-at-home housewife, and Tommy worked at one of the cotton-gin factories on the outskirts of Raymondville. They say that every evening around seven o'clock, she'd wait out on the porch for him to get home from work. One day in November, on his way home from work, poor guy must have been exhausted. I mean, why else would someone attempt to beat a speeding train? His little pickup truck was crushed like an eggshell, and she witnessed it all from afar. People say that Rose went crazy after the accident, because three months later, she put a pistol in her mouth."

I could feel myself choking up, so I had to pause before I could continue with the story. I quickly cleared my throat and carried on. "No one in their family ever came to claim the house. Supposedly all of their belongings are still in there. Some people say you can still hear her cries every now and then in November, but that's bullshit. It's pretty sad how people use her tragedy to invoke fear into this town," I said as I gazed at the old house.

Suddenly Jaceil started walking toward the road. She looked both ways as if she were planning to cross the street.

"Where are you going?" I shouted.

"I'm gonna check out the house!" she replied. "Come on, let's go!"

Before I knew it, Ruby and Kenny started trailing after her.

"I guess that means I'm coming too," I muttered to myself.

When we sneaked into the old, abandoned house, we had to use the light from the screens of our cell phones to see in the darkness. As we made our way around the house, Kenny stopped and, looking at me with a pair of sad eyes, said, "Looks like the rumors are true. I can't believe all their stuff is still in here." He sighed.

We found some unopened mail and a pair of keys on their kitchen counter. Their books and photos were scattered all across the dusty floors. All of their furniture had been vandalized. There was graffiti covering most of the walls, a mixture of gang signs and a few unkind words that endorsed Rose as an insane lunatic. I could feel my heart breaking as I gathered their photos from the floor. People say a photo is worth a thousand words, and although I'm sure that's true, I could only think of a few. Because the only thing I saw was a hope, a love, and a kind of happiness that hit so close to home. I turned to Ruby, who was shuffling through a stack of photographs beside me, and said, "Rose wasn't crazy; she was heartbroken. I could never imagine my life without Antonio."

Ruby shook her head, looking grief stricken, and said, "This isn't right. This was someone's home, and now people come in here whenever they want and piss all over it like it ain't shit."

"There's gotta be something we can do." Kenny's voice echoed in the darkness.

Without letting my brain process my words, I said, "Let's burn it down." The three of them looked at me like I had gone mad. I looked around the house and said, "Think about it. If we burn down the house, Rose and Tommy can finally rest in peace, because no one will ever be able to violate their home again."

Kenny slapped my ass and said, "I like the way you think!"

Moments later, while Jaceil and Ruby ran over to the Quickie Mart for some lighter fluid, Kenny and I gathered up all of the Doyles' old photographs and piled them in the center of the living room. As Kenny added some of their other belongings to the pile, I constantly peeked out the window to make sure there were no cops nearby. When I saw the girls walking back from the Quickie Mart in their costumes with bottles of lighter fluid in their hands, I won't lie—it was quite disturbing. They looked like two psycho bitches straight out of a horror film.

Once the girls got back in the house, Kenny handed each of us a purple pill. He looked at me with the most conniving smirk and said, "What? It's for our nerves." After the four of us took our pills, we went mad with the lighter fluid, artistically splashing it about.

Once all the bottles were empty, Ruby handed me a pack of matches and said, "The honor's all yours, baby girl."

I smiled and said, "I wouldn't have it any other way."

She winked. "That's my girl."

Ruby took her red lipstick out of her pocket and quickly retouched her lips. Once she was done, she said, "Jaceil and I are gonna head back to the Caddy to keep watch. We'll have the motor running and ready to go."

Jaceil kissed Kenny before she headed out the door and said, "Hey, Frankenstein, take care of my girl." She looked at us nervously as she headed for the door, adding, "And make it quick. I need to take a shit."

Kenny watched from the window and waited for the girls to pull up to the block. Once he saw the Cadillac close enough, he signaled me to strike the match. As soon as I lit the match, I felt that little purple pill begin to do its magic. As I watched the flame twirl, I thought of the consequences my actions could cost me. It was a test. I had asked for a dangerous life, and now was the time to prove that I was truly able to ignore the warning signs. I looked at Kenny and said, "And so there was light…to separate the day from night."

As soon as I tossed the match into the pile we had made in the living room, Kenny and I hauled ass to the car. As we drove away, I looked back at the burning house and felt a sense of ease. I know some people might question what we did on that night, but you had to be there in order to understand why we did what we did.

A few minutes later, sirens dashed through the streets of Raymondville like angry bloodhounds on the hunt. I never told Antonio what we did that night. In fact, I never told anyone. It was our little secret, a secret that made the bond of our friendship stronger.

Every weekend was a new adventure for the six of us. We were always finding ways to top the weekend before. But no matter what predicament we got ourselves into, every night in Corpus ended the same. After the bars and clubs were closed, we'd head back to Antonio's apartment for our version of an after party. Antonio lived in a gorgeous apartment complex down Ocean Drive. Luckily for us, Seaside Cemetery was located right behind his apartment. We would jump the fence every Saturday night to play Ghost in that foggy old cemetery. Ghost is a bizarre form of tag usually played in cemeteries. The rules of the game are simple: once you are tagged by the ghost, you become a ghost, and the last person to remain human is the winner. We drew straws every time we played to determine who would be the first ghost. Once the ghost was selected, the rest of us would scatter all across the dark and eerie cemetery, anxiously awaiting our fate. Every time I ran past the tombstones in the graveyard, I imagined the dead rising up and joining me in alliance as I dashed into the darkness. And as they sang, my lungs filled with laughter, for they sang, "Come on, baby. Don't fear the reaper."

When I pictured the dead, I envisioned a mixture of pilgrims and founding fathers, victims of murders and diseases who were all draped in the colors of a warm vintage film. Ghost or human, Antonio would secretly come find me, and we'd quietly run off to hide under a large willow tree in the center on the cemetery, where we would ramble on and on about how much we loved each other. I loved him so much. In fact, I still love him. And I'll always love him. Do you want to know why? Because I believe that I was blind until I saw the world through his eyes.

And in spite of being completely intoxicated and incoherent on each occasion that we ended up at Seaside, I clearly remember one night in particular. I guess it's because it was one of my favorite nights that I spent with Antonio under that deep-rooted willow tree in that hoary cemetery. It was a cool, quiet night. The sky was darker than the feathers on a raven, and not a single star seemed to be worried that the histrionic clouds weren't present as they twinkled. There we were like we always were. Just two ordinary people affected by such an extraordinary love. And although it was nothing grand, it was those small and simple conversations we had that made us who we were.

"Baby, am I more of a Marilyn Monroe or a Jackie O?" I asked. The gentle breeze rattled through the leaves on the branches above as he held me securely in his arms while resting his back against the bark of the willow tree.

"Neither," he responded with a wise smile. "You're my Audrey."

"Good answer." I gave him a much wiser smirk.

"Why do you ask?" he whispered as he stroked his dry, rough beard his against my cold, soft cheek.

"I don't know. Earlier today I was watching a documentary on the life of John F. Kennedy, and it made me sad."

"Why?"

"Because it reminded me a lot of us." I sighed the same way I do whenever I hear a Christmas song in the middle of June. "Boy, did she love him. You could see it every time she was around him, the way she looked at him, the way she held on to him. To the world he was just a president, but to her he was the world. If that isn't a perfect example of love, then I don't know what is. And I know it sounds silly, but I like to think that I love you in the very same way that Jackie loved her Kennedy."

He kissed the side of my head and said, "Well, even if I am your Kennedy, it doesn't change the fact that you're still all Hepburn, because you're wildly witty, eccentric, and drop-dead gorgeous."

I smiled in the way only he dared to make me smile. "Wanna know a secret?"

He gently rested his chin on my shoulder. "I'd like you to tell me a secret."

I carefully laid my head against his and sighed. "These are my favorite types of nights."

"You know, you got me asking why quite a lot tonight, and I don't know how I feel about standing in a conversation with nothing to give but a *why*. It makes me feel kind of aloof, but just so you know, I am interested in everything and anything you ever have to say, my little Morgan. So, with that being said, here goes one more. Why?" He chuckled.

"Because I don't believe there is anything more beautiful than your drunk eyes full of love under a sky full of stars." I nodded, gesturing for him to look up at the sky.

He gasped. "Wow. I didn't even notice how awfully bright the stars are shining tonight."

"They sure are," I uttered as I buried myself much deeper in his arms.

And just when things got too quiet, he began to sing to me like he always did, like I always expected him to. There was no song better fit to describe such a night than "Yellow." Once more he dared to make me smile like only he could.

"I love that song."

"Me too, kiddo," he said as he repeatedly kissed the side of my head.

"Ah, Coldplay." I sighed in awe. "They are truly a God-given gift to Earth."

"They sure are, baby," he agreed. "They sure are."

We usually spent most of our weekends in Corpus Christi partying downtown, hitting up every local pub, and eventually finding ourselves at the Wall. But every other weekend, whenever Sam threw one of his theme parties, we hopped the choppers and rode out to Raymondville. Every now and then, we needed our quiet nights, and on those quiet nights the gang would gather at Antonio's, where the girls and I would stir up baked goods while the guys played their video games. Ruby baked the best brownies ever, and Jaceil's oatmeal cookies were to die for.

I loved staying in, just hanging out with my girls and our boys, dancing and singing along to Frankie Valli and The Four Seasons as we dressed up in the most ridiculously hideous outfits, high as the stars and drunk on love, happiness, youth, and Pabst Blue Ribbon. Oh, those nights always reminded me of late December back in '63. Toward the end of the night, we would scatter across the living room for a movie that we were all too tired to watch. Jaceil and Kenny would always pass out with their mouths wide open halfway into the movie. I always knew Antonio was fixing to pass out as soon as he would ask me to play with his hair. I loved watching him sleep, because he always looked so peaceful for such a troubled man.

When I look back on those nights, I think about the random chats I had with the girls while we waited for Natalie to dress our beers at the Wall. I think about how crazy Jaceil and I must have looked dancing and grinding on stage with Mercedes while Ruby gambled a few balls at the pool table for gas and meals. I think of the sloppy table dances we gave our guys after they sang karaoke. We swore they were rock royalty and that we were a bunch of hot-shit groupies.

However, my fondest memories are the times when we were on the road to Raymondville. There was something about being on that chopper that made me feel like I was running with a pack of wolves or a pack of outlaws whose only desire was the freedom of the open road. It was something sensual and erotic. After all, what girl hasn't dreamed of being a biker's old lady?

There used to be a diner in Kingsville called Gem's House where we would occasionally stop on our way to Raymondville. Gem's House served the best hotcakes ever. In fact, there were times during the week that Antonio and I would randomly drive to Kingsville just to cure our cravings. There wasn't much to do in Raymondville besides party and dream, but that was more than enough for the six of us. The gang loved Raymondville, which I found strange, because not a lot of people I know are too fond of my hometown. But then again, there aren't too many people who can appreciate the simple things. Our nights in Raymondville usually started at Sam's. After a few beers, the gang and I would walk over to a nearby railroad track that was supposedly haunted by a weeping woman dressed in white. The only reason we even went over to those tracks was because we had high hopes of seeing the weeping woman, but she'd never show. I'll admit I'm still deeply disappointed that she never did, because I would have loved to have heard directly from her how much she loves the night.

Meanwhile, as we waited for the sight we'd never see, we played on the train tracks, telling scary stories, constantly attempting to scare the shit out of one another. Whenever a train would pass, the other two couples would lean in toward the moving train, getting as close as possible without being hit, only to feel its power. As much as I love a midnight train, I was more than happy to keep my distance. I would use Antonio's back to drown out the noise from the loud train and also to keep him from playing their dangerous games.

We were never at the old train track for too long. Before I knew it, we were on our way to The White Wing, an old, run-down hotel that had been abandoned since my mother was a teenager. When I was younger, I would beg my mother to tell me as much as she could remember about the old hotel, because she actually had the privilege of going inside several times when it was still up and running. She once told me that it was so beautiful and luxurious that people often referred to it as Hotel California. She said that only the wealthiest of people passing through Raymondville would stay there, because they were the only ones who could afford it. And I could see why. Even though it was completely ruined when I saw it, you could still clearly see the luxury it once carried. The White Wing was a two-story building with fifty rooms. It had a huge indoor pool and a fancy driveway laced with palm trees. The hotel was a block away from my parents' house, so it was no surprise when the gang insisted we should check it out.

We would always park the choppers at my parents' house and quietly walk over to the hotel. We'd usually sneak in through the back of the hotel to avoid being caught trespassing. As soon as we got into the hotel, Jaceil and Markus would run off and disappear into one of the rooms, where they would bone like wild animals while the rest of us chilled by the empty pool, using a Coke can for a pipe. Ruby always had a pack of brand-new batteries for her boom box packed in her JanSport, because she loved a good dose of music with her weed. The two of us would sit and talk about where we'd been and where we wanted to be in the next ten years while we listened to Tom Petty and the Heartbreakers, The Zombies, The Animals, The Mamas and the Papas, Seals and Crofts, Pink Floyd, Guns N' Roses, Led Zeppelin, Lynyrd Skynyrd, and, of course, my beloved Blue Oyster Cult. The guys would meanwhile be attempting ollies on old skateboards that local junior-high kids had left lying around the pool.

We went to the old hotel on several occasions. The last time we were there, we had a little run-in with the cops. Sam had thrown an Indian-themed party that weekend, so we were all covered in face paint and wearing feathered headbands. We just went on with our regular routine. Antonio was throwing back a few warm beers he had snagged from Sam's while Kenny snorted his party favors off the pool rail. I was huffing and puffing away while Ruby spun the records. We had only been there for about twenty minutes, when suddenly Jaceil and Kenny ran through the pool doors, shouting at the top of their lungs, "Shit! Let's go! The fucking cops are here!" They were both half naked, with face paint running down their faces. And although they tried warning us, the cops were right behind them. We quickly gathered what we could and charged toward the back entrance.

I remember the cops continually yelling, "Freeze!" as we continued to run, laughing at the top of our lungs, and mimicking Indian battle cries. We spent that entire night making fun of one another, laughing about the reactions we all had on our faces when the cops barged in on us.

Those were the good ole days. I remember every single conversation I had with Ruby. She was a profound girl with big dreams of living like a rock star until the day she died. She called herself a nomad, because she couldn't stay in one place for too long. In fact, Corpus Christi was the place that claimed her longest residency. She usually only stayed four to five months in a town, but she was already going on her ninth month in the Double C. I knew it would be just as hard for her to go as it would be for me to see her leave. I envied the way she lived her life, because although she was anchorless, she was carefree. But in the end, I guess she realized that having that much freedom could be quite lonely, because before she left Corpus Christi, she asked Markus for his hand out on the road, and of course he said yes.

On May 22, 2010, we all met at Antonio's for Ruby and Markus's farewell party. She had us all sign her JanSport, just like the rest of the people she found fascinating who she met along the road. The gang took turns with her whiteout pen, signing along the straps. When my turn came, she looked into my eyes and said, "Hey, can I talk to you?"

I smiled. "Of course."

She pulled me aside into the kitchen, away from everyone else in the living room. "I just wanted to let you know that I'm gonna miss you...I'm gonna miss you so, so much." She sighed. "You're all right, chica." She giggled and looked over at Antonio, who was in the living room sitting on the couch next to Kenny. "I hope you and Antonio live a long and happy life together, because there are no two people better for each other than the two of you. I hope the two of you have lots of cute little beauty queens and biker babies," she said, somehow still managing to make us laugh in such a bittersweet moment.

Although the next thing she said didn't make much sense then, it makes so much sense now. "Morgan, you are a very special girl; don't you ever forget that. No matter what happens in life, don't ever stop writing, because that little soul of yours is way too beautiful to be silenced. The way you envision the world is brilliant, and brilliance is a gift, and a gift should always be appreciated, no matter how big, no matter how small."

That day the evening sky was the perfect shade of gray for such an unpleasant good-bye. As Markus loaded a few last things onto the chopper, Jaceil begged Ruby not to go. By the time Markus put the key in the ignition, the night was all running mascara and tear-soaked beards. We each said one last good-bye. Jaceil and I hugged Ruby with all our might, hoping that she would change her mind. Before Ruby hopped onto the chopper, she turned back to look at me and said, "Hey, I'll see you on the dark side of the moon."

I chuckled, with tears in my eyes, and said, "I love you."

She smiled. "I love you more."

They drove away into the sunset and disappeared like they were never here, like they never even existed. She was his Bonnie, and he was her Clyde. In my mind they were a pair of outlaws on the run, with nowhere to go, with nowhere to hide—my Billy the Kid and my Annie Oakley. Last I heard, they had made their way up to Nevada.

A few weeks later, Jaceil and Kenny decided to end their so-called relationship. After all their fights, they had finally realized their chances of finding a healthy happiness would be better if they divided rather than remaining united. Besides, Jaceil wasn't born to belong to just one man. She was a gift to Earth, to men, and to the party. She moved to Austin to start a new life, and I haven't heard from her since. As for Kenny, well, he decided to give fame a shot. He assembled a band of three, and they moved to New York City, where they played in underground clubs and bars. But once he saw that music wasn't paying the rent, his passion dissolved, and he soon realized that some dreams just aren't meant to come true. Last I heard, Kenny had become a born-again Christian, spending most of his time as a youth mentor in Lower Manhattan.

And just like that, all my friends left in the end. But I gotta say, when we were together, those were the good ole days.

Part 4

I now know that drugs and love are a dangerous combination, because they're both hallucinogens that play mean tricks on the human mind. You see, they both have the power to make you believe you are invincible, and being so, you start daring yourself like a foolish child. And that, my friend, is what you call a lethal dose.

On the Fourth of July in 2010, Antonio and I had quietly climbed up the rooftop of an old, rundown motel downtown to watch the Corpus Christi firework display. I remember swaying in his arms as he hummed "Can't Take My Eyes off You."

That night, in his blue jeans and leather jacket, my baby boy looked cooler than 1954, and I felt as sexy as a rock 'n' roll song in my daisy dukes and Chuck Taylors. I remember a vague conversation we had about change while waiting for the fireworks display to start. At the time I didn't really understand why Antonio was so consumed with the concept of change. So I begged him and begged him to promise me that the good things would never change, and what's so sad is that he promised they wouldn't.

I'll always remember how the lights from the sparks of the fireworks came down from the sky, illuminating his smile and drizzling like rich icing on a french-vanilla cake. His smile—it chokes me up every time I think of him. It hits me like a train, without warning, without mercy. When it was time for the grand finale, he made his hand into the shape of a gun, pressed it against the side of my head, and shouted, "Bang!" I felt a cold shiver come over my body.

Suddenly the noise around me turned to silence, for I had foreseen a fickle fortune, one that made me realize I could lose him at any moment. Perhaps it was a form of intuition, a premonition, or just a realization of how quickly things can change. There was no way I was going to tell him what had just crossed my mind and risk ruining a great night. So I did the only thing I could do. I played it off. I took his hand from the side of my head, ran it down my cheek, and then pressed his fingertips against my lips, giving his thumb a quick suck.

Do you want to know a secret? Even though I never said it, even though I denied ever thinking it, deep down inside I knew that things were too good to be true. But whenever those thoughts would surface, I would drown them out with Christmas carols, seagull songs, and fireworks. And so I say, there are some warning signs that should never be ignored.

On August 26, 2010, Antonio took me out to Mustang Island, where we spent the day drinking cold beer and hunting for sand dollars. We talked about the crazy year we'd had and all the people we had met along the way. When it was time for us to leave the beach, we rinsed off in the public showers and changed into dry clothes. We had made dinner plans at a local outdoor seafood restaurant called Skippy's. The old surf shack was one of my favorite restaurants in Corpus Christi.

I waited for Antonio in the car as he packed up the ice chest and beach umbrella. We had taken the German car, as usual, because there was no way we'd ever take Arson anywhere near the sand or saltwater. As I waited, I began to notice that Antonio was taking an awfully long time to get to the car, so I looked through the rearview mirror to see what he could possibly be doing. I saw him sitting in the sand, looking out to the sea. When he heard me getting out of the car, he briefly turned to look at me over his shoulder. As I walked toward him, I asked if everything was OK. He simply nodded and continued to look out to the sea.

He sat there quietly for a moment, until he finally turned to me and asked, "Can I ask you something?"

"Of course." I sat down beside him.

He bashfully smiled. "When I'm old, can you promise me you'll always make sure I never skip a buttonhole and that every button is fastened where it's supposed to be?"

I smiled and said, "I promise I always will."

He smiled as he gazed over at me. "OK." He began to play nervously with the sand near his feet as he looked straight at me. "Promise me that you'll sew patches onto all the things I tear."

"I promise."

"OK," he softly uttered. He closed one of his eyes as he squinted at the sunset. "Do you swear, Scout's honor, that you'll always make sure that I never mismatch the socks that I wear?"

I laughed in response. "Yes, I swear. Why so many questions, tiger?"

He laughed too. "There is a point to all this. I swear."

"OK." I smiled.

He took a deep breath. "Last but not least, promise me you'll never get annoyed or upset when you have to constantly remind me of the things I keep forgetting, because I'll be an old man whose memory isn't what it used to be."

I brushed his hair out of his face. "Yes, of course I promise."

"OK." He stood up from the sand, quickly dusting himself off. He then picked up a nearby twig and began writing in the soft grains of sand. When he was done, he threw the twig aside and stared down at what he had inscribed, as still as a man made of stone.

I couldn't understand why he was acting so strange. He had been like that for the last couple of days too. He would not move from where he stood staring at the ground. So I decided to take a look at the message, which was obviously for me. When I leaned over to view the sand in front of him, I came across the sweetest thing he had ever written for me. It was a question that would change things forever, a question that only had one answer.

"Yes," I said.

His eyes opened wide, and he began jumping around for joy, like a little boy, screaming at the top of his lungs, "She said yes! She said yes!" He lifted me off the ground and spun me around. I could hear his heart beating loudly as he slipped the ring onto my finger and whispered, "I guess we're gonna finally find out what forever feels like."

After dinner we decided to head back to his apartment to call everyone we knew and tell them the news. As we left North Padre Island, I turned off the radio, as almost every station was on commercial. I remember looking over at the clock on the display. It was only 9:33 p.m. I turned my head to look at Antonio, to admire every single detail of the man behind the wheel, the man I was going to spend the rest of my life with.

"What?" he asked as he looked at me with a hopeful smile.

I smiled back. "Nothing. I'm just looking."

As we crossed the JFK Causeway, I looked up at the crescent moon and, deep in thought, played with my engagement ring in the shadows. "Look at the moon. She's so beautiful," I murmured, enchanted.

"Yeah," he whispered. "Almost as beautiful as you."

I smiled while trying not to blush, because I'll tell you, that man had a way of making me blush when he was sweet on me.

"Sing for me," I requested.

"OK. Any requests?"

"Hmm…How about a love song?"

"You got it, baby."

He cleared his throat, shook his head, licked his lips, and began singing "Moon River," the song Audrey Hepburn sings in *Breakfast at Tiffany's*. And as he sang, I thought, *How can people say fairy tales don't exist? Of course they do. Look at us. We're all the things that are prettier than gold.*

Life is the most fragile thing in the world, because once it's gone, there is no way of getting it back. So you should enjoy the time you have with the people you love, because in a matter of seconds, everything can change. Although I don't know where God was at the time, there we were, halfway across the bridge, dreaming of tomorrow and the years to come. Then suddenly, out of nowhere, there was another man too.

When I came to my senses, I heard the cops telling each other that the man in the truck had one too many. The road was covered in debris from the accident. For a second the only thing I could hear was the sound of my own heavy breathing. As I slowly began looking around, past the group of unfamiliar people hovering over me with blue gloves and stethoscopes, I saw flashing lights, tons of flashing lights, the bad kind, the ones that only shine when something is wrong; and I could tell by their numbers that something was terribly wrong.

I managed to escape the medics, looking for Antonio, like a madman searching for the slightest piece of sanity. When I first saw him lying on the ground, I was unable to identify him until I recognized one of the tattoos on his right arm. He was covered in so much blood. He looked like a plum that had been smashed against the floor, so disfigured that I knew there was no possible way he could be OK. I tried running over to where he was, but I was too injured to move much. Somehow I managed to make it about halfway to his still, lifeless body before the paramedics were able to restrain me. I couldn't stop myself from kicking and screaming like a lunatic. I was in shock, and what's worse, I was in denial. For some reason I felt like if I begged hard enough, cried loud enough, God would eventually have no other choice than to return him to me.

He didn't see us, baby. He didn't see the heart behind our history, the dreams we had turned into plans for our future. He didn't know I had promised you that I would take care of you always. He didn't know that I said yes because I was counting on you to love me forever.

I knew there was nothing I could do, but for my peace of mind, I still had to try. I fought with all my might to get the medics off me, but I was so weak, badly bruised and losing blood from a gash on the side of my stomach caused by a large piece of glass, that I didn't stand a chance against them. The harder they held me down, the louder I screamed. "Please, let me go! Please! I just want to hold him! Please just let me hold my baby!" I begged.

Everything happened so fast that I wasn't even able to grasp what had just occurred. Next thing I knew, they were covering him up with a white sheet, hiding him from view the way someone might sweep dirt under a rug. They picked him up off the ground like a piece of debris, without a care, without any sense of compassion, as if he were only an object. I became so enraged that I somehow managed to escape from the medics' grasp. I quickly ran to the careless coroners and began beating the shit out of both of them for being so insensitive with my baby's body.

Eventually the paramedics sedated me in order to get me to the hospital. As the anesthetic ran its way through my body, I remember wishing for death. I remember praying to God while on the edge of unconsciousness, begging Him with all my soul to either give Antonio back or to take me too, because my heart kept me alive, and he kept my heart alive; and without one of the two, I served no use.

Once my tears had run dry, I was able to process how selfish I was being for welcoming death. I was so consumed by my misery that I did not stop to think about how my death would affect the people around me. I knew my family needed me, and so I found the strength to accept my fate.

They took you away from me twice that day: first the drunk driver who had his few and then the medics and coroners. I counted a third time when they buried you, and I pinned that one on God.

When autumn came around that year, my grief robbed me of my colors, like a thief in the night taking all the things that make a flower beautiful, taking my armor and shield and leaving me defenseless against the long, cold winter that lay ahead. I dropped out of college and never went back. I became a zombie. I became a machine, unable to function on my own. Although I had physically survived the accident, emotionally I was left for dead.

I gave up the blue skies, the sunsets, and the sunrise and traded them all in for a dark room that made me feel the closest to him. I no longer cared for all the simple things in life that I once loved. When he left, all those little things no longer mattered, because they no longer existed.

Room 314 in the Wicker Palace became my old bedroom in my parents' house on Christmas Eve 2010. I now realize it was all of those moments, from when Antonio and I met to the night he was taken from me, that I relived in room 314 in the Wicker Palace. I was given the opportunity to revise those delicate and intimate moments so I could remember that true love may be rare but that it is real.

I found myself lying in bed with my eyes wide open. The darkness felt like a heavy presence possessed by sadness. I had neither an appetite nor the will to move. As the cold sneaked in through the cracks in my window, I began to wonder why: *Why did we have to come in contact with that inebriated driver? Why not someone else? Why couldn't he have been someplace else, some other time? Why did an innocent man have to lose his life in order for a reckless man to appreciate his? Why Antonio? Why not me?*

As if signing off on his will wasn't painful enough, Christmas and all its sentimental reminders arrived too soon. I spent that entire December locked in my room without any contact with the outside world. I didn't want to hear Christmas carols or see Christmas lights. I wanted nothing to do with all the things that made our hearts be light. In the midst of attempting to steer clear of anything that could trigger the slightest memory of the Christmases I once had, I heard a midnight train passing through in the distance. The sound shot through my heart like a bullet blasted by friendly fire. The pain was as excruciating as cutting through a wound that's on the verge of healing. It was as cruel as ripping the wings off a fly that's seconds away from its death.

I curled myself into a ball, feeling tender to the touch. And before a single one of my tears had a chance to land on my pillowcase, I was teleported once more; but this time, I found myself back at his parents' lake house, back to a time I swore I would never forget. I could feel the warmth of the sunrise shining through the large glass windows. I could hear the birds tweeting morning songs out by the calm, steady lake. The house smelled like lavender with the hint of an old pot of chai tea. The clock on the stove reminded me to be very quiet, for it was only seven in the morning. It had been so long since I'd been here, and yet nothing had changed. It was exactly how I remembered it being eight years before—because it *was* eight years ago, if the calendar was correct.

I made my way to the master bedroom, where I came across something so beautiful that it made me want to cry. Lying on the bed of the master bedroom was an apparition of the past that I often wished would've lasted. Somehow I had become a third person looking down at a seventeen-year-old girl intertwined with the twenty-seven-year-old man she would come to love until the end of time. His big arms were wrapped around her as they slept on one pillow and a few messy sheets. Her face was glowing with such peace that I came to envy her. I wished she could hear me so that I could tell her to brace herself for that kind of love. I wouldn't have ruined the ending. I would simply have let her enjoy all the things in between, like a fool in love ought to. I would have told her to listen to him when he spoke, because he'd forever be her greatest inspiration.

I knelt by the bedside, where he was only a few inches from falling off the edge. He looked warm and full of life, and as much as I wanted to wake him up to see that smile one more time, I knew he was not mine but hers at that time. As I leaned forward to gaze at his face, I heard him breathing, and my heart began to cry. Memories are always bittersweet—good and bad, happy and sad.

How do you even begin to say good-bye to the one thing you wanted the most? How do you forget the things that were taken from you when you weren't ready to let them go? The times we spent together over the years began flashing before my eyes as I brushed my hand against his cheek. I couldn't take my eyes off him. He was so beautiful that even if I tried explaining, you wouldn't understand. To be quite honest, if I hadn't told you otherwise, you'd think he was an angel.

As I looked at his strawberry lips, I couldn't resist the urge of feeling them pressed against mine one last time. I lustfully licked my lips as I leaned forward toward his mouth, when suddenly I felt someone grab my arm with the will of restraint from behind.

"Shh," he said before I could act startled.

I quickly turned around to see who it could be, and there he was, with that smile as beautiful as heaven. "Antonio"—I sighed—"is it really you?"

He was exactly as I remembered him the last time I saw him: his hair, his beard, and that body. "Yes, it's me," he responded, with his arms wide open, waiting for my embrace. I swiftly made my way into his arms. I had never heard him cry the way he did as he told me, "I've missed you so much."

It broke my heart.

I began kissing him as if I were trying to smother him with my mouth, but I was only trying to make up for the years I had spent without the warmth of his lips. There came a point when I literally had to stop in order to breathe, because I was slowly suffocating myself with his kisses. And so we just held each other. And I'm not sure who held who tighter, but he held me with one hand locked to his wrist as I held him, clenching my fists.

His lips gently grazed my ear as he whispered, "You look great, kiddo. The years have done you good."

We held each other for a few minutes, and then he pulled away, turning toward the ghosts of our once upon a time, who were both still sound asleep. As we stood in silence looking at the past, waiting for an unreserved future to make itself present, he gently broke the silence with some words he had seemed to be carefully choosing.

"Morgan, what we had was beautiful because it was rare. And although in the end it may seem unfair, the purpose was complete because you saved me." His jaw seemed to stiffen as he pressed his lips together to keep them from trembling. "You saved me in every single way one person can save another human being. By simply loving me, you gave me something I thought I would never have. And I can only hope that I did the same for you, because you know very well that I sure as hell loved you. But it's time to let go." He heavily sighed. "I want to see you happy. You deserve it, kiddo. So I need you to let me go."

"You have no right to ask me to do that!" I lashed out in anger and grief.

He looked at me with sadness in his eyes and said, "I'm the only one who has the right to."

"Well, I can't," I said.

"Why not?"

"Because I don't know how." I began to cry hysterically.

"Come here." He took me into his arms and gently sighed. "You see, my sweet, little angel bird, the thing about love is that it allows you to love more than once. And although it never takes away your past, it never keeps you from a future." He kissed my cheek and left his lips pressed against my skin as he said, "Don't ever let the love you have to give die, because that kind of love is like magic in a world drained of enchantment." He gently brushed my face with the back of his hand. "Don't be afraid. It's OK to go on with your life. I want you to. After all, the world is such a sad place when you're not happy, bumblebee." He quietly chuckled. "Besides, there are still a lot of good men out there. You deserve one."

"I couldn't do that to you," I softy said as I turned away.

"Hey, look at me. Don't you ever feel like you owe me a damn thing, because you don't; you owe it to yourself. And don't ever see my life as something that wasn't complete, because falling in love with you was my only purpose."

With those words, for the first time, I did not want to wake up from this nightmare. I wanted to stay there with him forever.

"Wait here. I have something for you," he said and then walked over to the other side of the bed. He picked up a medium-sized blue box tied with a white ribbon that had been tucked under the bed. "Here." He handed me the box and smiled. "Open it."

I cautiously opened the box. Somehow I knew that when I looked inside, I would find the musical figurine he had bought me for our second Christmas together. He carefully took the musical figurine from my hands and walked over to the nightstand. He began winding up the figurine, and once the winder would no longer turn, he set it down on the nightstand and let it play. And as the music filled the room like rushing water, he made it a point to catch one long, last glimpse of our past selves. I quietly watched him as his emotions nibbled away at his soul. Then, before he could defy or curse anything or anyone, a tear conquered his face. He turned to me as his tear slowly glazed his rosy cheek, and when he felt his tear drop, he began sobbing like a lost child. It was unbearable. His loud gasps for air raped my willpower. Even after he managed to clear his throat, his voice was still a prisoner that trembled.

"Morgan," he whispered, "I never really got a chance to say good-bye, so I guess now is my chance to do so." He took a deeper breath. "Shit, where do I even begin?" He looked around the room, gathering his thoughts, and finally said, "I guess I'll start off with a secret, because I know you'd want me to tell you one. I never told you this, but the day we met at the coffee shop, I was actually already leaving as you were getting there. I remember sitting in my car thinking, 'Damn. She is the most beautiful thing I have ever seen.'" He chuckled.

I flirtatiously smiled and softly asked, "So would you say that I had you hooked from the get-go?"

He slightly smirked. "Of course. I mean, shit, I didn't even hesitate going back in there after you." He laughed. "I remember being scared, scared shitless as I stood in line behind you thinking, 'What the hell would a girl like this ever want with a guy like me?' But as soon as I smelled the lavender in your hair, it didn't matter. I just knew I had to have you."

He reached out for my hands as he said, "Isn't it funny how the chances we take end up working in our favor, one way or the other?" He took me into his arms. "Morgan, every day I spent with you was like falling in love over and over again for the first time. Your smile was a constant reminder that there were still a few beautiful things left in this ole dreadful world. I loved how you never backed down when I needed to be put in my place. I loved how you knew exactly what to do with me when I had no idea what to do with myself." He laughed. "Morgan, Morgan, my beautiful little Morgan," he whispered, "you showed me the true meaning of one plus one. Because the truth is I always thought it was two, but whenever you were away, I was so incomplete without you." He sighed, releasing his warm breath on my hair.

"I miss the way you used to calm my nerves by sedating me with a warm cup of chai tea and reading me one of your short stories while I interrupted by stealing a few kisses here and there. I miss the late nights when the whole world was asleep but we were wide awake and dreaming. The late nights when the rain was pouring and I'd intentionally move away to my side of the bed just so you could come find me. It was always my way of telling you to hold me without actually having to ask." He smiled sadly and began to choke up. When he pulled away slightly to wipe the tears from his face, I could see that his eyes were glossy and his lips were trembling. Once he was able to get ahold of himself, he continued. "I have never, ever loved someone the way I loved you. And I'm so sorry that I didn't fight hard enough to stay here with you, because I know I hurt you. I hurt you, and it kills me because I feel like it's my fault that you feel so alone, so alone that you have given up on the two things we humans need in order to be human: dreams and love."

He began to sob like a child once more, without control, without hope. "I'm so sorry," he repeatedly uttered. "This isn't how it was supposed to be." He took a deep breath and then cleared his throat. "But in spite of everything, I want you to know that I'm OK. In fact, the day of the accident, when I was looking out to sea, not only was I thinking of the future; I was making things right with God. I asked Him for forgiveness, for another chance so that our children would be blessed with the life we never had. I wanted Him to be a part of our unity so that it would indeed be sacred. And I guess that's why He took me that day. He must have seen that I was as ready as I'd ever be." Antonio rubbed the palm of his hand against my cheek. "I don't have much time, kiddo. It took a hell of a lot of convincing to get them to open up those gates. I'd hate to make them regret their decision. So before I go, can you promise me one thing?"

I nodded, in tears. "Yeah."

"Don't ever be afraid of love, not of one aspect, especially when it comes to believing in it, welcoming it, allowing it. Because it's out there, and it's waiting just for you, maybe even closer than you think." He smiled. Then he looked around the room one last time before walking over to the bed, where he knelt to kiss the seventeen-year-old girl good-bye. As he pressed his lips against her forehead, he closed his eyes and quietly sobbed. He gazed down at her, admiring the girl he remembered, the girl I used to be.

When he finally got up from the bedside, he made his way over to me and kissed me. And as I felt the warmth of his tongue, I began begging heaven to let me in, to take me away in his kiss. He gently pulled away and said, "I gotta go."

"No," I softly uttered. "Please don't go."

"I will always love you, no matter what. Don't you ever forget that." He bit down on his quivering lip, and then he scrunched his face in sadness and said, "Good-bye, kiddo."

His last words pierced me like a splintered arrow, penetrating my soul. He slowly took a few steps back from where I was standing. And as soon as I tried to stop him, he started to disappear. Then, before I knew it, he was gone—again.

I couldn't feel a thing. As much as I wanted to kick and scream, I couldn't feel a thing. I looked around the room thinking of all that time had changed over the years. And as my senseless eyes gazed into the face of nothingness, I noticed a tiny, golden funnel slowly descending from the chandelier hanging in the center of the room. The funnel twirled and swayed side to side as gracefully as a winter's first snowflake, and as soon as it hit the floor, it bloomed into a wooden door. When I saw the door, I knew it was the portal that would take me back to the Wicker Palace.

As I stood at the door, torn in two, looking at who I used to be and well aware of who I was now, I realized that my biggest mistake was ignorance. Antonio and I got so caught up in the beauty of things that we were absolutely convinced that life could be predictable if we wanted it to be. I slowly reached out for the knob of the magical wooden door, but before I turned the knob, I pulled my hand away. There was one last thing I had to do. I quickly ran to the bedside and picked up the musical figurine. I turned the winder, and when it no longer turned, I let it play.

I watched my feet become steps as I made my way back to the portal, steps that sluggishly moved across the floor, my feet feeling like shackled prisoners oppressed by their heavy chains. Once I got back to the magical door, I slowly turned the knob and then gently pushed the door wide open. Before I took one step further, I turned back and gently whispered into the room, "Good-bye, my love. Another may come, and we may fall in love; but there will always be a place in time where I'm still yours and you're still mine. And there we will live on and on, sound asleep on one pillow and a few messy sheets, without worry, happy as can be. I love you, Antonio. I always have, and I always will."

As I headed out the door and made my way back to the Wicker Palace, I could still hear the musical figurine playing faintly in the distance.

7

MERMAIDS

When I stepped into the hallway, the entire hotel was filled with fog so thick that it was hard to distinguish anything. It was the kind of mist you would normally find layered over a swamp or lagoon. It had a light scent of lavender that wasn't harsh like smoke or heavy on the lungs. I had no idea where all the fog could possibly be coming from. As I slowly walked down the hallway, the fog began thinning out. Not only could I now see my surroundings a little better, but I was also able to see the source of the fog.

The Heart of Wicker, the fountain, had flooded, and somehow a small lagoon had formed. The lagoon looked like something ripped out of a nightmare. It was as enchanting as a myth. Strings of Christmas lights floated on the surface of the water along with hourglasses and strange pieces of debris. The water shimmered in a beautiful shade of purple, and it looked colder than a thousand knives. I could feel something drawing me closer, but I wasn't sure what. It felt like I had been placed under a spell that was slowly luring me to the lagoon.

I began making my way down to the first floor. When I got to Wick Oasis, I noticed that the floors were shallowly flooded. I could hear my feet splishing and splashing as I made my way toward the edge of the lagoon. Although the floor around the fountain was flat before, it now had a shore. Had I taken one more step forward, I would have plummeted to the bottomless unknown. I carefully knelt near the edge of the lagoon and started to think of all the disappointments that had chipped away so many pieces of the whole I once was. Then suddenly a loud splash came from the center of the lagoon, and although it did startle me, I was too consumed by my own thoughts to let any sort of curiosity linger.

I thought of my life and what it used to be with Antonio, and then I thought of what it has come to be without him. As I thought, a tear managed to escape from my eye, landing in the lagoon, causing a series of glowing ripples. I watched the ripples as they traveled toward the center of the lagoon, and where they stopped, four heads emerged. The four heads belonged to four familiar faces that were always on time when I needed them to be there for me. Each had small braids entwined in their long, slicked-back, wet hair. They didn't look completely human. In fact, they resembled the beautiful, mystical sea creatures we hear of in folktales as children. One by one, Jesta, Derya, Emily, and Cleo submerged themselves in the water and began swimming toward me in the most bizarre manner. Their silhouettes looked like speckled and blurred images glowing underwater. When they finally got to where I was, they pulled themselves up onto some nearby rocks that had magically appeared along with the lagoon. And that's when I saw their true form for the first time.

"Mermaids," I whimpered.

"Yes, mermaids with the ability to surface but a tendency to dwell in the depths because of fear." Emily's voice rang like silver clinking against crystal. She looked directly at me with those big, dark-brown eyes and said, "Isn't it astonishing what fear can do to us? We are too scared to surface from the sea because we fear that humans will have no mercy on us, but not every human is the same, right? Yet we deprive ourselves of the beauty and wonders of the world above because of this fear."

Their fins glistened like diamonds in the darkness, and their scales sparkled and shimmered like billons of stars from afar. Their chests were bare, solely covered by their long, wet hair, and their skin was pearl kissed. As I gazed at them in fascination, Derya gazed back at me with her own interest. "Why didn't you ever mention him before?" she asked.

I looked out onto the lagoon and softly replied, "Because suffering in silence is a beautiful thing. It makes the people around you believe that you're happy." I tried to find some peace of mind being in their presence, but I couldn't stop my tears from flowing. "I just want to go home," I murmured.

Jesta looked at me, seeming annoyed, and said, "How do you ever expect to witness something mystical if you don't even give yourself the opportunity to believe?"

A silence cloaked the atmosphere. No one said a word. No one moved a muscle. Just then, I noticed Cleo's eyes anxiously moving side to side, and before I knew it, she dove into the lagoon. She began swimming toward me like a serpent gracing the water. When she emerged, she wiped the tears off my face and said, "Your tears show me that you still have hope. After all, we never cry for the things we don't have hope for. Don't be afraid, because not only is love patient and kind; it is also infinite. Since the beginning of time, the measures of love have been tested and manifested. It has created, it has punished, and it has sacrificed. Love has been here since long before you walked this earth, and it will be here long after you're gone. So what makes you think all your cards have been dealt?"

I looked into Cleo's eyes. They were full of hope, the kind of hope I once had in mine. "The world isn't what it used to be," I said, "and it's just getting worse. People these days don't look for what's kind and patient; they look for what's convenient. Believe me. I've tried. I looked for pieces of him in other men, but the more I looked, the less I found. And I am so scared that the only love I'll ever have will be the one that exists only in my memory." I sighed.

The other three mermaids then dove into the water and began swimming toward me as well. They glistened distortedly through the ripples they had caused. And once the four were all united, they rested their elbows on the edge of the shore and began to sing:

> When the moon is full and the clouds roll by
> Waves die trying to kiss the sky
> Because all they want to do, all they want to do is fly
> When the moon is full and the stars are high
> I wish I could leave this all behind
> Because I just want to hear, I just want to hear your heart beat one more time
> Because I miss your heart beating, your heart beating next to mine
>
> But I'm a shadow of the sea
> Cursed with a tail
> Longing to be human again
> But neither silver nor gold
> Can set me free
> 'Tis a pirate's life for me
>
> When the moon is full and a ship sails by
> I sing a song, a song of love
> It's a love I can't possess, only dream of
> Because when they took my feet, they took my heart
> But left the memory of his arms
> Because when they took my feet, they took the best of me
> Now a thousand leagues keep us worlds apart

> Now I'm a shadow of the sea
> Cursed with a tail
> Longing to be human again
> But neither silver nor gold
> Can set me free
> 'Tis a pirate's life for me
>
> Yeah, I'm a song of the sea
> Because this is what you've made of me
> Just a song of the sea
> Boy, look at what you've done to me
> It's too late to save me now
> So don't try to save me now
> 'Tis a pirate's life for me

A drop of water dripped from Jesta's scaly skin into the lagoon, echoing throughout the entire hotel. "Morgan," she uttered, "love is the greatest gift God has given to humankind. Don't deprive yourself of it, because then you might as well suffer the ramifications of being a mermaid. You will love again, for I have seen the future, and I have seen that your love will be of pure fantasy. So enough with the pity party. Let's get down to business." Jesta then gave me an evil grin and said, "I hope you can swim."

Suddenly the four mermaids grabbed ahold of me, each holding on to one of my limbs, and pulled me into the lagoon. I kicked and tugged, but I couldn't break free. The harder I fought, the deeper they took me into the depths of the abyss. I could no longer breathe. The cold water entered my lungs, turning them into water balloons, and then everything around me became hazy.

I remember their bone-crushing grip. I remember thinking, *This is it. This is how I am going to die, in a dream, sound asleep.* I could smell death. I could no longer move. My eyes began giving out, slowly at first and then all at once, leaving me in complete darkness.

Darkness. Pitch black. The sky was so dark that I was either lost in a starless space or in a dream within a dream. In the sky, two angels made of fire were crossing blades in the sheer darkness. I gazed at them vigilantly, without fear, while walking down a narrow concrete path that bore no mercy on either side, toward a man off in the distance standing by a bright white willow tree. And as I got closer and closer, the angels fought harder and harder. Their clashing blades set off sparks that reminded me of fireworks with no color, of ghost rain. I could see the angels growing weary from their war as the man by the tree slowly turned in my direction, but I could not see his face. The willow was too bright, blinding like the sudden light of a UFO. There was no sadness in the man's presence, just a sense of rapture, a pure happiness. And just when I was only a few feet away from him, the angel fighting in my favor abducted me, taking me much farther into the darkness. Darkness. Pitch black.

8

PORCELAIN

Part 1

When I woke up, I found myself lying on the ground in an open field, gazing into a sky the color of snow. I felt as if I had been in a deep sleep for hours. The land around me was stranger than fiction, like the result of a bad acid trip. The grass was the color of wheat. The trees were all made of porcelain, and their leaves were made of ice. It looked like winter but felt like summer. There was not a single cloud in sight. In fact, there was nothing green or blue to prove that this was Earth. The air smelled like strawberries, and the wind felt like an embrace.

I sat up and found a ruby-red apple off to the side of me that had been bitten into. *Was I drugged, or was I poisoned?* In the distance I spotted two nearly all-white leucistic chinstrap penguins wobbling toward me. When they finally got to where I was, they both reached out for my hands, obviously suggesting I come with them. I joined them, and we walked through the field for almost ten minutes until we finally came across a brick road. The bricks on the road were made of pure silver. As we stepped onto the road, the penguins began wobbling rapidly ahead of me as I slowly strolled behind, allowing the land to astonish me.

Off on the sides of the road were the oddest things. There were scarecrows, windmills, and strawberries sprouting along the grass like wildflowers. There were silky-smooth lavender *Cattleya* orchids growing like weeds between the cracks on the road. There were beehives and owls infesting the white oak trees that fenced the sides of the road. Almost every plant and animal was in some way inlayed with porcelain.

We walked for several miles, and not once did the penguins talk. Finally we came across a small, white castle with a large moat at the entrance. It was clear that the castle was our destination. The only problem was there was no drawbridge to get us across, so I knew we were fixing to get a little wet. Once we got close, I could see this wasn't an average moat. The water was a light shade of brown and smelled like tea with a hint of honey. The water wasn't too deep, only about waist high, and there were fish the color of sugar swimming around my feet, leaving trails of pure cane and making the water ever so sweet. Scattered all across the moat were purple flamingos smoking from long, wooden pipes, blowing smoke rings aimlessly into the air.

When we were midway across the moat, three large figures began circling me in the water. I panicked and yelled, "Sharks!" but the penguins didn't turn back to save me. I yelled again, and this time the entire flock of flamingos in the moat began laughing at me. "Why are you all laughing? Help me!" I shouted at the mad birds.

One of the flamingos nearby blew a smoke ring my way and said, "Help you from what, my dear? Those are literally lemon sharks. The only thing they do is keep the moat zesty. Besides, they have no teeth, you stupid girl."

One by one, I gently pushed the lemon sharks away, and sure enough, they swam off like three playful puppies, without giving me any trouble. I tried to plow my way through the water to catch up with the penguins, but running in water is easier said than done. All the commotion from the splashing water eventually caught the penguins' attention. They waited until I caught up with them before they continued grazing the surface of the water, whispering in honks to one another. It wasn't long after we reached the castle when I realized it was made entirely of porcelain. Hanging high above in its tower were two cathedral bells that never swayed in the same direction. Their sound was as sweet as a Christmas carol and as soothing as a midnight train. The penguins pointed their flippers toward the large double doors, signaling me to enter the castle, and so I did, leaving them at the door.

Everything inside the castle was so white it hurt my eyes. I had never seen so much porcelain. The furniture, the utensils, the walls, and the floors were all porcelain.

But the strangest part was the number of clocks in the castle. There must have been thousands of ticking clocks scattered all across the walls. A white butterfly landed on my shoulder. Once she knew she had my attention, she flew right in front of me and began twirling around while batting her wings. I knew very well that she wanted me to follow her, and so I did.

She led me down a long hallway that led into a room where three women were having tea. The women were beautiful. Their skin was pale, their hair was platinum, and their dresses were made of fog and stardust. I locked eyes with all three, one by one, noticing in amazement that their pupils were literally diamonds that glistened and twinkled like morning stars. Their lips were frosted in a light shade of lilac. Needless to say, they were fierce and flawless. As I awkwardly stood at the doorway, one of the women steadily put down her cup of tea and politely asked, "Are you the girl with the broken compass?"

"Excuse me?" I pondered.

"Yes, my dear. Your compass is broken, is it not?" she asked. "Why else would you be here looking for directions?"

"I don't have a compass," I responded, feeling severely agitated. "In fact, I've never even owned one. And I am not here looking for directions, because to be quite honest with you, I don't even know where I am or how I even got here."

"You're in Porcelaind," she responded with a warm, welcoming smile, "and you're in far greater need of direction than you think. After all, you can't even find your own future. So, my dear, to answer your question: yes, your compass is broken. How else would you explain why you keep circling your past? Now then, stop being foolish and come sit down and join us." She smiled once more.

I pulled out a chair and properly introduced myself as I nervously took a seat. "My name is Morgan, aka the girl with the broken compass," I said as I awkwardly tucked my hair behind my ear.

"Ah, what a lovely name. My name is Jewel, and these are my sisters, Diamond and Gem. We will each be taking you on a separate journey to Then, Now, and Soon. I will start off by taking you to the past to revisit one of your most imitate moments, to refresh and hopefully restore your belief. Gem will then take you to the present to show you the opportunities your negligence can cost you. Last but not least, Diamond will provide you with a glimpse of the future."

Gem softly smiled at me and said, "Hello."

Diamond, however, did not glance once in my direction. She simply swirled her spoon around in her teacup, obviously avoiding me.

Jewel stood up and said, "Are you ready, love? It's time to take a little trip to the past." She looked me up and down, studying every detail, and anxiously said, "My goodness, dear. Is that what you'll be wearing to the past?" She scrunched her face in disgust. "And what is with your hair?" She began shaking her head in disapproval. "I am sorry, my dear, but you cannot travel through time looking like that. For goodness sake, you're dressed like a peasant."

She snapped her fingers, and fog instantly began ascending from the ground around me. The fog became thicker and thicker as it began funneling around me. Once I was completely covered in it from head to toe, the funnel popped like a bubble, and I was magically transformed into the belle of the ball. Jewel had given me the curls of a beauty queen and the most beautiful dress to go along with my new hairdo. It was an outstanding cocktail dress that shimmered like a pearl in the sun. And although my heels were a little too high, they were simply gorgeous, for they were as pale as the moon and made of porcelain. Jewel then looked me up and down again with a smile and said, "Much better! But let's add a little color to you."

She blew a kiss that sent a lavender mist into the air. The mist slowly twirled its way toward my lips, and when it touched them, it painted them with a light shade of lavender. Jewel seemed pleased, and, smiling, she reached for a wooden box in the center of the table near a giant teapot. She opened the box, which was nearly the size of a shoe box, and pulled out a large, yellow toad.

"Lick it," she said as she held the toad out toward me.

"I beg your pardon?"

"Lick the toad, my dear."

"No, thank you," I said.

"But you must. It is the only form of time travel in this land."

When I looked at the fat, slimy toad, I almost gagged, but I knew it was now or never. I snatched the toad from her hands and raised it to my mouth, but before I could lick it, she quickly interrupted. "Oh, and Morgan, just one lick for a trip. Otherwise it can be deadly."

I shut my eyes and gave the toad a quick lick. When I opened my eyes, I felt like I had been drugged. As Jewel's features began to blur, my balance began to abandon me. The clocks on the walls began melting and dripping like wax. Everything around me started spinning so fast that I felt like I was in the center of a twister. I reached out for Jewel and held on to her as I waited for my clarity to settle in. When the spinning finally stopped, I found myself in a very familiar place.

We had landed in Antonio's apartment on July 9, 2008, just a little past midnight. That night there was a really bad thunderstorm that had caused all the power to go out. Antonio had lit a tobacco-scented candle on the coffee table in the middle of his living room, where we sat Indian style on the carpet across from each other. As soon as I saw that candle burning, I knew exactly what to expect, and so I braced myself as Jewel and I stood off to the side and watched the past take its course.

"OK, kiddo," he said, "we can either tell scary ghost stories or play with our favorite narcotic."

I giggled. "Ew. You know I don't like ghost stories. I scare easily."

"*Las drogas* it is." He quickly stood up and went off to find a blunt that he had rolled earlier with some blueberry dro. I could hear him in the distance, stumbling around in the darkness, scrambling for the blunt and a lighter. When he came back, he sat beside me with the blunt in his mouth and the lighter in his hand and said, "Before we do this, I just want to remind you that drugs are bad, OK? And I in no way, shape, or form approve of this lifestyle." He laughed.

I raised my eyebrows and said, "I completely agree. It's a filthy habit. And not to mention it kills brain cells."

"It sure does. I've seen it firsthand." He playfully tapped my nose with his finger.

"You are so annoying," I said as we both chuckled. I took his trucker hat off his head and leaned in for a kiss. After he kissed me, I put his hat back on his head with the peak facing backward and whispered, "Light her up."

He clamped the blunt between his lips as he flicked the lighter. When the blunt caught a light, his eyes lit up too. My old man was so handsome. There was something about his eyes behind a lighter's open flame that drove me insane. I watched as the ring of fire gracefully rode up the blunt as he took a hit big enough to fill every inch of his lungs. And as I watched, I lost myself in thought.

She looks so beautiful when she burns, because when she burns, she'll burn for you and anyone else who wants her too. And although she has no wings, her halo makes her an angel. And although she is far from heaven, she can still comfort your soul. But don't pray to her, for she will not grant your prayers unless your requests are measured in ounces and paid for in full. Aye, she sells herself along the streets by vandalized stop signs and unfriendly neighborhood sidewalks. Aye, she is an outlaw but also a noble citizen who eventually gives back to the community for taking so much. Enemies have bonded because of her, whereas friends declare war during acrimonious disputes she single-handedly instigates. She can be deadly, but she can also save a life. She can be ugly, but she can also be the most beautiful thing. She may not belong to you, to me, or to anybody, but when she burns, she will burn just for you, for me, for anybody.

He passed me the blunt, and as I took a hit, he walked over to his old, battery-powered boom box, which was only a few feet away, and began rifling through his collection of CDs. "Ah." He picked up and waved a CD he had burned with all of his favorite Red Hot Chili Peppers songs. He quickly threw the CD into the CD player and hit play. As he sat back down, I passed him the blunt. He took a huge hit and then passed it back to me. I could feel my Zen kicking in. Everything around me was suddenly amplified. I could hear his heart beating through his shirt. It was louder than the rolling thunder outside the window. I swear I could hear the gushing rainwater calling out my name. I don't think anybody will ever truly understand what my eyes saw when I looked at him. I was in love. There was no doubt about it.

After I took a hit, I passed him the blunt. And as I held out the blunt, he firmly grabbed my arm and gently kissed my wrist. He continued kissing my wrist and then slowly moved up my arm until his kisses were at my neck. He finally took the joint from my fingers and placed it off to the side in an ashtray. And at that very moment, I knew I was ready. I began to kiss him heavily, pressing myself into him as if I were trying to become one with him. I reached for the button on his pants and unbuttoned it, and then I slowly began pulling his zipper down. He looked at me, clearly concerned, and asked, "Are you sure you're ready?"

"Yes. I'm as ready as I am sure that I love you." That was the first time I had ever told him that I loved him. And I did, in every single way a human being could possibly love another human being.

I could feel him gazing deep into my soul as he looked into my eyes and said, "I love you more."

While a song called "Porcelain" played softly in the background, I took off his shirt, and after he took off mine, I unhooked my bra and tossed it aside. I laid myself down on the bristly carpet. Once I had made myself comfortable, he placed his body over mine, and I could feel the warmth of his bare chest against my naked breasts. He nervously removed my shorts and then bashfully took off my panties. He began rubbing his big hands up my bare thighs. I was so nervous. I could hear and feel my heart beating like a drum as he placed my legs over his shoulders and cunningly sunk his face in between my thighs. The feeling of his warm breath on my innocence was exhilarating as he passionately kissed the part of me that separated me as woman.

Suddenly Antonio stood up and seductively dropped his pants down to his ankles. He then took them off and threw them aside. He wasn't wearing any underwear, so I couldn't help but stare. The truth was I had never seen a naked man before, but I can tell you this: if inches really do matter, then he was beyond average, beyond perfection.

He stood there in front of me, completely naked, unafraid to bare what he had to offer. After a while, I reached for his hand and dragged him back down toward me. I carefully placed him between my thighs, and as he sank in deeper and deeper, I experienced a pain I had never felt before. His penis was so thick that I could feel it pulsating inside me. As we made love, I could feel a light layer of sweat covering my body. The candlelight caused our shadows to flicker on the walls, giving off the illusion that we were two people in the midst of a brawl. But in reality he was so gentle, so considerate. The louder I moaned, the louder he grunted. My innocence was no longer mine. He now held it, and it was his to maintain. If he ever broke my heart, left, or cheated, my innocence was his to answer for.

Once we were both done, we cleaned ourselves up. I put on one of his old T-shirts, which draped on me like a gown, while he slipped into a pair of boxers. He placed a couple of pillows and a blanket on the living-room floor, where we lay for a few minutes in silence. As he held me in his big arms, he sensually ran his fingers through my fingers while I listened to the wind howling like a pack of hellhounds, watching the candle burn on its last few minutes. He gently pressed his lips against the side of my head and said, "It's an ugly world out there, my little porcelain doll, but it's people like you who give people like me the chance to still call it beautiful."

He briefly paused to kiss the side of my forehead then said, "I'll never fail you—I promise you that. Because as much as I want you, I need you more. Because as much as

I need you, I love you more. And as much as I love you, I am hoping that one day you'll love me more."

I turned over and kissed his cheek for being so sweet. He was always so sweet, yet it never failed to surprise me. "Antonio, can I tell you something?" I asked, trying to avoid direct eye contact.

"Sure."

"OK, but promise me you won't laugh, you asshole." I giggled.

He smirked. "I'll do my best."

I took a deep breath. "OK, here it goes. I've never had a real dance before, but if I ever do, I'd want my first dance to be with you." I bashfully smiled. "So, promise me that you'll take me out for a real dance one of these days." My cheeks were redder than roses, and I began nervously playing with his hand as I continued to ramble on. "I know it sounds silly, but ever since I was a little girl, I've dreamed of the day that my prince would come, and we'd spend the rest of our lives dancing the nights away. And although we may not be the world's perception of Prince Charming and Aurora, I'm yours and you are mine. And I like to think that's better than any other title I could ever have."

Before I could say anything else, Antonio quickly stood up with his hand extended, reaching out for me. He gently pulled me up from the ground and put one of his hands on my waist while his other hand held one of my hands up in the air. He looked so silly that although I tried, I couldn't help but laugh.

"Wait!" I sniggered. "Something's missing."

"Ah, but of course," he said and then smirked. "First we have to create the mood." He walked over to his boom box and switched it over to FM mode. He began flipping through radio stations until he came across an oldies station that had just begun playing "If You Leave Me Now" by Chicago. He looked at me with the biggest smile and said, "Perfect."

He quickly ran back over to me and placed his hands around my waist as I wrapped my arms around his neck. He softly began singing along to the song, gazing into my eyes while I lingered on the fact that I was in love. Without the sound of a single word, I mouthed a silent "I love you," which was shortly followed by his "I love you more." I placed my head against his chest as we rocked from side to side, swaying to the remarkable lyrics of such a beautiful song. It was a bittersweet moment, because the nostalgia lingering behind the song reminded me that I was no longer the little girl I used to be. I was now a woman in the arms of a man who believed in everything I wanted to be, in everything I could be. And even though my aspirations only could make sense in the stars that existed in my mind, somehow he saw them shine.

When the candle finally burned out, we laid ourselves down in the darkness, lost in the awareness of our love. The mixture of the rolling thunder and the refuge of his arms put me sound asleep that night, without a worry, without regret.

Then before I knew it, Jewel and I were back in the porcelain castle. When I looked at her, I knew that she was just as emotionally drained as I was. I could see it in her eyes.

"Come," she said, and we slowly headed out to the garden, where Gem was waiting for me with a wooden box.

Part 2

There was so much life and color in the garden, in contrast to all the white porcelain in the castle. The bark on the trees was ivory, and the leaves were as rich white as milk. Every time a leaf fell from a tree, it gracefully hit the ground and then dissolved into the gentle breeze. The shrubs were the shade of a Pacific sunset; but these were no ordinary shrubs, because the leaves were actually thousands of butterflies in an evening slumber. There were hummingbirds, lovebirds, and sparrows nesting in the trees. Their colors were so vibrant that they resembled the scattered pieces of a rainbow. The grass was the color of wheat and was as soft as silk. In the center of the garden was a large willow tree. It was the only tree in the garden that produced fruit. Its vines carried the burden of blueberries that were almost the size of walnuts.

When I first saw Gem, she was feeding some fish from off the side of a bridge that crossed over one of the small ponds in the garden. As Jewel and I approached her, I noticed a wooden box in her hand. It was the very same box Jewel had presented earlier, so I knew exactly what to expect.

Gem smiled at me, and I embraced her.

"Back so soon?" she said.

I nodded. "Unfortunately."

She took my hand and said, "Well, don't get too comfortable, because I will be showing you the things in your life that are fairly present. Life has so many opportunities in store for you, but it also many consequences if you choose to deny its opportunities. The stakes are high, and the risks are low, but the only way you'll see those odds is from the outside looking in."

I looked down at the box in her hand and said, "One lick for a trip."

"Precisely." She laughed.

When she handed me the wooden box, I quickly pulled out the toad, and without hesitation, I gave it a forceful lick. I was so curious to see what she had in store for me that my curiosity had suppressed my repulsion. My vision began to blur, making me feel dizzy. My whole body was tingling in a cold sweat. The entire garden became holographic. As I stumbled toward Gem, the butterflies on the shrubs woke up from their slumber and transformed into vicious crows. They flew toward me at full speed, ready to attack. As soon as I covered my face with my arms and closed my eyes, the sound of their wings fluttering around me stopped.

I opened my eyes and found myself standing in the center of a fancy restaurant, where a very familiar gentleman was sitting alone at a table waiting for his date to arrive. Gem placed her hands on my shoulders and whispered in my ear, "He's very handsome, isn't he? Do you know him?"

"Yes. His name is Chris. He works at the Wicker Palace with me." I stared at him, losing myself in a daze.

Gem continued to investigate the situation. "Do you have any idea who he could possibly be waiting for?"

"Yes. He's waiting for me," I replied.

"And where are you?"

"I'm not coming."

"Why?" She examined him, obviously looking for a flaw.

He looked so dapper in his button-up shirt, swishing the ice around in his bourbon. He looked more anxious than angry. He was constantly checking his phone and brushing down his shirt to prevent the slightest wrinkle. There was absolutely nothing wrong with him. He was perfect, and so I couldn't help but feel sick to my stomach as I responded to Gem's question. "I have no idea."

The waiter brought him another drink and asked if he was ready to order. Chris hesitated and told the waiter to give him a few more minutes. Another ten minutes went by before Chris finally realized that I wasn't coming. He asked for his check and headed for the door, hanging his head in complete humiliation. As he walked by a small group of waitresses, I overheard one of the waitresses telling her other two coworkers, "You'd have to be pretty stupid to stand up a hot piece of ass like that."

Gem and I quickly followed Chris to his car in the pouring rain. We sneaked into his backseat. The drive home was awkwardly quiet. I wanted to tell Chris I was sorry, but I knew he couldn't see me, let alone hear me. His apartment was warm and cozy. It smelled like strawberries with a light hint of weed. He took off his wet shirt and threw it on the ground. He was clearly agitated, and I couldn't blame him. After all, I'd be lying if I said I never gave him any signs of hope. He picked up a well-packed doobie that was lying on his kitchen counter next to a stack of hospital bills and then proceeded to his room. He must have just rolled the joint earlier that day, because there was still a small pile of stems and seeds from the weed on his counter. He took off his jeans and then released a big sigh as he threw himself onto his bed. His TV was the only thing illuminating his dark room. He reached over for the lighter sitting on his nightstand and used it to spark the joint that was firmly clamped between his lips.

"Don't his eyes look so beautiful behind that flame?" Gem whispered from behind my shoulder.

"Yes. They really do, almost baby-blue."

After the second hit, Chris was deep in his own thoughts. He released the smoke along with some words I would have never expected him to say. "Morgan, Morgan, Morgan…" He pondered. "I don't know what else to do to show you I care." He sighed while gazing at his joint. "I've done everything in my power, and it's been one failed attempt after another. God, it sucks. I know that she feels the same way. I just wish I knew why she is so scared." He inhaled another puff and then blew a cloud of smoke into the darkness. "I just need her to trust me. I just need her to know that when I think of the future, I think of her. When I think of all the things I've been through, I know there's not one chance I wouldn't take if I could wake up to that smile every morning, because I'm so tired of being alone. Boy, am I tired of being alone," he murmured.

His big, blue eyes looked like two glazed doughnuts fresh out of the oven. And although he was high, his thoughts were not compromised, for his whispered words were deeper than the ocean. "Freedom can be a blessing or a curse, but no matter what, in the end it is the worst form of imprisonment. Because a soul without a muse is a soul without a mate, and without both, a soul is just a ghost carrying around body weight."

He huffed, but this time when he puffed, he was no longer speaking to himself. It was clear that this discussion was between him and God. "Look"—he sighed—"I may not be the best person, but I know I'm not the worst. The faith I was able to maintain after all I've lost must be worth something. I still believe I have the power to change this nothingness into somethingness, because when the past wakes me from my sleep, it's the future that sedates me. I know I can be the man she needs me to be. Please, give me a second chance at happiness."

In the midst of his plea to God, he began to cough uncontrollably. He quickly grabbed a half-empty bottle of water that was near his bedside and drank what was left in it. He then launched the empty bottle into the wall across the room. It wasn't long after clearing his throat that he broke down in tears. His voice shook with anger and pain as he demanded to be addressed by God. "Why didn't You take me instead? She was just a baby! It should have been me! It should have been me."

He reached for one of the framed pictures near his bed. It appeared to be a family portrait. In the portrait his arms were wrapped around a young woman, and their blissful smiles fell on a beautiful baby girl. The woman's gorgeousness piqued my curiosity. "Who's the woman in the picture?"

Gem kept her sights on Chris as she replied, "That was his wife and his baby girl."

"Was? What happened to them?"

Gem put her head down in sadness. "About two years ago, Chris had some neighbors who got involved with the wrong people. They owed a Mexican drug dealer by the name of Don Juan Pablo some money and had failed to pay up. On the night of May 22, 2011, Juan Pablo sent two of his men to make an example of the neighbors and show the consequences that come from double-crossing him. Don Juan gave his men specific orders to set the neighbors' house on fire while everyone was sound asleep, and the two men went through with his orders. However, they got the wrong house. Christopher's baby died at the scene from smoke inhalation, and his wife died at the hospital from severe burns. Chris was the only one to survive. He lost everything in a fire that wasn't even intended for him, yet unlike you, he did not lose his faith. Everyone has a story lurking behind their silence. You're not the first to have loved and lost, but if you keep playing the victim, loss is all you'll ever have. He needs you, and I know you need him too. After all, it takes a broken heart to mend a broken heart. You hold the power of the chance at happiness that he deserves. Don't let your fear of loss keep you both from being loved."

Seeing Chris curled up like a baby with tears streaming down his face made me realize how selfish I was being. *What am I doing?* I thought. *A pursuit can only go so far if ends don't meet. If I keep running, one day the man of my dreams will only be a man in my dreams.* I began to make my way over to Chris, to make ends meet. I managed to reach his bedside, but before I could put my arms around him, everything began to swirl. I felt like I was being sucked into a black hole, and before I knew it, I was back in the garden of the porcelain castle once more.

When I arrived at the garden, I had a rough landing, falling face first in the grassy knoll.

"Clumsy girl." Jewel giggled as Gem helped me up. I dusted myself off and couldn't help but laugh as well. I had gone to the past, I had visited the present, and it was now time to journey to the future. I immediately began to look for Diamond, but she was nowhere in sight. When I asked after her, the other two avoided the question. Instead of answers, they offered me soft smiles and pitiful looks.

Jewel quickly broke the awkward silence, saying, "Sometimes we feel that life isn't fair because things don't go our way, but if things went our way, life would not be as it should, and the beauty of fate would be put to death. Everything happens for a reason, and as much as I hate to use that cheesy phrase, it bears truth. Love is a form of innocence, and like innocence, love can't be lost if it is maintained."

In the distance I saw Diamond wandering through the garden. When I attempted to approach her, she stopped dead in her tracks like a deer in headlights. She looked me up and down and then walked right past me. I felt like shit, but I held back my tears until she was completely out of sight. "Why won't she acknowledge me?" I asked, strangely hurt, wiping the tears off my face.

Gem quickly responded, "How do you expect the future to acknowledge you if you haven't even acknowledged the future?"

"Any more questions?" Jewel teased me cheerfully, for the point was well proven.

"What's next?" I laughed.

Gem smiled. "Ah, I'm glad you asked, because what happens next is completely up to you. You can continue to embark on this journey and learn more about how you can make ends meet with your future, or I can end this entire dream right now, and you can go back to the life you had before all of this."

"Can you do that?" I scrunched my face, baffled by her proposal.

"Of course, my dear. There is tea that contains a powerful potion made from the berries of the willow tree. One sip of this tea has the power to return you home safely. However, if you consume this tea, you will have no recollection of this dream when you wake up. You will not remember what you saw or who you met, and the whole purpose of this dream will have been in vain. After all, without a cause, there can be no effect; and without a memory, there can be no epiphany."

Jewel cleared her throat to get my attention. "However, if you choose to complete your journey, your memory will not be touched or tainted. Just give the toad one last lick, and you'll be on your way." She tilted her head, shrugging her shoulders with a peer-pressuring smile, and said, "So what will it be: tea or toad?"

I looked at Jewel and nodded. "I've come too far to quit now. Where's the toad?"

Gem handed me the toad, which looked much fatter than it had before.

"As much as I am going to miss the both of you, one thing's for sure: I certainly won't miss this toad." I chuckled.

Right before I licked the toad, Jewel stopped me and said, "Before you go, I want you to know that we will be cheering for you." I gave them both a hug as a sign of my gratitude for their support, and as soon as I licked the toad, I began to break into tiny particles that dissolved like vapor, until the last thing I saw was darkness.

9

GRANDPA

I awoke to the sound of crashing water and found myself lying in the middle of the hallway of the second floor. I felt hungover even though I wasn't. My head was throbbing, and my bones were aching. I had to use all my strength just to get myself up off the floor. I was able to shake off the discomfort for the most part, but I was still a bit hazy.

The entire first floor was submerged by the mermaid's lagoon, and the water was still quickly rising to the second floor. My train of thought was scattered. I didn't even realize I was still wearing the dress Jewel had squeezed me into until I could no longer bear the porcelain heels. I threw the heels over the railing into the rising water, and the splash echoed throughout the entire hotel.

There was nothing left to do but wait for a sign or a clue to indicate my next move. I began lurking through the shadows, like an untamed creature, looking for a sign;

but the more I looked, the less I found. I eventually lost count of how many times I had circled the second floor. I was exhausted. I had literally pressed my ear against every single door, waiting to hear from my next venture, but I heard nothing. There had to be a reason why I woke up on the second floor, and I was not giving up until I found out what that reason was.

Minutes went by, creating an hour, and I had managed to collect nothing but more silence. My eyes had grown heavy from the solemnity I felt, so I decided to get some rest. I would have been perfectly fine with resting in front of one of the elevators, but the water had risen from the first floor and was now above my ankles. I was longing for one of the beds in the suites, but I was so scared of entering a room without being summoned by it. Eventually I could no longer take the distress. I needed some sleep. Room 210 was just a few feet away, and I persuaded myself to simply deal with the consequences if there were any ahead. I quickly made my way to the door before I could change my mind. As soon as I placed my hand on the handle, I heard a loud banging coming from down the hall.

Bang! Bang! It was continuous, and I had no idea what was causing it. To be quite honest, it frightened me. It sounded like something or someone was on the verge of a forced entry. I began to walk, perking up my ears, using only my sense of sound, until my hunt ended at the door of room 222. The hinges on the door were splinters away from breaking off the wood. Fear began running all over my body like tiny insects. My attention had been sought and surely gotten. I knew I had to face whatever was on the other side of that door. The banging continued until I reached for the handle.

It was January 7, 2005, and my grandfather was lying on his deathbed. I'd only been granted a few minutes to say good-bye. He was vaguely conscious and almost unrecognizable in his fragile condition. I had no idea what to say to him, because I had no idea how to say good-bye to the man I thought was invincible my whole life. Hearing the weakness in his breath caused me to lose my strength. There's nothing more painful than seeing a hopeless hero, especially when that hero is yours.

I leaned over and gave my grandfather a kiss on his cheek, and then I released the best good-bye a whisper could carry. "I'm gonna miss you so much, Papa. I'm gonna miss sitting out on the porch in the summer watching you cut through a cold, sweet watermelon while you rant about your wild escapades, because I don't think there is anyone who can tell a story quite like you. Thank you for everything that you've done. Not only are you leaving this earth as a great man, but you are also leaving as my hero. I promise to do everything in my power to lead a life as great as yours. I love you, Grandpa."

He smiled as he collected a tear from my face, and that was the last time I ever felt his warm embrace.

In the blink of an eye, I was transported to paradise, surrounded by a white light. It was so bright it was blinding. It was nearly impossible for me to open my eyes. For a second I thought I was standing on the sun. Although I could not see a thing, I could feel nature surrounding me. The flowers were potent, and the bees were buzzing. A gentle breeze sent a peace flowing over me. Once my eyes adjusted to the change of scenery, I was able to behold the beauty of the paradise. The sky was a marine blue, and the sun stood next to the moon. I found myself in a harmonious meadow filled with wild daisies, which aroused a sense of nostalgia from the winter of my soul. It was impossible to determine where the meadow ended and where it began. The plains were as green as the New Zealand countryside. The clouds in the sky were clustered and silver lined. My past felt so present, and my future felt so clear, because a truce was settled between them; and it was so beautiful it made me want to cry.

Aye, my spirit hence thy dewy eyes, for if this is not my illusive state of mind, this must be paradise. I took my sights off the beauty for a second when I noticed a man sitting under a blossom tree about a mile due east. It was the only tree in the meadow, and he was the only person around for miles. It only took me a few seconds to realize who he was, and when I did, I ran to him like a prisoner running to freedom. When he saw me, his smile became as solid as concrete. I immediately threw my arms around him and said, "I've missed you, Papa."

Before he could say a thing, he started sobbing like a baby. I held him tight, because I wanted him to hold me forever. He smelled like ice-blue aftershave, just as he always did. He was exactly as I remembered, strong and full of life. Words cannot even begin to describe how much I'd missed those mysterious green eyes. I could not believe I was standing in the presence of that carless scruff and cowboy hat. We didn't say a thing. We just stood in silence. As the wind blew past us, the smell of cherry blossoms filled the air. All that mattered was that we were both here.

a&

Born and raised in San Luis Potosi, Mexico, Vicente Juarez spent most of his childhood surrounded by poverty, but instead of seeing indigence as a disadvantage, he saw it as an opportunity. He saw it as a chance to become a man of prosperity, and through that dream, he became a man of faith. And it was by his faith that he became a man of his word.

On one of his travels to Concepcion Del Oro, Zacatecas, he stumbled across a beautiful young girl named Virginia Rivera. Although he was only twenty-one, he knew the very moment he laid eyes on her that she would change his fate forever. As they fell in love, they began dreaming of the life they wanted for their love. They both knew the only way to have the kind of life they aspired for was to flee Mexico. In the middle of one summer night, he stole Virginia away from her father's house, and because she decided to leave it all behind, he decided to make her his wife. They lived in the city of Rio Bravo, Tamaulipas, for several years before coming to America. It was in Rio Bravo where they welcomed my father into this world.

Not only was my grandfather a man of vision; he was also a man of action. He proudly shed his blood and sweat so that his children could have good lives and so that his grandchildren would have even better lives. The greatest thing about my grandfather was his fear of God. It was this fear he placed in all of us. He told us that the greatest relationship we'd ever have as humans was the relationship we shared with God. He showed us that anything was possible with a pinch of faith.

Once our emotions had settled, my grandfather and I sat under the large cherry tree to comfortably carry on a conversation. He reached into a bag of apples he had off to the side of him. He handed me an apple and then reached back into the bag and grabbed one for himself. He tossed his apple around from one hand to the other as he stared off into the distance. Though his eyes had so much to say, his mouth was hesitant. I laid my head on his shoulder to make him feel more comfortable, but there was still so much tension. I had to do something to lighten the mood, and what better way to break ice than with a joke? "You know, they say an awkward conservation is better than an awkward silence."

He smiled and took a deep breath. "I'm so sorry."

"It's OK, Papa. I'm just glad that I got you to say something." I laughed.

He looked at me seriously and said, "No, that's not what I meant. I mean I'm sorry about what happened." A breeze blew the through blossom tree and gently rattled the branches. "Morgan, I begged the heavens for Antonio's life that day. Please believe me when I tell you that I tried, because I did, but there was nothing I could do. Death does not negotiate, and the will of God answers to no one."

His voice was so sincere and his eyes were so apologetic that it took all my strength to hold back my tears. I gave him a pouty smile. "Thank you, Papa. That really means a lot."

He bit into his apple and said, "I would like to share something with you, if you don't mind."

"No, not at all. Go ahead."

He took another bite of his apple and then tossed it aside. "The day I stumbled across your grandmother, I was just a young man, and for a young man, love at first sight can be a lot to bargain for. I didn't have much, and I most definitely didn't have anything to offer her. I knew it wasn't gonna be easy, but it's the sacrifices we make that reward us in the end. We had our good times and bad times, but we never laid down our weapons. We took on those challenges and overcame those obstacles, until our love became a force to be reckoned with. We took a chance on love, so love would take a chance on us." He sighed and kissed my forehead. "'It's better to have loved and lost.' That is a powerful statement that only those who have truly loved and have truly lost can justify." He sighed. "Aw, kiddo, why did this have to happen to you? You didn't deserve this."

I took a huge bite out of my apple before making any assumptions. The taste of my apple combined with the smell of the grassy plains was so therapeutic. I had to pause my chewing just to take a deep breath of the meadow's fresh air. I'd be lying if I said I could remember the last time my thoughts had this much clarity. A gust of wind blew some leaves off the blossom tree. I watched as the leaves danced and twirled like dust until they disappeared into the meadow, forever gone, forever lost. I sighed. "When did life become so difficult?"

"Life became difficult the moment you were old enough to realize that you had the choice to make it difficult," my grandfather immediately responded.

"Touché." My laughter coursed its way past my smile. I took a few more bites from my apple and then tossed it into the meadow.

My grandfather looked at me like he could not believe I had just done that. "Hey, Johnny Appleseed, I have a special pile for the apple cores."

"Oops. I'm sorry."

I got up quickly to go retrieve it, but before I could go, he stopped me. He looked me up and down, and his eyes sank in sadness from all the changes he saw. He sighed and rubbed his brow in disbelief. "I can't believe you're already twenty-five years old."

I sat back down underneath the shade of the blossom tree and whimpered, "I can't believe it either. Time goes by so fast."

He raised his eyebrows and said, "Too fast...I still remember the first time I carried you. You were so tiny. I loved you the moment I saw you. Now look at you. You're all grown up."

Suddenly, two blue jays flew near our feet from the meadow. They began to chirp as they skipped around us, inviting us to join in their shenanigans. They were absolutely adorable, the female so fearless and the male so charismatic. Where she went, he followed. He was never too far from where she was, looking out for her well-being and forgetting his own. He constantly tweeted for her kiss, and she never denied him one, for she loved him. I was sure of it. My grandfather laughed as the blue jays chased each other like two kids too young to know any better.

"I think he likes her," he said, clearly emphasizing his perspective.

"I think she likes him too," I said.

As I watched the blue jays frolic, all I could think of was Chris. I had been thinking about him a while since I arrived at the field. For some reason I couldn't get him off my mind. Just thinking about his smile and those baby-blue eyes made me all warm inside. My grandfather looked over at me with a curious grin and wasted no time in asking, "Who's the lucky guy?"

"Grandpa!" I playfully groaned, soon realizing I unknowingly had a smile too big. It was clearly uncommon.

"Come on..." He laughed.

"I have no idea what you're talking about," I awkwardly responded.

He busted out laughing. "Oh, please. Look at that smile. The only time I ever smile like that is when I'm thinking of your grandmother."

"I assure you I have no idea what you're talking about, silly man." My flushed cheeks were tingling with pain from the smile that pulled them from ear to ear. I even felt feverish from the truth that lay behind his cornering accusation.

"Uh huh...Well, I think he's a great guy. In fact, I see a lot of myself in this Chris fellow." He smiled. His sharp statement was more of an approval than a remark. I was so embarrassed.

"Grandpa!" I giggled. "How do you know about Christopher?"

He gave me a devious smiled. "I've got my ways, kiddo."

I playfully shook my head with dismay and then rested my chin on my knees. "He really is a great guy, Papa."

"Then what are you waiting for?"

I looked for a good excuse, but nothing was coming to me except the truth. "I'm scared."

"Scared of what?"

"I'm scared that I'll lose him, just like I lost Antonio. I'd rather not risk putting myself through that again. You can't lose what you don't have. Besides, it's better to be safe than sorry."

I could tell that my grandfather was getting agitated. He took a deep breath and exhaled. "That's not being safe; that's being a coward. Life is too short to be living in fear. After all, regret is the real enemy. Look, I'll be honest with you. I don't know if Chris is 'the one,' but you shouldn't be afraid to find out, because the chances you don't take are the answers you'll never have."

"It's not that easy."

"It's not that easy?" He raised his voice. "You think I don't know what it's like to lose someone? You think it was easy for me to leave your grandmother behind? Do you think it was easy for her? Well, it wasn't! She could have given up just as easily if she wanted to. She's old, Morgan! The heartbreak alone could have claimed her life, but she forbade it. She knew she still had a purpose to fulfill on Earth, so she fought to be the strength and support her family needed. You need to stop feeling sorry for yourself. It's pathetic. You are a beautiful young woman with an unimaginable purpose, but in order to embrace that purpose, you must sow a seed. There are two kinds of people in the world: victors and victims. A victor never utters an excuse for the impossible or complains about an obstacle. He simply takes on his task and makes a miracle out of it, and therefore he is victorious. However, a victim will use any justification to excuse himself from a matter that requires any determination. He solely sees his task as the cause of his unfulfilled life, and therefore he is a failure."

He was absolutely right. I had been living off of my excuses for the last two years. I set my dreams aside because I chose the role of the victim over the role of the survivor. I knew that I was wrong, but it is easier to justify than to hope. Who the hell was I to victimize myself as though I were the only person who had ever suffered from a broken heart?

Vain…selfish and vain I had been, for I had no concern for the suffering that suffered outside of my suffering. I felt my sense of disappointment like one would feel a cut or a burn. It was a dissatisfaction that was necessary, for without dissatisfaction there could never be a desire to be satisfied.

Our silence was so loud that it made the gusting wind sound like a mere whisper. I was so caught up in my revelation that I didn't even notice that the blue jays had flown away. My grandfather softly put his hand under my chin and turned my head toward his apologetic eyes. "I'm sorry. I didn't mean to be so hard on you, but you are selling yourself short. There are great things in store for you in life. Don't be the fool who buries her own treasure."

I smiled. "It's OK. I know you meant well, and I know there is a bigger purpose for me. I can feel it in my soul. It's been knocking at the door for some time now, and it's about time I let it in."

"Yeah, it's about time you do, because—let's face it, kid—you aren't getting any younger." He laughed. "Besides, you made me a promise. And I quote: 'I'll do everything in my power to lead a life as great as yours.'"

He raised his left eyebrow as he playfully scolded me. "But in all seriousness, I'm holding you to that promise. If you break it, you'll break my heart."

"I won't. I promise. I would really hate to disappoint you, let alone break your heart." My eyes glazed over with tears as I reassured him.

He smiled—I could tell it was a smile from the heart—and then he leaned over and wrapped his arm around my neck. He kissed my forehead and said, "Do you remember saying there was no one who could tell a story quite like me? Well, you were wrong, because you can. You got this old man's gift. Don't put it to waste, because I can guarantee you that you're gonna have one hell of a story to tell after this dream is over with." He laughed.

"It's a start." I nodded. "I'm pretty sure that people will demand a drug test before they believe this was an actual dream though." I laughed. "But yes, it is definitely a start."

"You're one crazy kid, and I have no idea where you get it from—but it's definitely not from my side of the family. Must be your grandmother's." He smirked.

"Oh, whatever! I don't know who you are trying to clown, because I am just as crazy and stubborn as you are." We both laughed.

"I don't know. Some of the things you did with Ruby and Jaceil kind of put my wild escapades to shame." He giggled. Then he looked me straight in the eye and said, "Oh, and by the way, Ruby says hi."

"I miss her." I smiled and gently sighed as I began to grasp what he was saying.

"She misses you too."
"When did it happen?" I asked.
"About a year ago, late December."
"How?"
"A head-on collision. They both died on impact."
"They?"
"Yes," he hesitated, "both she and Markus."

I put a fist over my mouth to silence my cry, but it was useless. I gasped for air, and my tears burned my eyes like lemon drops. It hurt so bad, not only because it had happened but also because I hadn't even had the slightest idea that it had happened. I felt so guilty for allowing myself to have lost touch with her over the years. I felt like a monster, even worse, a horrible friend. My grandfather pulled me into his arms and tried to console me. "You're OK. You just need some sleep. Close your eyes," he whispered.

As soon as I closed my eyes, my cries slowly faded. I felt like I had been sedated. I began to lose control of my body as it slowly shut down. I tried fighting off the haze, because I knew my grandfather would no longer be there when I woke up. But it was as pointless as trying to count to a hundred once the anesthesia starts kicking in. I didn't even get a chance to say good-bye to the old man.

10

WES

I tossed and turned a few times before realizing that I was sleeping on the coziest king-size bed I had ever been on. Unfortunately it wasn't mine. It was one of those moments when you forget you're not at home and wake up confused by your surroundings for a split second. I rubbed my eyes, dreading the thought of getting out of bed, but I knew the longer I stayed in this bed, the longer I'd be away from my own bed. I sat up and stretched my arms out toward the ceiling. I yawned and then muttered, "Come on, Morgan. Get your ass out of bed."

Peeling the covers off of me, I quickly made my way to the door and out of room 222. When I walked into the hallway, the air in the hotel was as humid as I would imagine a jungle to be after some rain. I could not bear the heat. My pores were bleeding sweat, and my mouth was dry from dehydration. I felt like I was slowly being suffocated by the lack of oxygen in the atmosphere. However, I did not suffer alone from the merciless climate. The entire hotel was in the grasp of its wrath. There was mold on the damp carpets and on the now-peeling wallpaper. It was everywhere, like an epidemic, a disease that the Wicker Palace had come in contact with. The mold was spreading faster and faster by the minute, as though it were some sort of alien life form.

I leaned over the railing for a glimpse of the first floor, completely baffled by the power that still lay in the element of surprise, for I could not believe my eyes. The flood caused by the salty lagoon had completely drained away. It looked like a monstrous hurricane had swept through the first floor. Pieces of debris were scattered all across the hotel from the loose furniture in the suites. The railings were rusted, and the pillars were covered in barnacles. The doors had been knocked off their hinges by the water pressure. The plants had been ripped from their roots and were left like soggy, lifeless sea creatures littering nearly every inch of tile. Menus, brochures, and registration cards added a magic touch to the haunting rubble. However, the strangest thing was the amount of seaweed layered in the atrium. All in all, the hotel looked like a really bad shipwreck after a huge storm.

I made my way to the nearest elevator and carefully slid myself down the cables to the first floor. I figured I might as well explore a bit, because there was no better time for a scavenger hunt. After all, they say big storms bring big treasures. I walked over to where the mermaid lagoon once was, but all that remained of the magical lagoon was a giant hole that led to an abyss beyond measurement. As I looked down into the abyss, my curiosity quickly turned into nerves, and I felt my body shut down. I immediately stepped back from the edge, shaking off the shiver. I have a fear of heights, and this gaping hole wasn't anything I was too eager to get close to.

Just then I heard a strange noise stirring in the distance. It startled me, as it was not a pleasant sound. It sounded like smothered cries for help. I stood still in silence, trying to pinpoint the source of the faint cries, but it seemed like the work of an evil ventriloquist, for I could not trace it. The only thing left to do was to put my full faith in my ears. I began walking toward the Oasis kitchen, my ears perked like a hunting dog's. I cautiously pushed open the kitchen door and then made my way through piles of broken dishes and tarnished silverware. I could hear the muffled cries growing louder as I took the exit to the patio right behind Wick Oasis, the location of our infamous little bar.

The patio was a big lounge where all our rich asshole guests gathered to compare wealth and chattels while doing a shitty job at handling their liquor. The lounge was in the midst of a beautiful botanical garden that provided the horny drunks with the illusion of a tropical getaway. Although the garden was completely destroyed by the flood, kudos to Wes for at least keeping this part of the hotel green for as long as he did.

Being in the midst of all the rubble felt so surreal, and remembering the Wicker Palace as it was compared to how it looked now gave me goose bumps like a morbidly twisted lullaby. My love for the hotel made all the damage hard to swallow. I lingered around the patio, recovering what I could. I could still hear the muffled voice drifting through the air, but my heart was focused on restoring some of the garden's beauty. I picked up a few overturned tables and placed them in their proper locations. I then gathered the chairs that weren't completely damaged and neatly arranged them near the tables.

Suddenly an unsettling feeling swept over me, a feeling that I was being watched. However, I did not make any indication that I knew I was under surveillance until the muffled voice clearly called my name. I stopped dead in my tracks and began to look around, investigating every corner and eerie shadow while still keeping guard over my own shoulder. I finally spotted the figure of a man in the shadows. He was sitting on a raised brick flower bed by the bar. The image was extremely creepy. I realized how twisted I was, though, when I began walking toward the figure instead of running away from it like a normal human being would. As I got closer, I began to shed my fear, because I soon recognized that handsome face.

"Wes!" I shouted with glee.

He was covered in weeds from head to toe. He looked like an ancient artifact buried in ruins. The color of his skin had lost its sun-kissed glow and was now completely sea green. His soft, plump, smooth lips, which were usually in perpetual motion, were sealed shut. He was still, apparently unable to move his limbs. His entire body appeared shocked into a state of paralysis. As crazy as it sounds, he looked like a dried-up plant that had been deprived of water and sunlight. Wes began to grunt, using his eyes to direct my attention to his mouth. It didn't take a genius to figure out what he wanted. I ran my fingers across his lips. They looked like they had been glued together with a thick goo. I didn't want to hurt him, so using my bare hands to rip his mouth open was out of the question.

"I'll be back," I said. "I'm gonna go find something that'll cut through all this glop." I hopped over the bar and began scavenging for any tool sharp enough to prop Wes's mouth open. I found a tiny knife behind the bar that belonged to Kim. The blade looked pretty dull, but if she was still using it to cut through limes, it should still have some nick. I ran back to where Wes was and gently pressed the dull blade against his mouth. His grunts became louder as I cut through the gunk between his lips. "I'm sorry, dollface. I know it hurts, but I'm almost done."

His lips began to bleed, but his blood was not the color of human blood. I realized then that Wes was not human. He was a living, breathing plant in the form of a human being. Once the knife had cut through most of the goo, he forced the rest of his mouth open by stretching it in a wide yawn. Once his lips had regained their full movement, he gasped. "Morgan, grab the fertilizer and the chemical pump from my shed. Hurry!" he shouted, sounding pained and panicked.

I ran quickly to his shed, which was located just on the other side of the bar. When I got to it, I couldn't get the door open. It was jammed. The wooden door had soaked up some of the water from the flood, causing it to expand into the door frame. "Great," I muttered.

I could hear Wes shouting in the distance, "Morgan, hurry!"

I panicked and went apeshit, banging on and kicking at the door with all my might. When it finally flung open, I rushed into the shed and gathered the items Wes had requested. The pump was full and extremely heavy. However, the bag of fertilizer was nearly empty.

I ran back to Wes and anxiously asked, "What do you want me to do with this shit?"

"Spray me down with the chemical!"

"What?"

"The weeds," he shouted, "spray them! They're eating me alive!"

"OK."

I began spraying him down with the toxic chemical until he was completely drenched. I covered my mouth to keep from inhaling the harsh fumes. I could hear the weeds screeching like wild animals as they dried up and died. I watched as they shriveled up one by one until the very last one hit the floor. "What now?" I asked.

He looked at the bag of fertilizer. "Grab a handful of fertilizer."

"OK..." *What the hell could he possibly want me to do with a handful of fertilizer?* I wondered.

"Put it in my mouth," he begged.

"What the hell?"

"I'm weak. I need food."

I reached into the bag, grabbed a handful of fertilizer, and shoved it in his mouth. He scarfed down the compost like a starving man would scarf down a piece of steak. Slowly but surely, he began to regain movement in his body. I gave him another scoop of fertilizer, and with his mouth full, he requested some water.

I ran to the kitchen and fetched a pitcher of water. When I got back to where he was, he had already regained most of the strength in his arms. I handed him the pitcher, and he quickly began to gulp down the water. Once the pitcher ran dry, he tossed it aside and then wiped off the water that had spilled over the side of his mouth. "Ah." He sighed. "Thanks, sweet-cheeks. I feel a lot better now. Come help me up." He positioned himself to stand, and I put his arm over my shoulder to keep him stable. But even with my help, he was struggling to keep his balance. If I didn't know any better, I'd say the man had been kept from walking for over a thousand years. His steps were as paced and cautious as a child's who was learning to walk for the first time. He was naked but tastefully covered in all the right places by the vines that had grown from and across his body. I helped him make his way to the atrium. Once we passed Wick Oasis, he stopped, sliding his arm off my shoulder.

"I can take it from here," he said, smiling. "I was just a little rusty." His jaw almost hit the floor as he took a good look around the hotel. "Oh, shit. Did I miss the party or what? My God, it's a mess in here." He gasped. "I heard you were a bit wild, but damn, girl." He smacked my ass, biting down on his bottom lip.

I pushed him away and said, "Look, if you touch me again, I'm gonna rip off your tiny botanical balls. Capeesh?"

"Whoa, no need to get fussy, sweet-cheeks. I'm just messin' with ya." He laughed, wearing his infamous playboy smirk.

"And stop calling me sweet-cheeks! I'm not one of your little bimbos," I snapped.

He rolled his eyes. "Yeah, thank God."

"You are such an asshole," I muttered.

"Yeah, yeah, yeah. You know, for not being one of my bimbos, you sure sound like one." He grinned.

I looked at him up and down. "I should've just let the weeds do away with you."

His mouth dropped in mock offense. "Oh, now who's being an asshole?"

"You're right. I'm sorry. That was a little harsh." I honestly did feel bad about my careless remark. I mean, sure, he was a douche, but I wouldn't wish anything bad on him. After all, he could actually be really sweet in the rare moments he wasn't worried about how his kindness would benefit his dick.

"Aw, it's OK, sweet-cheeks."

"You are so annoying."

"Oh, come on. You make it seem like I use that term on all my prospects. Nope, I came up with that one just for you, because you're such a pleasure."

"Well, don't I feel like the luckiest girl."

"Anyway, enough bullshitting. Let's get down to business." He began walking away and then hunted for my eyes from over his shoulder. Once he had his desired contact, he seductively whispered, "Come. I wanna show you something." We made our way to the lobby. When we got close to the front desk, he made a sharp turn to the nearest elevator. He looked in the elevator and then looked at me, completely puzzled. "Where's the cab?" he asked.

"There is no cab, buddy. We're climbing." I laughed in amusement.

"Ah, well then, ladies first." He grinned.

"Yeah, I don't think so." I pushed him toward the elevator and made him go up the cable first. I stood back and watched as he struggled to pull himself up. As amusing as it was, I felt bad, because I knew deep down inside he must have been embarrassed by his lack of strength. I didn't want him to feel pressured, so I used a little dark humor to distract the tension. "It's hard to believe that this is what society finds sexy." I sniggered.

"What is that supposed to mean?"

"That men these days are so focused on being pretty, they forget what it means to be a man."

"What are you trying to say?"

"That you better thank God for that pretty little face, pansy."

He looked down at me from over his shoulder and said, "What did you call me?"

"Nothing. I simply said you have the prettiest little face I've ever seen." I looked up at him with cartoon eyes and batted my lashes.

He scrunched his brow and playful scowled. "Whatever. I heard you, asshole. And for the record, I would have already been on the third floor if it wasn't for you."

"Me?"

"Yeah, you. You keep staring at my ass, and it's making me uncomfortable."

I busted out laughing. "Oh, please. I couldn't be happier that those vines are covering more than enough. You really are something else, you know that?"

After what felt like an eternity, we finally reached the third floor. We both rubbed our palms to soothe our irritated hands and then shook some circulation into our agitated limbs.

"Give me your hand," Wes said, taking a closer look at our surroundings. I extended my hand to him, and as soon as my palm touched his palm, he locked his grip. "Come with me."

We didn't go too far. In fact, he led me into the center of the balcony only a few feet away from the elevator. He rested his arms on the metal railing and looked down over the ledge. I snuggled up beside him and shared the lonely view, like sharing a cold cup of tea. As we stood in silence, gazing at the disaster that had swept over the Wicker Palace, he whispered, "You still don't get it, do you?"

"Get what?"

He looked at me and then pointed down at the atrium. "This hotel represents you. It represents how your fear of being disappointed has destroyed you on the inside. You have let your past consume you for so long that your future now feels unwelcome." He sighed. "Morgan, I want you to close your eyes and clear your mind of everything. I want you to think back to the very first time you stumbled onto the Wicker Palace. Do you remember the alluring feeling in your gut that made you come into the hotel and apply? Well, that feeling was fate tugging at your heartstrings. On that very day, fate had scheduled a wake-up call for you. Why else do you think you were so drawn to this place? You were destined to come across the Wicker Palace. This place needed you as much as you needed it. The longer you live suppressed by the past, the longer the abuse goes on, and over time the damage can become permanent. However, there is still hope for you. You've got a lot of people rooting for you. It'll be a damn shame if you let us down."

I looked at Wes, but before I could even open my mouth to assure him that I wasn't planning on letting anyone down, including myself, a loud howl ricocheted throughout the hotel. The sound was so powerful that it caused a power outage, and we were now standing in complete darkness. I had no idea where the howl came from, and it scared the shit out of me. I reached for Wes's hand and squeezed it tight to let him know that he had to be brave for the both of us. I then noticed a red light flicker in the distance. It appeared to be coming from the center of Wick Oasis. "Wes, what is that?" I asked, pointing at the light.

He squinted into the distance. "It looks like a fire."

I tugged at his arm. "Let's go check it out."

He immediately jerked his arms out of my grip and cowardly commented, "Well, aren't you a brave little pup?"

I looked at him in complete disappointment. "Fine. If you won't go with me, I'll go by myself."

"I didn't say I wouldn't go with you. All I'm saying is that we need to figure out what we are walking into before we go charging in like Galahad."

"Fine then. You lead the way, Philip Marlowe."

When we got to the first floor, I noticed a strange, ghoulish glow on our skin. I could have sworn that we were in the presence of a full moon, but there was no moon present, only an ambient luminescence. The entire atrium was basked in the pale light, and I felt like I was in the midst of a dark fairy tale. It was absolutely gorgeous. I latched onto Wes's arm as I trailed behind him. Gently squeezing his bicep, I sighed like a hopeless romantic. "Doesn't the hotel look so beautiful?"

His eyes wandered from side to side in paranoia as he softly said, "Beautiful? Nah. Creepy? Yeah."

As we got closer to Wick Oasis, we were able to confirm that there was indeed a fire. As we neared the fire, it grew bigger. However, this wasn't a wildfire blazing out of control but a man-made campfire in the midst of a deserted campsite. As we cautiously made our way around the campsite, I had a feeling that something wasn't right. Enough

THE WICKER PALACE

belongings for several people were scattered across the floor, but there was not a soul in sight. Enormous piles of gold and silver circled the fire, resembling miniature mountain peaks. We stood before the blaze, hypnotized by its colossal flames that fluttered like the wings of a phoenix.

I clearly heard a twig snap in the distance, and my heart stood completely still when I realized we were no longer alone. Before I knew it, we were ambushed by twelve barbaric-looking men. I had no idea who these men were, but I knew they were not friends. They immediately pounced on us, tied us up by our hands and feet, and placed us in the center of the camp. They kept a close watch on us, never uttering a single word. As they huddled around the fire, the men reminded me of the homeless trying to keep warm on a cold and starless night. However, unlike the homeless, they didn't use wood or newspaper to keeping the fire going. Instead they fed the savage flames pure gold and silver.

Wes gently nudged me and quietly said, "Boy, are we in trouble now, kid."

By the tone of his voice I figured he knew who these men were, and he didn't sound too fond of them. "Who are these bandits?"

"They're not bandits," he whispered. "Believe it or not, they're kings."

As I analyzed the men, I tried to comprehend how kings could be weighed down by cracked lips, bear beards, chipped teeth, callused hands, and Viking hair, by lack of poise and posture in their animalistic mannerisms. Their faces were covered in dirt, and the rags on their backs showed no signs of riches. Wes nudged me again, but this time a little harder.

"Ouch. What was that for?"

"Stop staring. You're gonna get us killed."

"I'm sorry. I didn't even realize that I was staring. It's just hard to believe that these men are kings."

"The road to greatness is never easy. It requires a substantial amount of sacrifice and determination. However, the sacrificial sense is not to test our extreme ability but our humility; for a modest heart is a mature heart, and a heart that is mature is ready to take on the responsibilities of its purpose. Meanwhile, the act of determination is to prove our self-worth. If we cannot value ourselves, we are not ready to value our purposes. These men were all destined for greatness but failed because they couldn't comply with those two components. They made the same mistake a lot of people still make today. They mistook their dreams for wishes, but dreams, unlike wishes, are not granted without pursuit. You can't expect everything to just fall into place; you have to create the ripple. Everyone is meant to be who they are. A destiny never changes. A destiny just goes unfulfilled. Therefore you have kings without kingdoms and storytellers without stories."

I honestly would have preferred Wes to just slap me, because I'm pretty sure it would have hurt less. "Touché." I sighed, and he quietly sniggered as he wobbled around on his ass for comfort. "What do they want with us?" I asked.

He looked at me and said, "They want us to feel their pain. They want us to fail as they did. They want to see your gold and silver disintegrate in the fire until ash is all that remains of your dreams and desires."

Suddenly I felt someone grab me from behind. It was one of the kings. He began to laugh at the top of his lungs as he dragged me closer to the fire. I cried out to Wes, but he was just as helpless as I was. The barbaric king held me out inches from the scorching flames. I could feel my sweat pouring. The heat wave must have caused me to hallucinate, because I could have sworn that I saw Abidah, Cyrenius, and the mermaids dancing in the midst of the flames. I was losing consciousness. I could hear the kings laughing like they were intoxicated. Just then a loud howl silenced every breath in the room. It even caused the fire to blow out, leaving us in the pale shadows. The king quickly tossed me aside like a piece of luggage.

When I turned over to look at Wes, he smiled at me, and I watched as he turned to stone.

11

THE WOLF

Neither my muscles nor my nerves had any instinct to move. Everyone in the campsite stood still in fear. I watched as the kings looked from side to side as if they knew exactly what they were looking for. I, however, had no idea what to expect, and it didn't help that I was still trying to regain full consciousness. The moon-like light reflected off figures lingering in the shadows, and even our own silhouettes became hard to distinguish. As I began to prepare myself for the worst, I heard one of the kings shout in fear, "It's the beast! He is here!" Then all hell broke loose.

The kings scattered like ants in terror, quickly retrieving their torches and arming themselves with weapons. One by one, twelve torches were ignited, and as the shadows subsided, I could now see the chaos behind the commotion. The kings squirmed into a circle, turning their backs to one another. Meanwhile, I lay low by one of the piles of gold, where I watched and waited. The silence made me nervous. This was the part of the movie where you brace yourself, because you know you're fixing to jump out of your seat. Once again the bone-chilling howl rang throughout the hotel, a cry of midnight terror. I could hear the weight in my breath as I anxiously waited for this creature to present itself, but as the old saying goes, be very careful what you wish for.

The creature soon emerged from the shadows into the flickering light of the torches. Although the beast had the characteristics of a man, he clearly was not human. As he approached the kings, he taunted them with snarls and growls to remind them that he was the predator and they were the prey. Though wolflike, this wasn't one of those cute, cuddly little werewolves you read about who get caught up in a cheesy love triangle. This was a full-on demon sent from the depths of hell.

He stood erect with big, black eyes, hands for paws, razor-sharp claws, and—by God—what big teeth he had. His coat was the color of a moonless night, and his pointy ears resembled horns in the darkness. He flaunted his bloodthirsty snout, looking directly at me; but I did not feel a single chill, for I was not afraid of the big bad wolf. In fact, I had the strangest feeling that the creature was there to save me.

A spear slipped through of one of the king's hands, and the reverberation of the weapon against the cold marble tile bestowed the lycan's undivided attention onto the king. The king quickly and carelessly reached out for the spear, alarming the beast. But that was a bad move, because everybody knows that when an animal feels threatened, it attacks. The wolf hunched down on all fours and pounced in full fury. After ripping the flesh from the king's neck, the wolf released a thick layer of smog from his nostrils and then quickly clawed through three other kings. The beast looked around, observing the remaining men. I could tell that the creature was deliberating his plan of attack, as tactical strategies seemed to be running through his eyes. Apparently making a decision after his quick halt, the wolf then went on a roaring rampage.

The battle between the men and the lycan was graphic and brutal. And although it happened fast, it probably wasn't fast enough for the men, who had no hope against a demon who showed no mercy. They swung their swords and launched their spears but failed to land a single blow. The creature was too fast, too cunning. He leaped around the kings like a flea. I watched as the lycan mutilated the kings one by one, ripping off their limbs and gnawing the features off their faces. I could hear his claws shredding through their torsos.

I had never seen so much blood in my entire life. The sound of crushing bones and gasping guts made me wriggle like a worm on a hook. The mixture of cries and roars sent me shivering, and I nearly went faint as the king's royal, red blood streamed through the cracks between the tiles, forming a small puddle around my feet. It was only a matter of seconds before I felt the human tar crawling up between my toes. I was utterly disgusted.

Before I knew it, there were only three kings still standing. Two of the men had spears, while one carried a sword. They circled around the beast, agitating him more than intimidating him. After a few minutes of rallying their battle cries and dancing with the devil himself, one of the kings finally decided to take charge. He ran at the beast, aiming his spear to kill, but the beast quickly snatched the weapon from the king's hands and tossed it aside. The lycan then grabbed ahold of the king and sank his fangs into the man's face, shattering every bone in the man's skull. Once the king was dead, the wolf threw him so hard against the wall that he exploded like a watermelon against the concrete.

Only two kings were left, but they were not going down without a fight. The king with the sword began swinging the blade around as a diversion while the other man sneaked up behind the wolf with his spear. "Look out! He's behind you!" I shouted, trying to aid the wolf, but it was too late. The king had managed to pierce the wolf's rib cage with the spear. The beast whined in pain, and then it quickly turned to the king, whose spear was still stuck in the wolf's side, and sank his teeth into the top of the defenseless man's skull. Once his grip became deadly, the wolf vengefully tugged the king's head right off his neck.

Although there was only one king left to kill, the beast was injured and too weak to do it on his own. I knew I had to help. I picked up a sword that had been dropped nearby and ran toward the king. Our blades crossed paths a few times before the beast sliced the skin off the king's face.

The man slowly dropped to his death, and I was now alone in the presence of the wolf man. And you know something? I had never felt so safe in my entire life.

The wolf looked me up and down as if making sure I wasn't hurt. Once he saw that I was OK, he reached for the spear stuck in his side and removed it with a loud growl. He quickly lost consciousness, and after falling straight to the floor, his body began to change. I watched as the creature transformed into a man, which was somehow exactly what I had expected to happen. However, what I had not expected was for that man to be Chris. I watched his hands and feet shrink to their normal size. I watched as his coat slowly disappeared, leaving his beautiful body completely naked. And I must say, it was a relief to see not only that he was fine but also that he was well endowed.

Even though Chris's body was quite the vision, I felt obligated to cover him up and began scavenging through a pile of items the kings had left behind. I was looking for anything I could use to keep him warm, finally coming across an old suede blanket. It was a beautiful shade of red, a color truly fit for a king. I tossed the large blanket over Chris and neatly tucked the edges underneath his body. I sat beside him and placed his head on my lap, brushing my fingers through his hair as I patiently waited for him to regain consciousness.

After a few minutes, he slowly began to open his eyes, smiling bashfully as he gazed up at me. "Morgan..." He sighed, looking relieved and happy.

I gently brushed his cheek with the back of my hand. "Hey there, tiger. How are you feeling?"

He playfully pouted. "Eh, it's just a scratch. I'll be all right."

Even though he tried to act like he was OK, I knew he wasn't. He was hurt. He couldn't lie to me. I was there. I saw the spear pierce him. He moaned in pain as he tried lifting himself off the floor.

"It's just a scratch, huh?"

He pressed his hand against his rib to keep his wound from throbbing.

"Here, let me take a look at it," I kindly suggested.

I pulled the blanket down to his waist to examine the wound. It actually wasn't that bad. I guessed that during his transformation the wound must have shrunk as well. It was now merely a minor gash. However, it was obviously tender to the touch. I gazed into his beautiful, blue eyes and said, "I'll be right back. I'm gonna see if I can find something to wrap around your wound."

Before I could even get up off my ass, he stopped me. "No! Don't go," he begged. He grabbed my arm. "Stay here with me. I'll be fine. I just need a minute. Please don't go. Please don't leave me."

I kissed his lips and then whispered, "I'm not going anywhere."

He smiled, and in a matter of seconds, laughter emerged from that very same boyish beam. "You know what? I just might need you to get up after all."

"Why is that?"

"Well, to be honest with you"—he paused for a brief moment—"my nuts are freezing." He chuckled, blushing and biting his lip in the most alluring manner.

"Hopefully I share the same pant size as one of these guys," he sighed.

As I helped him up, he carelessly let the blanket covering his naked body fall to the floor. My eyes unknowingly began to admire his chiseled physique. He had several tattoos running across his upper body that only seemed to amplify his Greek-godlike figure. He looked at me and cleared his throat. His grin was the sole sign I needed to know that he was aware of my admiration. I was so embarrassed that I quickly looked away and pretended to keep searching for the pair of pants I hoped we wouldn't find. Unfortunately it wasn't long before I saw him wriggling the pants off of one of the corpses. He immediately slipped into the old, raggedy pants and said, "Ah, perfect."

He approached me, smiling from ear to ear. I could feel my heart beating like an African drum. When he finally kissed me, his lips reminded me of the first time a seventeen-year-old girl I used know paid her first visit to an old coffee shop. Being in the presence of his starry eyes reminded me of a simpler time, when things were easy and life was innocent. And it felt nice to be back in such a familiar place.

I leaned in for another big kiss. And before our lips separated, making a smacking sound, tiny flakes of snow began to descend inside the Wicker Palace. Then before I knew it, I was in the midst of a winter wonderland. Chris was trying so hard not to laugh as he said, "I don't know if you've noticed, but there's a lot of strange things going on around here."

"You don't say." I chuckled.

He simply gave me a wink and acted like he was too cool to say anything else. I began rubbing my hands against my arms to keep the shivers away. Meanwhile, Romeo was acting like it was the middle of summer in Saint-Tropez. And although I was freezing, I wasn't about to desperately throw myself into his arms. I wanted him to make the first move, as I began overexaggerating my "Brrrs" until he finally got the hint. "Oh, shit. You're freezing." He briskly rubbed his rough hands up and down my arms and then quickly ran over to retrieve the suede blanket I had used to cover him earlier. He tossed the red blanket over my shoulders like a cape.

"Aren't you cold?" I asked as I snuggled up in the blanket.

He shook his head. "Nah, I'm good."

I looked at his bare torso and raised my eyebrow. "Are you sure?"

He flexed his chest and said, "Yes, I'm sure. After all, I am the big bad wolf." His eyes turned completely black as he flashed his fangs.

"Well, aren't you a lucky little fur ball. I can't even feel my feet." I looked down at my bare feet, which were suffering from the cold of the snow-laden ground.

Chris mischievously pouted. "Aw, poor baby." An impulsive shiver followed his laughter. "I'm just kidding." He nervously chuckled. "I can't feel my feet for shit either. Let's get the hell out of here."

"Where are we going?"

"Stand back" was his only response, and he arched his back and huffed and puffed. The warmth of his blow melted the snow, leaving the ground both warm and relieving and clearing a trail all the way to the lobby. We quickly made our way down the trail, sneaking through the shadows like two thieves in the night. And no matter how dark and twisted this was, it was my fairy tale, for I was the damsel in red and he was the wolf man with claws as sharp as shining armor.

Our palm-to-palm grasp and lovers' kiss was as natural as the change of the seasons. Oh, hear me now, for I swear on the moon and the stars and any other light that might inflame the night that if I were made to suckle honey, then he would be made to sting like a bee. If I had truly been living in the winter of my life, I had no other choice than to call him spring, for he was the fire below my heart and above my thighs. My tears were no longer prisoners to the fall that came before that winter—that fall when I saw daisies without petals marching around the meadows like horses without hooves, that fall when I witnessed freedom genuflect before self-imprisonment. But hear me now, for I say unto thee, many battles have been lost, but the war has seen victory. A northern wind caused a shift in the tide, a northern wind caused by the bravery of one woman and the patience of one man.

When we finally reached the hotel lobby, Chris picked me up from my waist and sat me down on the front-desk counter. It wasn't until his second attempt that he was finally able to get himself up onto the counter as well. He took my hand and began to trace the lines on the inside of my palm with his finger. He then pressed my hand against his to compare their similarities and admire their differences. I know you shouldn't wish to live in a moment forever, because it is the nevermore that makes a moment beautiful, but I vainly wished and wished for our hands to live on like this.

And although I couldn't tell you what was going through his mind, I can tell you what was running through mine: infatuation. I was visually spellbound by the beauty of this man. And why wouldn't I be? His nose was just right, not too big or too small. His eyebrows were perfectly arched to fit his cynical personality. He was all lashes surrounding those baby-blue eyes. The ink on his skin looked like poetic lacerations made from the experiences that had altered his life. His teeth were neatly aligned behind those luscious lips. To be quite frank, the guy was a total babe. But above all, what made him the most intriguing was that he fought to have a place by my side.

He immediately broke my train of concentrated infatuation when he asked, "What are you thinking about?"

I allowed his question to linger for a while until I finally replied, "The future...for once."

"Does it scare you?" he asked.

"It terrifies me."

He rubbed the palm of my hand. "Well, if it helps, it scares me too, but together we can be fearless." He turned my face toward his until his eyes were able to look deeply into mine. "Don't ever think you're gonna be in this alone, because I will be here every single step of the way, good or bad, happy or sad."

I could feel his eyes holding my soul for ransom as he waited to hear me say the words that would become his anthem. I took a deep breath and begged my heart to be steady. As I looked into his eyes, I saw a broken man, a man who did not need to be pledged a false allegiance or flattering, flimsy promises. After all, in life a broken promise can be compromised, but in love a broken promise does all the compromising. This was the start of something unpredictable, so I only guaranteed what I seemed capable of.

"Chris, I don't ever want you to feel like you're alone, because you're not, not anymore. As long as you're with me, I will be here, and we'll be together."

He kissed my cheek and said, "That's my girl."

I looked around the hotel. "So, where do we go from here?"

He raised his eyebrow. "Home." He placed his forehead against mine.

Gently pushing him back with my forehead, I said, "Well, I'm ready whenever you are."

He pouted and squinted as he playfully analyzed me. "OK, but I need you to promise me something before we go."

"I've been making quite a few promises tonight. I just hope I can remember them all. After all, I hate making promises I can't remember to keep. But I guess one more wouldn't hurt." I grinned.

"Good. Promise me you won't forget what you've witnessed here tonight," he whispered, with a fearful fire in his eyes.

"Believe me; I couldn't even if I tried." I chuckled.

"Well, with that being said, I'll be waiting for your kiss tomorrow morning by the sugar and cream." He smirked like a mischievous child.

I shook my head, as I couldn't believe him. "Come on, Chris." I sighed. "You and I both know this is just a dream. Your presence here is just a part of my subconscious. And as much as I wish you could remember this like I will, you can't be aware of dreams you don't dream for yourself."

When I looked up at him, I noticed I had lost his attention. There was something on his mind, the urgency of which was written all over his face. He cleared his throat as he directed his eyes away from me. "There's something I have to tell you." He paused as he gathered his thoughts. "This whole dream wasn't conducted by your subconscious. It was arranged. About two nights ago, Antonio paid me a visit through a dream that was very similar to yours. After sharing the story from his point of view, he asked me to assist him in saving you. So here I am. Morgan, this might be a dream, but I'm real. He made me promise that I would take care of you, and I intend to keep that promise. He was a great guy and still is, because he couldn't rest in peace until he saw you happy again."

My lips began to quiver as my eyes filled with tears. "Yeah, that sure sounds like that stubborn man. So how do we get home?" I asked.

Chris kissed the back of my hand and smothered his words with my skin. "It's easy. All you got to do is close your eyes and kiss me. But when you kiss me, you need to prove to yourself that you mean it."

I set my sights on his lips and pondered them as if I had never been kissed. I licked my lips as I slowly leaned in toward his. Then, right before our lips touched, I quietly whispered, "Let's go home."

Pressing my lips against his, I felt the heat of our breath collide as our mouths opened. I could feel his sensuality penetrating my soul as the warmth of his tongue became my heart's delight. I locked my arms around his neck with certainty, because there was no doubt that this was now mine. No more ifs, ands, or buts. And to prove it to myself, I sealed it with a kiss that nearly caused me to suffocate. Our bodies began to disintegrate into tiny particles that slowly evaporated into the air. Although my eyes were closed the whole time, I could see it happening. And before I knew it, there was nothing left but our two pairs of lips.

Ring! Ring! Ring! My alarm nearly caused me to fall out of bed. I quickly reached for my phone to silence the dreadful ringing. Although my snooze button and I usually have an unspoken alliance, I couldn't help but welcome this particular morning with open arms.

I didn't know whether to call it a sweet dream or a nightmare, but whatever it was, it was over now. I stumbled out of bed and made my way to the bathroom. The darkness was like fog, there to remind me that I could still count a few stars if I wanted to. My apartment was freezing, but I didn't care, because there was a warm shower calling my name. Once I got the water going, I began singing at the top of my lungs as if I were Mama Cass herself. I don't think I'd ever been that eager to get to work. And even though I was rushing, I still managed to put emphasis on the details that would make me look extra pretty that day. I applied a little more makeup than I usually did, using softer colors to indicate my change of heart. I twirled my curling iron through my hair to add some waves, and then I used a red ribbon to tie the front portion of hair back, tying the ribbon into a bow. I was so consumed by making an impression that I accidentally brushed my teeth twice in a row.

When I finally arrived at the hotel, Michael was the first to greet me. "Good morning, Morgan!"

"Good morning, Michael!" I cheerfully returned the gesture. "How are you doing today?"

He flashed his goofy smile and enthusiastically replied, "I am doing absolutely fabulous on this magnificent morning! How are you?"

I smiled and said, "I couldn't be better."

He was so animated that I couldn't help but smile while in his presence. And sure, Michael was a bit over the top, but hats off to the guy. I could not imagine having the energy he does every single morning. "Hey, Michael, do you by any chance know if Chris is here yet?" I asked nonchalantly.

Michael was unable to contain the sly smile that came along with his response. "Yeah, he actually just walked in a few minutes before you did. He was headed to the atrium."

I playfully scorned Michael's conclusive smile and bashfully shook my head as I proceeded toward the atrium. This was it. This was the real thing. I was sure of it. I even pinched the side of my thigh to confirm that this was reality and not another dream. As I made my way to the atrium, I could see Chris digging for a packet of sugar while pouring some cream into his cup. As I snuck up on him, I prayed that he would not turn around and catch me coming toward him, because I had the perfect idea of how I wanted this to play out. When I got close enough to him, I tapped his shoulder, and when he turned around, he had the biggest smile I had seen in a while. Then, without saying a word, we met halfway for a kiss.

And that's where this story ends. After all, this is not a tale about finding love or falling in love all over again, since the truth is no one ever really knows when love is going to happen. This is simply a story about finding the courage to take chances again, because the chances we don't take are the answers we'll never have. This is a story about a dream I had that is now a book you are reading. And although I may not know what the future holds, I am no longer afraid of finding out. So, take it from me: no matter how much a relationship consumes you, no matter how bad the hangover is, never let the disappointments or heartbreaks stop you from raising a glass for love. And please remember that love shouldn't feel safe or secure; there should always be some hint of mystery, a dash of danger, and a dollop of adventure.

And last but not least, before you ever completely give your heart away, ask yourself, is this everything I've ever wanted? If it's not, don't be afraid to give yourself more. "Settling" is just a word we use when we don't want to say that we've given up.

Love is a scary thing, because the truth is no one really knows how it works. There is a possibility that your first love is your only love. Then again there's a chance that the first is simply a preparation for your actual love, or maybe any love after the first is simply to forget. No one really knows, so all you can do is live. Live, enjoy your youth, be weird, be free, take chances, and always be wild at heart.

With that being said, I have a kiss to get back to.

Dedicated in loving memory to Ruby Ruiz and Vicente Juarez

Made in the USA
Charleston, SC
08 September 2015